THE
DREAM
HOUSE

BOOKS BY JESS RYDER

Lie to Me
The Good Sister
The Ex-Wife

THE
DREAM
HOUSE

JESS RYDER

Bookouture

Published by Bookouture in 2019

An imprint of StoryFire Ltd.

Carmelite House
50 Victoria Embankment
London EC4Y 0DZ

www.bookouture.com

ISBN: 978-1-78681-971-0
eBook ISBN: 978-1-78681-970-3

For survivors of domestic violence everywhere.

PROLOGUE

The night sky was a battlefield, brilliant with clashes of colour and flame. Crackling explosions kept jump-starting her heart. Her head was spinning so fast she thought it might shoot off into space and burst into a million sparkling pieces. She was a Roman candle, a banger, a glorious fountain of golden rain.

The air was thick with smoke, the sulphurous kind you only get on Bonfire Night, that seeps into your clothes and sticks in your hair for days after. The smell reminded her of being a kid – neighbourly get-togethers in back gardens, writing her name with sparklers, stamping the ground to bring the life back to her toes. Burnt sausages, fried onions and tomato ketchup. Dads carrying around biscuit tins and setting off weedy displays – Catherine wheels that wouldn't spin, rockets that spluttered then fell into the rose bush. They had been simple, innocent times, she thought. But now the smell of gunpowder would be forever associated with this extraordinary night.

The ground was soft after days of rain. She made her way to the end of the garden, the long wet grass licking her ankles, mud soaking into the soles of her slippers. It was strange that she couldn't feel the cold. Her breathing was quick and shallow – the baby was so large she couldn't fill her lungs. She steadied herself on a fence post. The child kicked out, pressing its foot against the wall of her womb.

Bang, whoosh, sizzle, wheeeeee … The sky was on fire. Hot sparks fluttered around her, illuminating her silhouette as she walked around the compost heap, testing the ground. She crouched down, letting the hem of her dressing gown trail in the damp earth, and picked up a few dead leaves, mulched by the rain.

Yes, this was the place. Nobody was around to witness; they were all at the park. They would watch the finale, have a few more goes on the rides and stalls, then drift slowly away, stopping off for chips or last orders. Everyone would come home and go straight to bed. She could be out here all night and not a soul would notice.

It had been a night he had predicted, that she'd been warned about a thousand times. The ultimate attack she'd strangely wanted to happen, but only because she could no longer bear the tension of not knowing when it would come.

Her fear of him was permanent, a tattoo on a part of her body only he had ever seen. Although the bruises, burns and bite marks had faded, they would never go away completely. She'd been a work in progress to him. 'One day I'll finish you off,' he'd often said, and there'd been no reason to doubt him.

A loud scream pierced the air. She looked up to see a huge rocket zooming towards the heavens. It held its breath for a moment, then exploded, spattering the sky with blood-red drops of fire.

The new human being inside her – she hoped it was a girl – drew her knees into her chest.

'It's only fireworks, silly,' she whispered, stroking her hard belly. 'No need to be scared. We're safe now.'

our clothes are hanging off hooks like dubious works of art. A pizza box from last night lies stranded on the desk; electric cables trail hazardously across the floor. The airbed we've been sleeping on is unmade, and dirty washing is heaped in the corner. I should have tidied up before they arrived, I suppose – not that there's anything to tidy stuff into.

While they're assembling the frame, I retreat to the kitchen to finish making the tea. Fingers crossed this will cheer Jack up, I think. He's been sulking since our row a few nights ago. One of those quick, nasty exchanges that came out of nowhere, fuelled by tiredness and alcohol.

'I'm sick of living like this,' he said. 'The airbed is crippling my back, I haven't had a proper shower in weeks, and if I have to eat another ready meal, I'm going to kill myself.'

'It's worse for me. At least you spend the day in a smart office – I'm stuck in this one room.'

'*You* decided to buy the place.'

'It was a joint decision!'

'No it wasn't. It was your money, I couldn't stop you.'

'Yes, *my* money because *my* parents are dead,' I said, then burst into tears.

I felt bad about using their deaths to trump the argument. The next day, I drove to one of those superstores in a retail park just out of town and bought the best frame and most comfortable mattress they had. It's a surprise. You could even call it an apology.

This evening I'm going to steel myself to clean the hob and cook a proper meal for once. It's only spaghetti bolognese, but I've bought fresh Parmesan and a bottle of decent Chianti. Tonight's going to be a fresh start. Proper food, proper wine, proper bed. Maybe we'll even have some proper sex for a change.

*

Five hours later, my heart leaps as I hear the sound of Jack's key turning in the lock. Rushing to the mirror, I check my lipstick and adjust my hair. I've changed out of my usual baggy jumper and jeans and put on a slinky black dress. I'm wearing the sparkly earrings he bought me for my birthday.

'Hi! I'm home!' he calls.

I quickly glance around the room. Fresh linen is on the new bed, nightlights are flickering on the mantelpiece, the bottle of wine sits expectantly on the desk we're using as a dining table. The atmosphere is almost romantic, in a tatty, bohemian kind of way.

Jack enters, unzipping his jacket. 'My God! What's all this?' he says, grinning.

'I decided enough was enough. It's queen size, bigger than the double we had at the old flat.'

'Yeah, so I see.' He sits and bounces up and down on the mattress. 'Not too hard, not too soft. Good choice, Stella.'

'I'm so glad you're pleased. I know we were going to wait until the new bedroom was finished, but—'

'No, no, you did the right thing.' He flops back in a starfish shape and sniffs the air. 'And do I actually smell cooking?'

I run off to the kitchen to serve up while Jack opens the Chianti and pours two generous glasses.

'Ta-dah!' I waltz back in with the steaming plates of spaghetti. 'Not exactly *MasterChef*, I know, but at least it's real food.'

'Anything's better than the shit we've been eating lately,' he says, then adds, 'I mean, I'm sure it'll be delicious.'

The pasta and the bottle of wine seem to do the trick, and before long we're snuggled up together on our new bed, watching a movie and starting some casual foreplay. His hand creeps along the front opening of my dress and slips under my bra. I feel my nipple harden and lean into him, gently caressing the back of his neck. It's been so long since we made love, we've almost forgotten how to do it. I stare into his dark brown eyes and grin mischievously. He gives me a slow, understanding nod and shuts the lid of the laptop.

Then everything picks up speed and we're tearing each other's clothes off and thrashing about, kissing everything we can get our mouths to.

'I love you,' I whisper. 'I'm sorry everything's so chaotic – do you think it was a mistake buying the hou—'

'Shut up,' he replies softly, opening my legs. 'I don't want to think about that now. All I want is you.' I pull him into me, clasping my hands over his small, tight buttocks as we rock together.

Suddenly there's a loud thumping noise. I start nervously. 'What was that?'

'Mmm … it's nothing. Kiss me.'

'No, listen! Somebody's at the door.'

'Who cares?'

Thump, thump, thump. It sounds like they're hammering with their fist.

'Who do you think it is? What shall we do?'

Jack lifts his head. 'Ignore it.'

The knocking continues, growing louder, more insistent.

'Maybe it's Alan. He might have forgotten something.'

'If it is, he can wait till tomorrow.'

'It can't be Alan, he's got a key.' *Bang, bang.* They're not giving up. I wriggle out from under him and grab my dressing gown.

'Don't answer. It's probably some delivery guy got the wrong address.'

Bang, bang, bang.

'Not at this time of night. It sounds really urgent. Maybe it's the police.'

'Why would it be the police?' he says, sitting up. 'That's ridiculous.'

But I know the banging's not going to stop until I answer. I run barefoot into the freezing hallway, quickly tying the belt of my gown.

'Who is it?' I shout. A dark silhouette presses against the wire-reinforced glass.

'Please let me in! Please!' A female voice.

I bend down and shout through the letter box. 'Who are you? What do you want?'

'I need help!'

Jack emerges, a towel around his waist. 'What's going on?'

'There's a woman out there. Says she needs help.'

'What? It could be a scam, Stella. Don't answer.'

But all I can think of is Mum and Dad, remembering how they lay bleeding in the road that dark rainy night. Maybe they cried for help but nobody came. If the driver had stopped, if a passer-by had witnessed the accident and called an ambulance, they might still be alive today. And then I wouldn't be carrying all this guilt around with me. Maybe, just maybe, this is a chance to make amends for the terrible thing I did.

Without another thought, I fling open the front door.

CHAPTER TWO

Stella

Now

The woman staggers forward a few paces, then falls headlong into the hallway, smacking herself hard against the cold tiles and rolling onto her side. For a second she's completely still; all we can hear is her heavy breathing. Jack and I stare down at her.

'What the …?' he murmurs.

Her face is badly bruised, her lip is swollen and blood is trickling from the corner of her mouth. There are streaks of dried blood down the front of her sweatshirt, her jogging bottoms are tatty and stained and she's wearing slippers. No coat, no socks. She's clutching a brown handbag to her chest. Behind her on the doorstep is a small black suitcase, the size I'd use for a weekend away.

'What happened?' I crouch beside her.

'Door,' she says through thick lips.

'What? Is somebody out there? Jack – shut it, for God's sake! She's terrified.'

He goes to the doorway and steps outside, peering into the darkness. 'I can't see anyone.' He comes back inside, moves the case into the hallway and shuts the door. 'Have you been mugged?' She shakes her head.

'Don't worry,' I say gently. 'We'll take care of you.' I look up at Jack. 'Should we call the police? Ambulance?'

'No! No police!' She shakes her head fiercely. 'No ambulance.'

'But you've been attacked.'

'No! They said it was okay … No police …'

'Who said it was okay? The bastard that did this?'

'No! No … Phone … On the phone.'

'I'm sorry, I don't understand.'

'Who are you?' asks Jack, hovering a few paces away. 'Why are you here?'

'Let's not worry about that now. There's a first-aid kit in one of the boxes,' I say. 'See if you can find it.'

He doesn't move. 'But we don't know anything—'

'It doesn't matter right now. She's hurt. Find some antiseptic cream, plasters, anything. Boil a kettle, we need hot water.'

'We should call the police.'

'She doesn't want us to. Please just find the first-aid kit. And get some clothes on.' He turns around with a huff and disappears into the front room.

I go back to the woman. 'Are you okay to sit up?' She nods. 'Let me help you.' I carefully ease her upwards. 'I'm Stella. What's your name?'

'Lori,' she mumbles. 'Ta.' She moves her head stiffly, looking around her with a puzzled expression on her face.

'Are you sure you don't want to go to A and E?'

'No. I mean, yes, I'm sure … Don't need hospital. No police.'

'But you've been attacked, Lori. You need to report it. How did it happen? Was it a stranger, or do you know them?'

She screws up her eyes. 'This is Westhill House, right?'

'Yes …' I say warily.

'You take anyone in, no questions, no police unless we ask for them. You never turn anyone away, that's what they said.'

'Who said?'

'The helpline.'

'What? I'm ever so sorry, I think there's been some mistake.'

'No, no mistake,' she says firmly. 'This is Westhill House. The refuge.'

'A refuge?'

'Yes! You know, for battered women.' My mind immediately goes to the bedsit units, the communal spaces downstairs, the cameras, the alarms, the security glass on all the external doors.

'Well, um, maybe, I don't know, maybe it *used* to be a refuge, but it's not any more, hasn't been for a long time. It's a private house now. I'm really, really sorry, but you've been given duff information—'

She grabs my arm. 'Please, love, please don't turn me away! I've nowhere else to go, I'm running for my life. He'll be out there looking for me. If he finds me, I swear he'll kill me. Please, I'm begging you, let me stay.'

My head spins with contradictory thoughts. I've just let a total stranger into my house; I must be crazy. How do I even know she's telling the truth? But then I look at the bruises on her face, her swollen bloody lip …

'Let's get you cleaned up first,' I say, gently lifting her to her feet.

I steer her into the front room and sit her on the edge of our new bed, where just a few moments ago we were in the throes of passionate lovemaking. Her glance wanders over the telltale scene. The remains of our romantic dinner are still lying on the table, flickering candles almost burnt down to stubs, our empty wine glasses stained ruby red. My clothes are lying on the floor where Jack threw them after he ripped them off me. The sheets are crumpled from our thrashing about.

'Sorry about the mess,' I say, quickly kicking my bra and knickers under the bed. My flimsy dressing gown barely disguises my nakedness, and my bare feet are freezing. 'We're camping in here while we're having the house done up.'

'Oh, right.' She pulls her knees together, clutching her handbag as if it contains her whole life.

Jack, now back in jeans and a shirt, brings me the first-aid kit and I tear open a packet of antiseptic wipes. She flinches as I try to clean the dried blood off her face. 'Sorry. There's a small cut on your cheekbone and the inside of your mouth seems to be bleeding.'

'He swung at me, made me bite my cheek.'

'You should get checked out at the hospital,' Jack says, hovering behind me.

She shakes her head. 'Nah, it'll be all right … I've had worse.'

'There, that's the best I can do.' I stick a plaster over the cut. She looks up and gives me a weak smile.

'Thanks, you're an angel. Don't know what I would have done if you hadn't answered the door.'

Jack is staring at her, his nose wrinkling in disgust. 'Who did this to you?'

'My husband,' she says quietly.

'Jesus … Why?'

'Let's not go into that now,' I say, shooting a glance at him. 'She's escaped, that's the main thing.' Turning to Lori, I add, 'You've been incredibly brave.'

'Oh, I don't know about that.' She looks down at her grubby pink mules. 'What must I look like? A total wreck. Didn't even put my shoes on.' Tears well up in her dull grey eyes and she wipes them on her sleeve. 'But at least I'm alive, eh? Just about.'

There's a pause. 'Would you like a glass of water? Or some tea?'

'Tea, please, if you're making.'

'I think we could all do with one.' I look meaningfully at Jack and he signals that he wants to talk to me. 'I'll be right back,' I say, following him out of the room.

We go to the kitchen and he closes the door behind us, his face puckered with annoyance.

'I know what you're thinking,' he hisses, 'but she can't stay.'

'Why not?'

'Because! We don't know who she is, or why she's here—'

'She's just told us. Her name's Lori; her husband beat her up so she escaped.'

'How do we know she's telling the truth?'

I fill the kettle and put it on to boil, hoping its roar will drown out our conversation. 'Look at the state of her! We can't turn her away. Her husband could have followed her. He could be out there now, waiting for her. What if he murders her in the street? We'd never forgive ourselves.'

'If he's outside, we should call the police. Let them sort it out.'

'She doesn't want them involved.'

'That's stupid. Why on earth not?'

'I don't know, Jack, she must have her reasons. Maybe she doesn't trust them.'

He huffs, unable to comprehend. 'Well maybe I don't trust *her*. I mean, why come here? Why pick on us?'

'Apparently this house used to be a refuge.' He stares at me blankly. 'You know, for victims of domestic abuse. Their locations are kept secret.'

'Oh. Right …' He thinks for a few seconds. 'If it's a secret, how come she knew about it?'

'She rang a helpline and was given this address.'

'What helpline?'

'I don't know. They told her to come here and she'd be looked after – they got it wrong, it wasn't her fault.'

Jack takes a breath. 'Okay, okay, that makes a *tiny* bit of sense, I suppose. But it's not a refuge any more, is it?' He looks at me hard.

I pop tea bags into three mugs and pour on the boiling water. 'It's midnight; she's hurt, scared, in shock. We can't turf her out now. She can have the air mattress and a sleeping bag in the other room.' I push past Jack to get to the fridge and take out the milk. 'It's no big deal.'

'Yes it is – it's a huge deal,' he fumes. 'We don't know anything about her.'

'It's just for tonight. I'll help her sort out a proper refuge in the morning.' I pick up two of the mugs. 'Be kind, Jack. Please, for me?' I leave him pouting furiously in the kitchen and go back to our guest.

'Do you take sugar?' I say as I enter the front room, hoping to God she didn't overhear us.

'No, that's fine, as long as it's warm and wet.' I pass her a mug, and she cradles it against her bloodstained top. 'I'm really sorry for barging in on you like this. They told me on the phone I could just turn up, no questions asked.'

'Don't worry, it's not your fault, you were misinformed.'

'I know, but I feel terrible …' She pauses, looking anxiously towards the door. 'I get the feeling your husband isn't too happy about me being here.'

'He's not actually my husband, but he's fine – it's okay, we both want to help. We've got a camping mattress you can sleep on tonight. I'll set you up in the other room. It's a bit of a building site, I'm afraid.'

'Anything's better than being on the streets. You're a diamond, thank you.'

'Please don't keep thanking me, it's okay. Try to get some rest and we'll sort it all out in the morning.'

It's nearly one o'clock before we get to bed. I lie in the darkness, listening to Jack's snuffling breathing and wondering about Lori in the room on the other side of the hallway. Has she collapsed with exhaustion or is she still awake too? I'd be surprised if she could sleep after what she's been through tonight.

I turn onto my side, listening to the noises of the house. It's as if it has woken up after a long sleep, rubbing its eyes and stretching its limbs. I can hear it gently breathing, the floorboards creaking like old bones, the rusty pipes gurgling and coughing. How many women have knocked on its door, battered and bruised, desperate for help? It could be in the hundreds, even thousands.

Jack's furious with me, but I couldn't turn her away, I just couldn't. Thank God we were at home tonight. What if we'd refused to answer? What if her husband had followed her and stabbed her on the driveway with a kitchen knife? Left her dying in a pool of blood? I shudder, banishing the violent image from my mind and replacing it with a picture of her wrapped safely in her sleeping bag in the room across the hallway. I did the right thing, I think. For once in my life, Mum and Dad would have been proud of me.

CHAPTER THREE

Kay

Then

It was mid February and the shop was heaving with symbols of love. Posters in the window, red bunting strung between the shelves, teddies with hearts stitched onto their tummies, heart-shaped key rings, foil balloons that brushed against her face every time she opened the till. The 'with sympathy' and 'get well soon' ranges had been put away in drawers, as if nobody would have the nerve to fall ill or die at such a romantic time of the year.

Kay grumpily rearranged the gift bags, which a customer had jumbled up. It was going to be her first Valentine's Day at the shop and she hoped it would be her last. By this time next year she was determined to have a different, better job, hopefully in Miss Selfridge. This was no place for a single mum without a love life.

She'd felt so envious these last couple of weeks, watching the young men shuffle in, as embarrassed as if they'd just walked into a porn shop. Although to be fair, the majority of their male customers were older, and even if they didn't wear a wedding ring, they had a married look about them. It seemed a bit daft, sending a Valentine's card to somebody you'd already bagged, but how wonderful to have a romantic husband, she thought. How wonderful to have a husband at all …

'No man will ever want you now,' her mother had said when Kay had confessed that she was pregnant. She was only fifteen. The father was a Spanish waiter she'd met on a family holiday in Torremolinos. He was breathtakingly handsome; all the girls staying at Hotel Cascada had fallen for him. His name was Miguel Angel, although he pronounced the *g* in Angel as a thrilling, husky *h*. He sneaked free shots of Bacardi into her Coca-Cola without her parents knowing and told her to meet him at the end of his shift. She pretended to go to bed at the same time as her parents, but crept back down an hour later, emboldened with alcohol, puffed up that he'd chosen her above the other English girls. It never occurred to her that he'd picked her out as the most likely fool.

He took her onto the dark, cool sand, and laid her down beside the pedalos, lifting her dress to her waist and taking her knickers down, scraping them over her sunburnt thighs. She was a virgin. Until that point, there'd been little more than a clumsy grope of her breast, an ugly love bite on her neck, a slobbering schoolboy kiss. But Miguel Angel was nineteen and reckoned she owed him more than just kisses. She didn't mean to let him go all the way, but she was drunk and her Spanish was limited to *por favor* and *gracias*. Before she could stop him, it was all over. More a devil than an angel, as it turned out.

'You're shop-soiled, damaged goods,' her mother said, but to her astonishment, they let her keep the baby. As time passed, she found it harder to remember Miguel's features, but she saw his gorgeous dark eyes and smooth olive skin every day in her daughter. Abigail was four now and had just started school.

Kay glanced at the clock and tried to work out what the little girl would be doing at this moment. It was morning break; she'd be running around the yard or playing games with her friends. She was a precocious little thing, surrounded by doting grown-ups. Mum and Dad had been very kind, Kay reflected, as she neatened up the cards, putting the ones that had wandered off back in their rightful places. She had disappointed them but they hadn't thrown her out. They adored their granddaughter – spoilt her rotten, in fact. But the second she started school, Dad had shoved the evening newspaper in Kay's face and told her to find herself a job.

She'd applied for several, mostly in clothes shops because they gave you a ten per cent discount, but Many Congratulations had been the first place to call her to interview and they'd offered her the job on the spot. They were good about letting her work around school hours. She did nine to three Monday to Friday and then a long day on Saturdays. Mum babysat, but she didn't want to look after Abigail all day and then all evening, so Kay hadn't had a Saturday night out for months. She couldn't help but feel she was still serving a punishment for that hot August night over five years ago.

Somebody behind her coughed. She turned around to see a young bloke holding up several Valentine's cards. They were spread in a fan, making her think of a magician. *Pick a card, any card …*

'Would you help me, please?' he said. He was tall, with a square jaw and beady blue eyes. Smartly dressed in a Crombie-style overcoat and a pair of stay-press trousers. 'I don't know which one to choose.'

'Wife or girlfriend?'

'Neither … not yet.' He went slightly red and undid the top buttons of his coat. If she wasn't mistaken, that was a proper Ben Sherman shirt he had on – pale blue with a buttoned-down collar. She guessed he was about the same age as her, twenty-one or two at the most. Far too good-looking to be unattached.

She looked at his choices. He was obviously the romantic type; the cards he'd picked out were all very similar – combinations of hearts, flowers and cute-faced teddies. A few had tiny satin bows stapled into the fold, and there was a lot of glitter, some of which had come off on his fingertips.

'What's she like?'

'Very pretty.' He screwed up his eyes as if peering at her through frosted glass. 'Slim but not skinny. Lovely hair. Great legs. Beautiful smile.'

'I meant what sort of personality has she got.'

'Oh! A kind one, I'd say. She's a very nice person, but to be honest, I don't know her very well.'

'Then I'd go for something quite tasteful, not too over-the-top – you don't want to scare her off.'

'Good point,' he said.

'That one would be my pick.' She pointed to the card in the centre of the fan. It featured a bouquet of wild flowers, pinks, blues and purples on a white background. Silver glitter sparkled between the petals and there was a small silver heart embossed on the top right-hand corner.

'Thank you. That's decided, then.' He plucked out the card and gave it to her to put in a bag.

She was glad when it was three o'clock and she could leave the shop. As she stood at the school gates waiting for the first glimpse of her daughter's little brown face, she thought again about the girl's father. What was Miguel Angel doing now, she wondered? Five years had passed; he could easily be married and Abigail might have half-brothers or sisters. Every so often Kay toyed with the idea of going back to Torremolinos and trying to find him. But for what purpose? She didn't know his surname or his address. He probably wouldn't remember her, and even if he did, he was bound to deny he was the father. She'd suffered enough indignities, thank you very much.

'Mummy! Mummy!' Abigail hurtled across the playground and flung her arms around her mother's legs.

Kay stroked her daughter's soft dark curls and banished her silly thoughts from her head. 'Come on, chipmunk, let's go home.'

It was Thursday, fish and chips night. Dad always picked them up on his way back from work. They ate them out of the paper on a tray in front of the new colour telly, washed down with a mug of strong tea. Then Kay would bath Abigail and put her to bed. She was a good sleeper, especially since she'd started school. Later on, Mum and Dad would pop out to the local pub to play darts.

All Kay's friends had boyfriends; a few were engaged and one had just got married. Abigail had made a gorgeous little bridesmaid, but the wedding itself had been excruciating. Standing on her own at the ceremony, creating an odd number at the table, looking like a spare part in the group photo. She had no intention of putting herself through that again.

'Grub's up,' shouted Dad as he came in, followed by a sharp waft of vinegar. He was holding a second bag behind his back. Her mother skipped down the stairs – she'd put on a fresh blouse and coated her mouth in sugar-pink lipstick.

'What are you hiding?' she asked teasingly. He always bought her a box of Milk Tray and a card on Valentine's Day.

'That's for me to know and you to find out,' he replied, kissing her on the cheek. 'All will be revealed tomorrow.'

Kay banged the cutlery on the counter. *Bloody Valentine's Day. Can't get away from it …*

Dad came into the kitchen and gave her the food to unwrap. Three cod and chips and a pickled onion. It was always the same; he never deviated, never asked anyone if they would like a chicken and mushroom pie for a change, or haddock instead of cod. Kay shared her portion with Abigail, which was fine because she was supposed to be watching her figure. She dished up while her mother poured out the tea. They trooped into the sitting room and sat down with their trays, eating in silence as the local teatime news blared out. Abigail bounced around on the sofa, picking at her chips and making greasy marks on her

Alan returns upstairs with promises that I'll go to the bank as soon as I get the chance. I give the clothes to Lori and she thanks me profusely before going to her room to change. The banging starts up again.

I escape to our room, then open the lid of my laptop and boot it up. There are a few national helplines for victims of domestic violence, and I call them all. The women who answer the phone are very kind and understanding, but I'm sure they think I'm the real victim and don't believe I'm enquiring on behalf of someone else. Annoyingly, none of them owns up to the mistake of still having Westhill House on their database.

After a fruitless morning spent on the phone and various websites, it becomes clear that a lot of refuges have closed in the last few years. The nearest one is twenty miles away and only accepts women in high-risk categories who've been referred by Social Services or the police.

But if Lori won't report the attack she won't get referred, and if she can't get into a refuge, where can she go? She won't have enough money for a hotel. If I make her leave, she'll have no choice but to live on the streets. Or return to her violent husband.

No, I can't have that. It's not fair, it's not right. She'll have to stay here for a few more days, just until we can sort something else out. Jack will understand. I'll call him at work and explain. I reach for my mobile.

Jack *doesn't* understand. 'I'm sorry, but it's her problem, not ours,' he says, irritatingly tapping away on his computer at the same time. 'She has a choice. If her life is really in danger she should go to the police and have him arrested. It's simple, isn't it? If he's behind bars she doesn't need to be in a refuge. The police can protect her a lot better than we can. I want her gone by the time I get home.'

'Please, Jack, have some compassion.'

'It's you I'm thinking about, Stella. What if her husband finds out where she is and comes after her? That puts you at risk too, and I can't have that.'

'I'm not worried about me. I'm used to strangers turning up in the middle of the night. I had it my whole childhood. Mum and Dad never turned anyone away.'

'But your parents were proper foster carers,' he reminds me. 'And the kids were sent by Social Services. This is completely different. I still think it could be some kind of scam. I know you want to help, but we're not experts. Anything could go wrong.'

'Okay, okay,' I mutter, silently mouthing 'heartless bastard' into the receiver. 'Have it your way.'

I finish the call and slam the phone on the desk. How am I going to tell Lori that she can't stay here when there's nowhere else for her to go?

For the next hour I stay hidden in the bedroom, unable to face her. My thoughts are in gridlock; there doesn't seem to be any way to turn. I don't want to fall out with Jack, but I really need to help Lori. For my sake, just as much as hers. It sounds ridiculous, but I have this strong feeling that she's been sent to me, almost as a kind of divine gift. I've been given a chance to make up in some small way for the sins of my past.

Jack doesn't understand, and why should he? He doesn't know what I did, and so far, I haven't had the courage to tell him. We've only been together a year; our relationship is too new, too fragile to tamper with. I love him like crazy and can't risk losing him. He believes I'm a good person; he has no idea about the darkness in my heart, the stain on my conscience I can never erase. Nobody knows the whole story – not my family, not even my best friend Molly.

I decide to call her and ask for some advice.

'It's up to you,' she says, typically. 'All I'm saying is, remember it's your house, not his. If you want this woman to stay for a few days, then put your foot down.'

'Yes, but I don't want a big argument with Jack. He hasn't settled here – doesn't like Nevansey much. He keeps complaining about the commute, and he's not very interested in the building work either. I need to keep him happy too.'

Molly sighs heavily. I can picture her sitting on the sofa with her legs up, baby Zara balanced on a cushion, suckling peacefully at her breast. She's been an amazing friend, stuck by me through some awful times, offered me sympathy, comfort, and a few harsh words of truth along the way too. When Mum and Dad were killed, she was the first person to get in touch. She knew how devastated I would be, how I'd struggle to cope. I couldn't have got through the last twenty-one months without her. There's only one problem with my friendship with Molly – she doesn't like Jack.

'What's he got to complain about?' she says. 'He's living in an incredible house right by the sea. Anyway, if you love someone, you don't care where you live.'

'It's not an incredible house at the moment; it's a building site,' I reply, trying to defend him.

'Well, whatever …' I hear the baby gurgling contentedly. 'Look, I totally get why you want to help this woman, I think it's a great thing to do. Looking after other people can be very healing. Don't worry so much about Jack. Trust your instincts, girl, do what you think is right.' We end the call with kisses for little Zara and promises to meet up soon.

It was good to talk to Molly, but I don't feel any clearer in my mind about what to do. It's easy for her to dismiss Jack's feelings – she thinks he only got together with me because I had money, which isn't true, although I did once overhear him referring to me as 'the heiress'. She's right that it's my house, not his – he doesn't even pay rent. Technically, if I want Lori to stay, there's nothing he can do about it. But our relationship doesn't work like that. We're building a future together and this house is at the centre of it. Once we're married, it will be jointly owned. This could be a forever home, where we can raise a family and grow old in each other's arms. I don't want to put all that in jeopardy, and yet ... I can't turf Lori out either.

learned the rules of the house, but my parents also took a lot of short-stay emergency cases. They often arrived while I was asleep, and I wouldn't know anything about it until I met the new faces at the breakfast table.

'Right, can't sit here all day, much as I'd like to,' says Alan, rising to his feet.

Lori looks up. 'Can I help? I don't mind what I do. Passing tools, holding things steady … I could strip some wallpaper if you like. Or do some painting.'

Alan hesitates. 'I'm better off working by myself …'

'And you need to rest,' I say.

'But I'd rather be doing something, take my mind off it,' Lori says. 'And it's a way of paying you back.'

'I don't need paying back.'

'I know, but I'd like to.' She twists a strand of hair between her nail-bitten fingers. 'I'm not a sponger, you know. I'm a good worker.'

Alan shrugs. 'You could do some wallpaper stripping in one of the back bedrooms, I suppose.'

'I won't get in your way, promise.'

'Okay,' I say. 'If you're sure that's what you want to do, but only if you feel up to it.'

'I'll be fine.' She gives me a swollen, lopsided smile. 'Be up in a minute.' She gathers the dirty plates and mugs and fills the washing-up bowl with soapy water.

Alan plods upstairs, singing an old Queen song. I put the pot of jam away, even though it's empty.

Back in the slightly more comfortable surroundings of the bedroom, I power up my laptop to do some more research into support for victims of domestic violence. At the moment, it's okay. Lori is safe and Jack's none the wiser. But she can't stay here indefinitely. Hiding her from him is hard enough during the week, but the weekend would be impossible. She *has* to be gone by Friday evening. If she won't go to the police, she should at least try Social Services or one of those charities for domestic abuse survivors. There are some fantastic organisations out there that offer help. I'm sure they'll do everything they can to find her somewhere else to live. But she has to ask.

Rising from my desk, I leave the room and go into the hallway. Banging sounds are coming from upstairs. The radio is blasting out even more loudly than usual and I can hear Lori and Alan calling out to each other above the music. I climb the stairs, rehearsing a few lines in my head.

Alan is ripping up the floorboards in what will eventually be our master bedroom, and Lori is in the room opposite. She's back in her bloodstained clothes, a bucket of water at her side, metal scraper in hand. One wall has already been stripped, revealing patches of crumbling plaster.

'It's nearly lunchtime,' I say. 'Come down when you want a break.'

'Don't worry about me, I've got my sandwiches, remember?' She nods in the direction of the foil packet sitting on the windowsill.

'Well don't work too hard. Anyway, I could do with talking to you about … well, you know …' I tail off, pathetically.

'I just want to finish this alcove.'

'Fine. When you're ready … I'm around all afternoon.'

Hurrying downstairs, I fix myself some lunch, then go back to my room. I'm not handling this very well. I need to be more assertive, but it's difficult when she's so much older than me. Maybe I should just go ahead and fix an appointment for her tomorrow.

But an appointment with whom?

I go back to the internet. Helplines are all well and good, I think, but it would be better if Lori could talk to someone face to face. The best place seems to be Citizens Advice. The nearest branch is in Laversham, about five miles inland; they run a drop-in

He brought a four-pack of beers for Dad and a bunch of flowers for Mum. Nothing for Abigail, though. The little girl didn't seem to notice; she was quite happy to help Grandma arrange her chrysanthemums in a vase.

'Eat all your veggies, sweetheart, and this afternoon we'll play hide-and-seek with Foxy in the garden,' Kay said. For the first time in her life, Abigail ate her carrots without complaining. But Foxy showed no interest in her. He was too busy concentrating on his charm offensive with Kay's parents. He complimented her mum's Yorkshire puddings and said her roast potatoes were the best he'd ever tasted.

'What line of work is your father in?' her dad asked. Kay winced inwardly. She already knew the sad story.

'I wouldn't know.' Foxy's voice began to falter. 'He abandoned us when I was six and my brother was barely two. My mum had a drink problem. I basically brought Micky up myself.'

'Oh dear, that's awful.' Mum ladled out another portion of crumble.

'Yes, they were difficult times,' he said. 'Still, I refuse to let my past hold me back. I've got a good job and I'm saving up for a house.'

'Good for you, lad,' declared Dad. 'Custard?'

After they'd eaten, the men talked football while the women washed up.

'What do you think?' Kay whispered, closing the serving hatch so they couldn't be overheard.

'He's lovely. Why on earth didn't you ask him over before? The poor boy has no mother to look after him. Next time you must invite his brother too.'

'I haven't met him yet,' she replied, omitting to mention that Micky was in prison for burglary. Apparently he'd only been the lookout, but he'd still been sentenced to nine months.

'He's obviously madly in love with you,' her mum added. 'You're a lucky girl, Kay. If I were you, I'd get a ring on your finger as soon as you can.'

He proposed on Valentine's Day – the first anniversary of their meeting. She was kind of expecting it because he was such a romantic. They went to a Berni Inn and ordered steak and chips and a bottle of sparkling wine. He got down on his knees in front of the whole restaurant and produced a ring from his trouser pocket.

'I love you with all my heart, Squirrel. Will you marry me and make me the happiest man in the world?'

She felt herself going pink all over. 'Yes, Foxy, you know I will,' she giggled.

As he slipped the ring on her engagement finger, everybody cheered and applauded. It was deeply embarrassing and wonderful all at the same time. Kay held out her left hand and wiggled her finger, making the solitary sapphire sparkle in the candlelight. She would have preferred a diamond – diamonds were for ever, after all – but it didn't matter. The ring would have cost him a couple of months' wages and was probably the best he could afford.

For the rest of the meal they discussed wedding arrangements and where they would live afterwards. Not that there was much to discuss – he'd already planned every detail.

'We don't want the fuss of a church service,' he told her. 'A registry office will do. We'll have a small reception at the social club. They do a good spread and there's a DJ I know who can provide the disco. I'll pop down there this week and sort out a date.'

'June or July would be best,' Kay said, trying to hide her disappointment about not having a white wedding. He was right, of course; she was hardly a blushing virgin. Her mother's harsh words – *shop-soiled, damaged goods* – still echoed in her head. She was lucky to have found anyone to take her on at all. But the best thing of all about getting married was that Abigail would finally have a daddy.

Her parents were thrilled and her father offered to foot the reception bill. But they couldn't get married until September, because Micky was still serving his sentence and he had to be best man. Kay told everyone that he was working on an oil rig in the North Sea and wasn't allowed any time off. It was touch and go that he was going to be released in time, but he just made it.

When Micky turned up at the registry office, Kay was struck by how similar the brothers looked. Both big men, they shared the same solid jaw, the same intense blue eyes. Together they looked like a force to be reckoned with.

'You're the luckiest girl in the world, you know,' said Micky, giving her a bear hug. 'Make sure you treat him right.'

Friday 10 September 1976, the day they got married. The day it started.

After the hottest, driest summer on record, September was a washout. They'd had to have their photos taken indoors because of the torrential rain. But it hadn't dampened anyone's spirits. Everything was fine until they arrived at the social club and Foxy went to the bar. Kay didn't clock how much he was drinking because she was busy greeting her guests and talking to aunts and uncles she hadn't seen for years. She was no longer the black sheep of the family and wanted to make the most of her new respectability. Her parents seemed happy too, relieved that she was finally off their hands. Dad was set to give his father-of-the-bride speech, and would no doubt come up with the old joke about not losing a daughter so much as gaining a bedroom – or in their case, two.

She moved on to a group of old school friends, Ruth, Elaine, Sue and Debbie, and their respective partners, Dave S, Dave W, Pete and Colin. She knew Ruth's Dave from school, but didn't know the other lads very well. They asked her where she was going for her honeymoon, and she told them that they were staying at a hotel in Nevansey for the night and catching a plane the next day for a week in Jersey.

'Where will you be living?' asked Ruth's Dave.

'We're renting a little house on the Fairmead estate,' she explained. 'It's virtually brand new.'

'You're going to be just around the corner from us,' said Sue, who was also newly married. 'You must come over for dinner sometime.'

'We'd love to,' Kay replied enthusiastically. Living with her husband, looking after her own place, dinner parties with friends – it all sounded so grown-up. 'As long as we can get a babysitter.'

Abigail was running around in her shepherdess bridesmaid dress, her jet-black hair and dark skin making her look anything but an English rose. Kay was briefly reminded of Miguel Angel, and metaphorically stuck two fingers up at him. If he could see her now … She hadn't let him bring her down; she'd overcome so many barriers and was proud of what she'd achieved as a single mum. But now things were changing, and a new, easier life was ahead.

She glanced across the room to Foxy. He was standing at the bar with his brother, sipping a pint and scowling in her direction. She blew him a kiss but he didn't respond. What was wrong? Had she done something to upset him? She weaved her way through the crowds, who were shuffling into a line for the buffet.

'I'm gasping,' she said. 'Can you get me a glass of wine, love?'

He frowned down at her, making her feel even smaller. 'You've had enough already by the look of it.'

'What? I've only had one glass.' She put her hands on her hips. 'Come on, I'm thirsty. I've been talking to our guests.'

'Talking? Flirting more like. We've been watching you, haven't we, Micky?' His voice was cold. Micky nodded sagely and downed his pint.

'I've been chatting to my aunts and uncles, telling them how great you are. Don't be silly, Foxy. Come and meet them.' She held out her hand, but he didn't take it.

'Who's that bloke in the red tie?' He waved his glass in the direction of her school friends.

'You mean Dave? He's Ruth's boyfriend, I knew him at school.'

'What do you mean, "knew him"?'

'He was in my class. We were ... he was ...' Now she was getting flustered. 'Nothing. He's been going out with Ruth for years.'

'We thought he must be an old flame,' said Micky.

'Well you're wrong, he's not even a friend ... Foxy, please, I'm telling the truth.'

He drew her close and pinned her against the bar, pinching her hard on the arm where nobody could see and keeping up the pressure. The pain stung sharply.

'I love you so much, Kay,' he whispered into her ear. 'You belong to me now. Don't you dare break my heart.'

CHAPTER EIGHT

Stella

Now

I'm up and dressed by half-seven, tired from yet another sleepless night but keen to get on with the day's task: Operation Help Lori. It's really important that I get her to Citizens Advice this morning. With a bit of luck, they might even be able to find her accommodation for tonight.

I make a bowl of porridge and carry it to the back of the house, eating it standing up while I gaze through the conservatory window at the frost-covered garden. Straggly bushes are crawling across the lawn; some extremely tall weeds are growing out of a lumpy mound where the vegetable patch used to be. The rockery is so overgrown you can't see the rocks any more. It's completely out of control, but who knows when we'll be able to tackle it. Alan has made a start on the inside, but it's far too big a job for one person. I feel overwhelmed by the thought of everything that needs doing and how much it's all going to cost. The claggy porridge sticks in my throat and I hurry back to the kitchen to spit it out.

Alan enters the house with a loud 'Morning!' addressed to the world in general. Wiping my mouth, I walk into the hallway to greet him.

'How's it going?' he asks. 'Is Lori still here?'

'Yes. At least I think so. Haven't seen her yet today. Why do you ask?'

'Only I half expected she'd be back with her bloke by now. She was making all kinds of excuses for him yesterday – he's been under a lot of strain, got an anger-management problem, takes it out on her because she's closest and he loves her the most. Load of bollocks. You don't hit someone you love, full stop.'

'I don't understand why she won't go the police,' I say. 'I mean, he's gone and attacked her mother now.'

'Maybe he's already on a suspended sentence or something. She could be scared of what he might do to her if he gets sent down.'

'But he won't be able to do anything if he's in prison.'

Alan laughs. 'You think? Ha. Men like that always find a way. You've no idea what goes on inside.'

'Yes I do,' I retort. 'I know there's a lot of violence and drugs and prisoners carry on committing crimes. I'm not stupid.'

He raises his hands in surrender. 'No, I know you're not. Sorry, love, I didn't mean to offend you. You're a lovely kind girl. If you were my daughter, I'd be very proud. Now, excuse me, I'd better get a move on.' He tips the brim of his cap in a mock salute and goes straight upstairs. Within seconds, the sound of his radio is drifting down to the ground floor.

Alan's kind words linger wistfully in my head. They *would* have been proud of me, I think. Proud, and a little surprised. Of course, the irony is that none of this would be happening if they hadn't been killed. Was it an accident? My thoughts drift back to those weeks after their death, when the police came to interview me. As the driver hadn't stopped, there was speculation that it might have been a deliberate hit. Mum and Dad followed the same routine every evening, taking the dog out after the ten o'clock news to give him a last walk before bed. They always took the same route around the village and had done so for the last twenty years.

'Did your parents have any enemies?' asked the detective.

'Quite the opposite,' I replied. 'They were very much loved.'

'Only one of the neighbours said there was an incident, about thirteen years ago. Some boy who tried to set the house on fire. Do you think it could be him, still bearing some kind of grudge?'

'I very much doubt it,' I replied. 'Kyle was just a troubled kid who'd got in with the wrong crowd. He didn't know any better.'

'Well, if you can think of any other candidates, please let me know.'

There *were* other candidates – a few former foster kids who'd grown up to follow in their parents' criminal footsteps – but the whole idea seemed far-fetched. The police made some enquiries but nobody fitted the frame. Kyle, the most obvious culprit, was serving a prison sentence.

I go back to the kitchen and clean the porridge pan, feeling increasingly uneasy as I scrape at the congealed mess. Why hasn't Lori surfaced yet? Yesterday we agreed that we'd leave as early as possible after breakfast to be first in the queue. But I haven't heard a squeak out of her yet.

The minutes tick by. I tidy up the bedroom and apply some make-up. I check my emails, although nothing interesting has come in overnight. I sit on the edge of the bed and think about Mum. Would she ever have deceived Dad in the way I'm deceiving Jack? I can't imagine it. The two of them were always a team, stuck together like glue. Although it was incredibly shocking, it was fitting in a strange way that they died together. If one of them had been left on their own, I don't think they'd have coped.

I hear footsteps coming slowly down the stairs and go into the hallway.

'Sorry I'm late,' Lori says, steadying herself on the banisters. 'I've been throwing up. Just nerves …'

I feel instantly guilty. She cuts a tragic figure in my ill-fitting patterned trousers and shapeless jumper. 'Oh God, you don't have

a coat, do you? And you can't go out in those slippers, your toes
will drop off. Let me find something for you … Um, what size
do you take?'

Her feet are a size bigger than mine, so she has to make do
with the floral wellies that I wear at festivals. I lend her my red
jacket – it's the only coat that will fit around her hips. Nothing
matches, and the colours are too bright for her mood. She looks
like a depressed children's entertainer; the livid bruises on her
cheek could almost be smudges of face paint. But she'll have to do.

I pick up my keys. 'Ready?' She nods, but looks terrified.

I open the front door and she emerges like a wary animal
venturing out of its den, sniffing the air, looking for predators.
We get in the car, and she immediately locks herself in. I back
onto the Esplanade, then take the first left, heading for the main
road that leads out of town. Lori slides down in her seat, head
lowered, her left hand shielding her face. But nobody is looking.

'What were you doing in the turret room last night?' I ask as
we leave Nevansey and drive onto the dual carriageway.

'I don't know what you mean,' she replies.

'The room on the corner with the pointy roof.'

'Oh, there. I was just exploring. It's a fantastic room; you can
see almost all the way around.'

'Yes, I know, it's my favourite room in the house. But you
should be careful, Lori. Jack saw you looking out of the window.'

'Oh no, I'm sorry,' she says. 'I didn't want to get you into
trouble. What did you say?'

'I didn't have to say anything; he thought it was a trick of the
light. We got away with it, but it could have been Darren out there.'

'You're right. I won't risk it again.'

'Well, with a bit of luck, Citizens Advice will find you somewhere safe to sleep tonight.'

'Your petrol light is flashing.' She points at the dashboard.

'Oh shit. Sorry, I'd better stop. Don't suppose you happen to know where the nearest petrol station is?'

'Not far. On the other side of the roundabout.'

'Great. I'll be as quick as I can. Sorry about this.'

I find the garage and pull up next to the pumps. Lori shuffles even further down in her seat and covers her face. I fill up and go inside to pay. The cashier is on the phone and makes me wait while she finishes her call. I tap impatiently on the counter.

'Okay, let's get going,' I say, climbing back into the car and switching on the engine. Just then, a battered blue car pulls in off the road. It doesn't go to the pumps, just stops in the middle of the forecourt.

'Oh fuck! It's him!' says Lori, looking into the wing mirror. 'Drive! Drive, Stella!'

'What?' I swivel round. 'You sure?'

'It's his car! It's Darren. Drive! Now!' Her tone is so insistent, I put my foot down and screech out of the garage. Luckily, there's a gap in the traffic so I can immediately turn onto the road.

As I drive on, my eyes dart between the rear and wing mirrors. 'Are you sure it's him?'

'Yes! Oh my God, I knew this would happen!'

'Where is he now? I can't see the car.'

She looks behind us. 'He's trying to turn out of the garage … There's too much traffic.'

'And you're sure it's definitely, definitely him?'

'Yes … Shit. Some idiot's let him out!'

'Even if it is him, he can't have seen you; you were virtually lying down.'

'I don't know how he knew, but he's following us. He's going to try and overtake. I can see him edging out. Can you go any faster?'

'Not really.'

'We've got to lose him! Can't you suddenly spin round and go back the other way?'

'I'm not a stunt driver, Lori.'

I'm trying to concentrate on the road ahead and look behind at the same time. There are several cars following me; I can't tell if the blue car is one of them. This is absurd. It can't be Darren. It's too much of a coincidence.

'I think you're just being paranoid.'

'I *know* it's him, I know it! He's going to hunt us down.' I glance in the mirror. A dark blue car is nosing out, trying to pick off the intervening vehicles. 'See? That's him, he's coming to get me. You've got to do something!'

Adrenalin shoots through my veins. The van in front of me is going too slowly. I'm going to have to overtake, but there isn't enough room.

'He'll ram us off the road,' cries Lori. 'You've got to go faster.'

'I can't!' I shout. 'How does he know where you are?'

'I think he must be tracking my phone.'

'What?! Then turn it off! Now.'

She digs into her bag and takes out her mobile, fumbling with the button. 'Sorry, I didn't know.'

Another look in the mirror tells me that Darren – if it *is* Darren and not just some jerk on a suicide mission – has sneaked forward. There are only three cars between us. A junction is coming up; the traffic lights are green. I've got to get across. Taking a deep breath, I put my foot down and pull into the middle of the road, overtaking the van. An oncoming car hoots as I squeeze past, darting back into the nearside lane just as the lights turn amber, then red. Without thinking, I shoot across the junction, narrowly missing a car turning right.

'Jesus Christ!' My heart crashes into my ribs.

'Ha! He's stuck!' Lori says. 'Brilliant! Nice one, Stella.'

'I nearly killed us,' I retort, feeling breathless and sweaty. 'I can't do this, it's frigging dangerous.'

'Turn left here, then we can double back,' she orders. 'I know the side roads, I'll direct you.'

'We're supposed to be going to Citizens Advice.'

'We can't, it's too risky,' she replies. 'He'll be looking for us. We should go home ... Next left.'

My pulse is still racing as I drive back to the house, looking anxiously in the rear-view mirror for Darren's car. But there's no sign of him. If it ever *was* him, that is ...

As soon as I pull onto the driveway, Lori gets out and runs to the front door. I let us in and she shuts it behind us with a dramatic sigh of relief.

'We made it,' she says. 'Safe at last.'

I take off my coat. 'This doesn't make sense, Lori. I mean, if Darren's had a tracker on your phone, he must already know where you're staying.'

She bites her lip. 'I guess.'

'So if that's the case, why did he go and smash up your mum's house? Why hasn't he come straight to find you?'

'I don't know. Perhaps he was waiting till I went out?'

'But nobody followed us to the petrol station. Are you sure it was him?' She nods insistently. 'You didn't just see a car that looked a bit like his and panic?'

'No! At least, I don't think so ...'

'Did you catch the registration number?'

She shakes her head. 'I don't know it. It's his car; he doesn't let me drive it.'

'Hmm ...' I can't stop myself heaving an irritable sigh. 'Well, we've missed the drop-in session now.'

'Sorry.' She sits on the bottom stair and takes off the wellies. 'We'll go tomorrow, yeah?'

'They don't run sessions tomorrow. Just Tuesdays and Thursdays.'

'I don't suppose they'd be able to help anyway.' She puts the boots neatly by the door. 'Probably just give me a load of useless leaflets.'

'The thing is, Lori, if that *was* Darren and he *is* tracking your phone, you're not safe here any more.'

'I don't know for *certain* he was tracking my phone,' she says quickly. 'I mean, I don't think he'd know how to do it. He's not very good at that kind of thing.'

'So it was just chance that he happened to be at the petrol station.'

'It's where he usually fills up. I was on the lookout, so when the blue car arrived, I instantly thought, oh shit, it's him.' She looks down, shamefaced. 'But maybe it wasn't. I don't know, I'm not sure now.'

I pace about the hallway. 'You made me run a red light. We could have had an accident.'

'I'm sorry.'

'That's how my parents were killed. Some wanker in a residential street driving twenty miles over the speed limit.'

Her hands shoot up to her face. 'I'm really, really sorry. I just got confused. I was scared. Sorry, sorry, please forgive me. I'm a mess, I don't know what I'm doing. I feel like I'm going mad.' She starts to cry again, pitiful tears streaming down her bruised cheeks.

I sit on the step next to her and put my arm around her shoulders. 'It's okay, Lori. It wasn't good, but we're okay, nobody got hurt. Just calm down, eh?'

This is impossible. What am I supposed to do? The poor woman's in a desperate state. If I turn her out into the cold, she'll probably jump off the end of the pier. There's no choice. Like it or not, I'm going to have to let her stay.

CHAPTER NINE

Stella

Now

Alan finds me in the conservatory – that's how the estate agents described it in the sales brochure. In reality, it's a rickety lean-to with a white plastic corrugated roof.

'Bloody hell, it's like a freezer in here,' he says. 'Everything okay, love?'

'Um, yeah … sort of.' I pull a blanket further across my chest, gripping it tightly. But things are not okay. It's Friday afternoon and Lori is still here. She's been stripping wallpaper in between running up and down the stairs to keep Alan supplied with tea. They seem to get on incredibly well. He brought her home-made sandwiches again, and I could hear them joking around during his lunch break. She seems to have recovered from yesterday's trauma, but my nerves are still frazzled. I'm constantly imagining Darren prowling the street outside, or sitting in his car waiting to pounce on me the moment I open the front door. Last night, I could have sworn I heard someone pacing about on the drive. When the wind rattled the window frames, I thought he was trying to break in.

I wanted to confess to Jack that Lori was still here, just in case Darren attacked the house. But I was worried that he'd chuck her out immediately with nowhere to go. If Darren *does* know where Lori is, it would be like handing her to him on a plate.

This subterfuge can't go on. I promised myself that I'd tell Jack this morning before he left for work, but for some reason the words refused to leave my mouth. Then I composed an email, admitting all, but was too scared to send it. He'll be home soon and I don't know what I'm going to do.

'I'm done for the day,' says Alan, breaking into my thoughts.

'Okay. Thanks.' I glance out of the window, and sure enough, the sun has sunk rapidly behind the houses and the jungle garden is bathed in an eerie blue light. 'Have a good weekend.'

He hesitates. 'It's, um, pay day?'

'Oh God, sorry, it went right out of my head.'

'Don't worry about it now, but if I could have it on Monday morning?'

'Of course, I'll go to the bank first thing.'

'And there's that five hundred quid for materials I spoke to you about?'

'Yes, sorry.' I smack my forehead. 'Doh! What with everything that's been going on, it slipped my mind.'

He hovers for a few seconds, hands stuffed into the pockets of his overalls. 'So, er … what's happening about Lori? I thought she was leaving, but now she's saying you're letting her stay on.'

'For a few more days, just until she sorts herself out.'

'It's very good of you.' He removes his cap and wipes his face with a handkerchief. 'Not many people would take someone in on trust. Everyone's so suspicious nowadays. They want police checks and references, five-star ratings, online reviews … They want to know all about your past, every little mistake you've ever made. Do one thing wrong and that's it, you're finished. Nobody gets a second chance.'

'Lori hasn't done anything wrong. She's a victim.'

'I think you'll find they're called survivors these days.'

I nod, impressed. 'Yes, you're right. Lori's a survivor.' *Or she will be, as long as she can stay safe.*

Jack doesn't arrive home until nearly midnight. Often I moan when he calls to say he's going to be late, but this evening I encouraged him to stay out as long as he liked.

'How was your day?' he asks me, sitting on the bed to unlace his shoes.

'Fine, thanks,' I say into the pillow. Guilt sits in the bottom of my stomach like a bad meal. I so want to tell him that Lori's still here – I spent most of the evening working out what I was going to say – but now it's late, we're tired and he's had a few drinks. It's not the right time for a deep chat.

He gets undressed and cuddles into my back. I smell beer and dried sweat and another, indefinable smell that is just him. I love him so much. It's horrible lying to him like this; it almost feels like I'm being unfaithful. I'll tell him tomorrow morning over breakfast. Then if he makes Lori leave, at least she'll have the whole day to find somewhere else.

'It's been one hell of a week,' he mumbles into my shoulder. His cheeks are still cold from walking back from the station. 'I'm so glad it's the weekend and we've got the house to ourselves.' I don't reply. He slips off the left strap of my pyjama top and cups my breast. 'We still haven't christened the new bed properly yet.'

'Not now, Jack. I'm tired.' I gently remove his hand.

'It was such a piss-off, that awful woman knocking at the door.'

'She's not an awful woman,' I snap. 'She was desperate, she needed help.'

He sighs. 'You're so like your parents, always taking in waifs and strays. I wish I'd met them; they sound like pretty amazing people.'

'They were,' I say.

'I'm sorry I was negative about it. I was worried for your safety, that's all. It could have turned out really badly. Next time some woman knocks on the door in the middle of the night, we're not answering, okay?'

'There won't be a next time. I rang all the helplines and told them this was no longer a refuge.'

'Good. The estate agents should have warned us. I mean, nobody said.'

'I *like* that it was a refuge,' I say quietly.

'Really? Why?'

'It makes me feel proud of the house.'

He laughs. 'It's not a person, it's a building.' He kisses me on the shoulder before turning onto his side. 'Sweet dreams.'

We make love in the bright, cold light of morning, diving under the duvet like we're in a tent. I want him so much and yet I can't stop my mind from drifting to Lori and the confession I've got to make. The thought of her upstairs is very inhibiting. What if she can hear us thrashing about?

'Shh,' I whisper as he groans with pleasure.

'Why? I can't help it if you drive me crazy with desire.' He sticks his head out of the duvet and shouts, 'My girlfriend is the most beautiful, gorgeous, sexy—'

'Stop it!'

He flops onto his back and groans. 'What's wrong, Stella? Why are you being so uptight?'

Tell him. Go on, tell him now.

'I don't know. Sorry … I'm just …' I feel a hard lump in my throat. 'Too stressed.'

His tone softens. 'Hey, don't get upset, babe. It's supposed to be fun.'

'Please, just make love to me gently.' I lean over to kiss him on the lips and we tumble into each other. Softly. Deeply. The knots of tension loosen, and at last it feels like I've come home.

Poor Lori, I think an hour later when we still haven't got up. She must be desperate for a cup of tea. At last Jack goes off to shower and I text her to say we should be leaving the house in the next half-hour. We've been in the habit of going out for Saturday brunch almost as long as we've been together, so he won't be suspicious when I hurry him out of the door.

However, it's not that easy to get Saturday brunch in Nevansey. At least, not the kind of brunch we're used to. It's all 'full English' here – heart attack on a plate. I'm afraid we're more the scrambled eggs and smoked salmon type. We've even been known to add slices of avocado. The only half-decent place is on the other side of the pier, where the beautiful old Georgian town houses are, although most of them have been turned into cheap hotels, their once elegant facades festooned with plastic banners offering discounts for stag and hen parties.

Fortunately, green shoots of new life are sprouting in one of the cobbled passageways that run between the seafront and the lower half of the high street. I found Back Lane a few weeks ago when I was trying to get my boots re-heeled. There's no shoe repairer, but it does boast a vinyl record shop, a tiny boutique selling vintage bags and hand-knitted berets, and Cathy's Café. It's where all the down-from-Londoners hang out, not that there are many of us. The café doesn't do cooked breakfast, but the croissants and pain au chocolat are home-made and the coffee's organic.

We walk down the Esplanade, his arm around my shoulders and mine around his waist, my fingers hooked into the belt of his jeans. Our hips rub together as we jolt along, still wanting to be one flesh. The afterglow of our lovemaking clings to us like perfume. If only I could bottle it and spray it over us every time we have a problem. It feels so good now, but when I tell him about Lori, I know the positive atmosphere is going to evaporate instantly.

'Mmm, good coffee,' Jack says. 'Well done for finding this place. We should come here every Saturday after we've had sex.'

I lick buttery flakes of croissant off my fingers. 'Shh! People can hear you.'

'So what? Why are you always so bothered about what other people think?' He leans across the table and snogs me.

'For God's sake, you're like a teenager,' I say, but it's good to know that he wants me, that despite all the recent disruption in our lives, we're fundamentally still okay.

'I think we should go home and do it all over again, don't you?' he says, as we come out of the café and retrace our steps to the seafront.

'Hmm,' I say, linking arms. 'Actually, I need to look at some flooring today.'

'Boring.' He catches my reproving look. 'Yeah, yeah, I know, it's got to be done. It's just, well, it's not my house, is it? I'm just the lodger – the live-in lover.'

'Yeah, but one day ...' I feel myself redden. 'One day maybe you'll be the joint owner.'

He laughs. 'You're only saying that to make me come to the DIY store with you.'

'No, I'm not. I'm serious.' The implications of what I've just said hang like a breath in the air, but he doesn't pick up on them. We walk on, our pace slackening. My stomach clenches and I re-taste the sweet almond croissant. I feel him slipping away from me, little by little.

He halts for a moment, turning to face the sea. The mist has lifted, and it's turning into a sharp, bright day. Horizontal blocks of mud, water and sky stretch before us like a contemporary landscape painting. 'Nevansey is a dump,' he says. 'No matter what you do to the house, you can't change its location.'

'But I love the location. The views are amazing; you can't get any closer to the sea.'

'The town sucks. It needs more nice cafés, an art gallery, an independent cinema …'

'I know, but it's on the up and up,' I insist. 'In a few years' time it'll be just as good as Whitstable, if not better.'

'Hmm …' he answers doubtfully.

He lets go of my hand and we walk up the hill in silence. My plan had been to text Lori to give her advance warning of our return, but there's no way I can do it now without Jack asking questions. My feeling of dread increases the nearer we get to the house. What if she's having breakfast in the kitchen, or sitting in the conservatory?

'Jack …' I start, then stop, not knowing what to say.

'What?'

'There's something I need to …' But it's too late. He's already unlocking the front door and stepping into the hallway.

My heart's in my mouth as I listen out for sounds of life, but the house is as quiet as when we left it. Jack walks into the kitchen and I follow him like a nervous puppy.

'God, it's icy in here,' he says. 'There's a gale-force wind blowing. Is the back door open or something?'

'Um, I'll go and check.'

'It's what my mum calls an invitation to burglars,' he calls after me, chuckling to himself.

I rush into the conservatory and see that the door is indeed wide open. But where's Lori? I step onto the patio and peer down the garden, catching a glimpse of my jumper moving between the overgrown bushes at the bottom. She must have gone down there for a cigarette, making sure she was far enough away for the smell not to drift into the house. I close the door without locking it and go back to the kitchen.

'Yes, the door *was* open,' I say casually. 'Sorry, must have been me.'

But Jack isn't listening to me. He's got a mobile phone in his hand. It's plugged into my charger on the counter. Its cover is pink and shiny.

'What's this?' he says. 'Some kind of secret phone?'

I feel my cheeks flame. 'No, no, it's … I, er … um … I can explain.'

He wrenches it free of the cable and passes it to me. 'I hope so. 'Cos somebody has just sent you a rather strange text.'

'It's not mine, it's …' The rest of the sentence hangs in mid-air as I stare down at the words in the tiny box.

Come back now or you'll be sorry. Love you for ever, D xxxxx

CHAPTER TEN

Stella

Now

Jack gives me a thunderous look. 'What the hell's going on, Stella?'

'It's nothing to do with me – this is Lori's phone,' I say, resting it on the counter.

He blinks several times, taking the information in. 'Right … So … what, she left it here?'

'She's in the garden, having a smoke.' I glance anxiously towards the conservatory, hoping she won't come back inside just yet.

'But how … I mean, how did she get in? When did she come back?' He sees the shame flooding my face and his expression darkens. 'Oh, I get it. She never left, did she? Jesus Christ …'

'Sorry. I was going to tell you last night, but—'

His voice rises. 'She's been here all week and you weren't going to tell me until *last night*?'

'I know. I'm sorry, really sorry. I wanted to tell you but I was frightened you'd chuck her out.'

'Yeah, because I don't trust her. When are you going to wise up? Remember that time that tosser got fifty quid off you – *fifty* quid – for a train ticket to go and see his dying granny?' He puffs out a breath. 'They must see you coming a mile off.'

'Lori's genuine. You can't fake bruises.'

'You're too kind for your own good, Stella.'

'No I'm not,' I say sharply. 'I know what I'm doing, I'm not a fool.'

'I get that you own this house, but I live here too. Don't I have *any* say in who stays here? I gave up living in London to move down to this dump. I did it because I wanted to be with you, because I thought our relationship was going somewhere. But you behave like my opinions don't matter; if you don't agree with them, you just go behind my back, do what you want regardless. You care more about a total stranger than me!'

I feel myself heating up. 'That's not true, you know that's not true. I've been trying to help her leave but it's not that simple. There's nowhere for her to go. A lot of refuges have closed—'

He bats my words away. 'I couldn't give a shit about that. I'm talking about *us*. About simple things like honesty and discussing things and reaching a joint decision.' I flinch as he bangs his fist on the worktop. 'We've been talking about getting married, for fuck's sake!'

'But you weren't being very understanding or kind. I felt, as another woman, that I had a duty to help.'

'What about your "duty" to me? You don't seem to care about that. You lied to me – you betrayed me.'

'I didn't betray you, that's ridiculous.' I feel my back arch with annoyance. 'I was just trying to sort out a difficult problem the best way I could. I'm really sorry I lied to you … well, I didn't actually lie, but I didn't tell you Lori was still here and I feel bad about that. But it was only because you were so unreasonable.'

'You're calling *me* unreasonable?' he fumes. 'I let you bring a total stranger into our house, I allowed her to stay overnight, even though I thought it was a really shit idea.' He comes right up to me and jabs with his finger. '*You're* the unreasonable one, you're way out of line!'

'Leave her alone.' We both turn around to see Lori standing in the doorway, hands on hips. 'Don't you dare touch her.'

'What?' snarls Jack.

'It's okay, Lori,' I say quickly.

'Keep out of it,' he barks. 'This is nothing to do with you. You shouldn't even be here.'

But she stands her ground. 'Your girlfriend's a really lovely person. She's been helping me. I don't know what I would have done without her.'

Jack draws in a furious breath.

'Please, Lori, would you mind? We need to sort this out.'

'My husband did this to me.' She carries on undeterred. 'Then he went around to my mum's and smashed up her place because she wouldn't tell him where I was. Stella looked after me, gave me clothes, food and drink—'

'Yeah, I know, she's the patron saint of good causes. It runs in the family.'

'She took me to Citizens Advice. Darren followed us but she helped me escape, even drove through a red light to shake him off.' Jack's eyebrows shoot up into his hairline.

Please don't go on, Lori. You're making it worse.

'Wha … what?' he splutters. 'You were in a car chase and you never told me?'

'It wasn't as bad as it sounds,' I say. 'Lori wasn't sure it was Darren, she just panicked.' But he stares at me like he no longer knows who I am.

'This is crazy. You're *both* crazy.' He takes his mobile from his back pocket. 'I'm calling the police.'

'No! Please don't!' Lori rushes forward, eyes wide with alarm.

'But there's a maniac prowling about outside my house …'

I put my hand on his arm. 'There's no evidence for that. She hasn't told anyone where she is, have you, Lori?'

'No, I promise.'

'Stella!' He shakes me off angrily. 'Get a grip. This is serious. We have to call the police – for our own sakes.' His finger swipes into the call screen.

Lori's hands go up in surrender. 'Please, please don't! I'll leave right now, okay? Just don't call them, I'm begging you.'

'Jack – please just hold back for a moment. This is getting out of control. We all need to calm down.'

'*I* need to calm down?' He paces up and down. 'This is insane.'

I turn to Lori. 'I don't want you to leave, but you have to tell us why you don't want the police involved.'

'Are you on the run or something?' says Jack. She shakes her head.

'Is it because you're frightened of Darren?' I try.

'Yes, but it's not that. If the police find out, it'll ruin everything.' She presses her eyes to push back the tears. 'I'm sorry, I'm sorry, you just don't understand.'

I go up to her, putting my arm on her shoulders and peering into her swollen face. The bruises are already turning green and yellow at the edges. 'We can't understand if you don't explain. Let's sit down in the other room and talk, eh? The three of us. You tell us what the problem is and then we'll decide the best thing to do about it.' I look up at Jack. 'Is that okay?'

He sighs wearily, putting his phone away. 'All right. I think you're mad, but yeah.'

I steer Lori into the front room and Jack follows. I lower her onto the bed, then sit cross-legged on the rug in front of her. Jack drags the swivel office chair forwards and perches awkwardly on its seat.

'Just tell us the truth, Lori,' I say, clasping my hands together.

She rolls her eyes upwards. 'Where do I start? Darren's got problems. He's always on a short fuse; you never know when he's going to blow. I try my best not to aggravate him, but he can't control himself ... It was starting to have a bad effect on the kids.'

'You've got *kids*?' I interrupt. 'You never told me.'

'A boy and a girl. Jamie's eight and Casey's six. I'm sorry. It's a complicated story, I didn't want to get into it. I feel so ashamed.'

'Honestly, Lori, you've nothing to be ashamed of. Has she, Jack?' I look to him for confirmation and he shakes his head slightly. 'So, what happened?'

'Jamie was having problems at school – being really aggressive towards the teachers, fighting in the playground. The school's involved in this family therapy scheme, and they offered us counselling. They had a good idea about what was going on at home, but there was no proof and I didn't want to get the police involved.'

'I still don't understand why not,' says Jack. 'Sounds like your husband needs to be behind bars.'

'The most Darren would have got was six months, and he'd have been out in three. I'd have got the blame and it would have just made things worse. He thinks the world of the kids, never lays a finger on them. It's only me he hurts.'

'I'm sorry, I still don't get it,' Jack says. 'Why stay with the bastard?'

I lean forward. 'So where are your children now? At home with Darren?'

'No ... I started having these therapy sessions, and when I admitted what was going on, they informed Social Services. They decided it wasn't a safe environment for the kids so they took them away.' She starts to cry. I snatch a tissue from the box and pass it to her.

'You mean they're in foster care now?'

'Yeah.' She sniffs. 'Darren's not allowed any contact yet but I get to see them once a fortnight. It breaks my heart every time.

They're really confused and unhappy; they don't understand why they can't come home.'

'I'm sure they're being well looked after,' I say. 'My parents were foster carers. I grew up with kids like yours.'

A host of childhood memories come flooding back. Traumatised kids huddled beneath their duvets, determined not to wash or get dressed, pushing away the plates of nourishing food my mother had cooked, refusing to speak. Some of them settled down after a few days, but others never accepted the situation, no matter how abusive their previous home life had been or how generous and patient my parents were. At the time, I knew nothing about the circumstances that had brought them to our house; all I was told was that I had to be kind to them and treat them as part of the family.

'Sorry if I'm being thick here,' says Jack, 'but surely all you have to do is leave Darren and then you'll get the kids back and you can have a much better life.'

She shakes her head vehemently. 'No, no, it's not that simple. Like I said, Darren loves the kids and they love him. I want us to be a family. I was brought up without a dad and I missed out.'

'But Jack's right. He's abusing you, Lori – you can't have that.'

'He's trying to sort himself out. He's doing this course at weekends. If he gets the certificate and proves to Social Services he's changed, then we'll get the kids back and we can have a fresh start.'

I can't believe I'm hearing this. 'But he hasn't changed, has he? I mean, look what he did to you.'

'I know, but he's really sorry. He's begging me for forgiveness. If I go to the police, there's not a chance in hell we'll ever get the kids back and I don't know what Darren will do. He'll go mad. He'll blame me for everything. I'm frightened he'll kill me.'

Jack swivels impatiently in his chair, clasping his hands together. 'You're not thinking straight, Lori. None of this is your fault. You should go to the police, tell them the truth, get Social Services to help you and the kids get away from him for ever.'

'But it won't work. He'll track us down.'

'So what's the plan, Lori?' I say, feeling the frustration rise. 'You're going to go back to him, put up with the beatings, lie to Social Services, get the kids back under false pretences ... Is that what you want for them?'

'He's a good father.'

'No, he's a violent abuser.'

'Only to me.' She pushes a strand of hair away from her face, unconsciously revealing the cut on her cheek, the flesh not quite knitted together. 'I had to get away from him, for his own sake. He needs some time to cool off and come to his senses. Once he's done this course and got the certificate—'

'Oh Lori, Lori,' I cry. 'Can't you see this is never going to work?'

'But it might,' she replies, eyes shining with tears. 'It might. I just need a few weeks away from him, somewhere safe, where he can't find me. I would have gone to a hotel but I don't have any money. The bank took all my credit cards off me.'

She pauses to blow her nose. Jack and I exchange a private glance. Finally it feels like we're on the same side, even if it's one of astonishment and disbelief that anyone could be so stupid.

'So how come you knew about Westhill House?' Jack asks.

'The helpline—' she begins.

'Don't give me that bullshit. It hasn't been a refuge for at least three years; all the helplines must know that.'

'I rang them all, Lori,' I add, 'and every one of them insisted their database was up to date.'

'I didn't want to lie,' she mumbles, 'I thought if I said a charity had sent me here, you'd be more likely to take me in.'

'Then who told you it was a refuge?'

She shrugs. 'Oh, just some woman who stayed here a long time ago. She saw my bruises and knew what I was going through. She told me there was this big house in Nevansey on top of the hill, overlooking the beach. They took women in and looked after them, no questions asked. It was where she found her freedom, she said. When I decided to run away, it was the first place I thought of.'

I get to my knees and grab Lori's hands. 'Why didn't you tell us the truth from the beginning?'

'Because the truth usually gets me into trouble.'

Jack stands up. 'Lori? Would you mind giving me and Stella a few moments to talk?'

She nods. I let her go and she rises quickly, almost losing her balance. 'Please, let me stay a bit longer. I won't be any bother. I'll help out with the building, I'm a good worker. I've got a few quid in my purse – you can have it towards my keep. I won't eat much. Alan's been making me sandwiches and—'

'I don't know, Lori, we need to discuss it,' I say gently.

'Just a week or two,' she pleads. 'Until Darren's calmed down. Then I'll go home and I promise you'll never hear from me again.'

CHAPTER ELEVEN

Kay

Then

Kay spooned liquid fat from the roasting tray over the chicken. It smelt good, almost like one of her mother's Sunday dinners. She put the chicken back in the oven. The potatoes were browning nicely and soon it would be time to put on the vegetables – Foxy only liked thinly sliced carrots and frozen peas. She crumbled an Oxo cube into a Pyrex jug, listening to the conversation coming from the lounge. Micky was there. All the brothers ever talked about was football; it bored her stiff. But at least cooking the lunch gave her something to do.

They'd been married for six months, and by and large all was going well. He was still incredibly romantic – scarcely a week went by without him buying her a bunch of flowers, a small box of chocolates or a copy of her favourite magazine.

'I spoil you,' he said, kissing her on the top of her head like she was a child.

Her friends told her she was very lucky. 'He's so devoted. When you're out with him, he never takes his eyes off you.' They thought it was brilliant that he bought clothes for her – dresses, tops, skirts, even lingerie – and admired his taste. It wasn't often *her* taste, though. She wasn't a fan of baby pink, or blouses with frilly edges that made her neck itch. He didn't like her showing her cleavage, and last summer he'd made her wear a one-piece swimsuit on the beach, even though it was the hottest July on record. She'd felt so self-conscious when other girls were wearing scanty bikinis. A few had even gone topless.

'There's no way I'd ever let you do that,' he'd said, and she'd felt herself bristle inside. Not that she particularly wanted to bare her breasts to the world, but they were *her* breasts and she would have liked a say.

She opened the freezer compartment and took out the bag of peas, her forearm scraping the frosty bed of ice. She never mentioned the nasty pinch he'd given her at the wedding. The mark had quickly faded, but the nip of pain had lodged itself under her skin and refused to go away. She shut the fridge door. He was just drunk, she told herself for the thousandth time. He didn't mean to hurt me. And maybe she *had* been a little flirty with Ruth's boyfriend, although she hadn't meant anything by it – it had been fun to be the centre of attention for one day. Foxy seemed to have completely forgotten about the incident; why couldn't she do so too?

The conversation in the lounge was getting louder. 'Trevor Brooking is who you want midfield, he's got class,' Foxy was saying.

'Nah, he's a poncey git, mate.'

'You're talking crap.'

She heard the hiss of another beer can being opened. They'd already been to the pub earlier; why did they need more booze? She poured water over the sliced carrots and turned on the ring. At home – no, *this* was home now – they had a gas cooker. She wasn't used to the electric rings; they took ages to heat up, and she'd burnt herself a few times wiping them clean before they'd properly cooled down.

'When's dinner, Squirrel? We're starving to death,' Foxy said, coming into the kitchen and putting his arms around her waist from behind.

'Won't be long now.' She stared down at the carrot water, willing it to come to the boil. He nuzzled into her neck like an animal, his lips reaching for her ear.

'Stop it,' she whispered. 'I'm cooking.'

'Spoilsport.' He gave her left breast a sharp squeeze, then pulled away, going back to the lounge.

She rubbed herself to disperse the pain. The honeymoon period was showing little sign of coming to an end, certainly not in the bedroom department. He was still very attracted to her – a bit too much, if she was honest. They had sex nearly every night. The one time she'd refused, due to a terrible cold, he'd sulked for days, and there were no presents that week. It wasn't that he was unkind; he just didn't seem to notice when she was ill or tired. In his mind, she was always happy and smiling, eagerly waiting to see him at the end of the day. She hated disappointing him. Even if she felt exhausted, she still refreshed her make-up before he came through the door.

'You're the perfect wife, Mrs Foxton,' he said. 'Always bright-eyed and bushy-tailed.'

But being bright-eyed and bushy-tailed all the time was becoming a strain. If she ever dared to moan about work, he said things like 'It's easy for you, you're only part-time' or 'Standing around in a card shop isn't a proper job. Not compared to what *I* do.' He was right, she supposed; selling insurance demanded financial skills and strong powers of persuasion. It was a responsible position. But she had responsibilities too. There was little Abigail to look after, not to mention all the cleaning, cooking and shopping to fit in. When you added it together, she worked longer hours than him, but they didn't count because they weren't paid.

What was Abigail doing, come to think of it? She was supposedly upstairs, playing in her bedroom, but they hadn't heard a squeak out of her for hours. Kay turned the carrots down to a simmer and went to the foot of the stairs.

'Abigail!' she shouted. 'Time for lunch! Go to the toilet and wash your hands!'

Her daughter's voice tinkled down the stairs. 'Coming, Mummy!'

'Good girl!' She popped her head around the doorway of the lounge. 'I'll be dishing up in five minutes.'

'Nice one,' said Micky, lifting his can in a toast.

Foxy rolled his eyes. 'About bloody time.' Neither man got up or asked if they could help.

Kay went back to the kitchen, put on her oven gloves and took the chicken out to let it rest. What next? Put the peas on, make the gravy, carve the meat, strain the carrots, take the potatoes out, dish up. Timing was everything for the perfect Sunday roast. She switched off the oven and put the plates in to warm. He hated her serving hot food on cold plates. It was one of the many things he insisted on.

Foxy believed that as the man of the house and the main breadwinner, he should be in charge. Kay was no women's libber, but secretly she thought his views were very old-fashioned. She wanted to challenge him, but it was difficult because he always made her feel she was on the back foot in the marriage, her debts still chalked on the slate. Abigail was the problem. Not the child herself, who was a darling, but the simple existence of her.

From day one, Kay had encouraged her to call Foxy 'Daddy'. 'Ask Daddy if he wants a biscuit'; 'Let Daddy put your shoes on'; 'Sit between me and Daddy and have a hug.' The little girl showed willing at first – most of her friends had daddies, and she'd asked before why she didn't have one. But 'Daddy' never came to school events, or answered if Abigail called to him, and when the three of them were out in public, he walked ahead on his own, like they were nothing to do with him.

'It's blindingly obvious she's the daughter of some greasy dago,' he complained.

'He wasn't a greasy dago; he was Spanish,' Kay wanted to say. 'And actually, he was the most gorgeous man I'd ever met.' But of course she never dared.

How long would this go on? she wondered. This continual punishment for that one reckless act when she was only fifteen years old. Her parents were the same, always going on about how lucky she was to have found someone prepared to take on another man's child. Kay wasn't proud of her mistake, but she was proud of Abigail. She was such a clever little girl, well behaved at school, popular with friends. They were a family now. What did it matter that she hadn't been made by his sperm? Kay darted between husband and daughter in a constant game of piggy in the middle, catching his filthy looks and nasty digs and secreting them in her heart.

'You can't expect him to love her like we do,' her mother said. 'What he needs is a child of his own – that'll set everything to rights.'

Abigail ran into the kitchen wearing her princess costume – lavender satin decked with yellow ballet net. Grandma had made it for a fancy-dress competition at last year's school fair, and she'd all but grown out of it.

'Mummy, can I sit next to you?' she whispered, glancing anxiously towards the lounge.

'If you like. Show me your hands.' Abigail solemnly held them out for inspection. They were covered in scribbles of pink felt pen and tiny specks of glitter. 'Hmm, did you wash them with soap?'

'Yes! Promise!'

'Try again. Use the nail brush.' Kay sent her scampering back upstairs.

She tore off the chicken legs and started to attack the breast with a knife. At her parents' house, her father always carved the joint with a tiny electric saw. Her thoughts drifted back to her mother's advice. For once, she agreed with her. If she and Foxy had a child of their own, all the separate ribbons of their lives could be tied into a beautiful bow. She would love a brother or sister for Abigail, but she knew Foxy wasn't ready for fatherhood yet. On the few occasions she'd broached the subject, he'd brushed her off, saying, 'It's bad enough sharing you with the gypsy girl. I don't want anyone else getting in the way.'

He'd had a difficult childhood, she understood and sympathised with that. He'd virtually been a father to Micky, who was still a great worry to him. It wasn't surprising that he couldn't take on any more responsibility. Not yet, anyway. So she carried on popping her contraceptive pill every night.

Micky had managed to keep himself out of prison, but he wasn't in a great state. Now that he had a criminal record, it was hard for him to get work. He'd had a week's trial at a petrol station, but when the takings didn't balance, he was accused of dipping his hand in the till. There was no proof, but he was still let go. His brother had marched into the garage like a mum going up to the school and demanded to see the boss. It didn't do any good; they said Micky was lucky they hadn't called the police.

He was signing on and hanging out with the old crowd, several of whom had been inside; it was only a matter of time before they dragged him back into crime. Foxy tried to keep him busy – they joined a darts team and went to the football together. And he came over every Sunday for lunch. Micky was a nice enough kid, but he drank too much and swore in front of Abigail. He needed house-training, frankly.

'Lunch is ready!' Kay chirped, her fingers stinging with the hot plates as she carried them into the dining area. They had a through lounge with folding doors in the middle.

'I'm sitting next to Mummy!' Abigail bounded over to the table and scrambled onto the seat.

'You'll sit where I tell you to sit,' Foxy growled, but he didn't make her change.

Micky plonked his beer can on the tablecloth and sat down opposite Kay, stretching his long legs into her space. The two brothers were side by side, and as they ate, she noticed how alike they were, how similar their way of eating. They shovelled the food into their mouths at an alarming rate, as if expecting the plate to be whisked away at any moment. Her gaze rested on Micky. He was too skinny and had a few spots on his chin, but when he grew up, he'd be just as much of a catch as his brother. He caught her looking at him and their eyes met briefly.

'Great grub, Kay,' he said, winking. 'Any more chicken going?'

'I'll see what I can find,' she smiled. 'Fancy a wing?'

'I always a fancy a wing.' He laughed coarsely, as if she'd just made a dirty joke.

Foxy usually had seconds, but her exchange with Micky seemed to have put him in a bad mood. He refused the dessert of tinned peaches and ice cream and left the table, sticking the telly on. An old black-and-white war film was playing – artillery fire and stirring orchestral music blared out. Micky pretended not to notice. Or maybe he *did* notice and played up to Kay to cause mischief. He made more remarks about her fantastic cooking and helped her clear the table.

Kay was cross with her husband for spoiling what had otherwise been a nice meal. When Micky offered to dry up, she let him. It made a nice change to have someone to chat to while she washed the dishes. He told a funny story about his mad old landlady and made her laugh. He wasn't a bad kid, she thought; he'd just lost his way.

After they'd finished clearing up, she made a cup of tea and then Micky went home to his lodgings. Abigail was upstairs playing princesses by herself. The war film was still droning on; the music sounded very sentimental, which meant it must be nearing the end. Kay washed the cups and saucers and laid them on the draining board. She wanted to bring Foxy out of his sour mood but she didn't know how.

'Flaming Nora! What did you think you was doing?' She turned around to see him standing in the doorway, as if she'd somehow conjured him from her thoughts.

'I don't know what you mean,' she replied, feeling her legs starting to tremble. His face was like thunder and he was glaring at her from beneath his eyebrows.

'You little slut. Virtually having it off with my brother while I'm in the next room – you disgust me.'

'Don't be silly. We were washing up, that's all.'

'You were leading him on all during lunch, winking and flirting, playing footsie under the table—'

'I was not!'

'You were, I saw you. Put me right off my food.'

He stepped forward and she backed away, only there was nowhere to go so she had to move sideways, clinging to the edge of the worktop.

'Please, Foxy. I didn't do anything wrong.'

'You never, ever, *ever* flirt with my brother again.'

He put his hand round her throat and squeezed. She opened her mouth, but the scream was trapped inside.

CHAPTER TWELVE

Stella

Now

'We're colluding in a very bad situation,' says Jack. We've come down to the beach to discuss what we're going to do about Lori. 'This husband of hers very obviously shouldn't be allowed anywhere near his kids,' he continues. 'Nor should she.'

'I agree about him, but not her,' I reply. 'Lori's not violent.'

'Not that you know. You're assuming she's telling the truth about why the children have been taken away from her.' He starts picking up stones and throwing them into the sea.

'It's only because she's still with Darren.' I lift my voice above the wind. 'We need to convince her that ditching him completely is the only way to get her kids back. We have to wean her off him, like a drug.'

He raises his eyebrows at the word 'we'. 'That's not our job; we're not professionals. I certainly don't know what I'm doing, and nor do you.' He hurls a stone and watches it skim across the water.

'Lori doesn't trust professionals, but she trusts us.'

'Leave me out of it, please.' He crouches down on the pebbles, picking up a few and turning them over, assessing their suitability for flight.

'But we – *I* – can help her, I know I can. I *want* to help her, Jack, it's important to me.'

He stands up and releases another stone with a flick of his wrist. It bounces several times on the surface before plopping into the sea. I can't skim stones to save my life, and Jack has never been able to teach me. I realise in that moment that he can't understand other people's problems unless he happens to share them. There's no point in trying to bring him around to my point of view, I'm going to have to be assertive.

'I know you're not happy about it, but I'm going to let her stay for another week or so. Don't worry, she'll keep out of your way; you won't even know she's there.'

He looks out to sea, his eyes fixed on the wind farm, its white sails whirring in the distance. 'Okay, Stella, do what you want, like you always do. Be a Good Samaritan, if you must. I still think there's something fake about Lori, something about her story that doesn't ring true. I can't explain it, it's just a feeling. You can ignore me if you like, but don't expect me to pick up the pieces if it all goes wrong.'

'There won't be any pieces.' I lean into him, kissing the small patch of beardless skin on his face. 'Thanks. This means a lot to me.'

Lori is visibly moved when we tell her she can stay for a little while longer. She can see that Jack's still unhappy about it, so she diplomatically makes herself scarce for the rest of the weekend, confining herself to her bedroom and only coming downstairs when she needs to make a drink or get something to eat.

We don't talk about her, but the subject lingers in the air like a bad smell. By Sunday evening, I'm desperate for a break and suggest we go to Whitstable to see a film. There's an arts centre there with a good programme of independent cinema. Jack's a sucker for subtitles.

As he drives us there via the coast road, I'm reminded that this is my car, bought with my inheritance money. Jack has very little of his own – a few bits of furniture, some sound equipment, a couple of guitars, some boxes of books. Even though he has a good job, he's not been able to build up any savings. That's not because he's extravagant; it's just impossible if you're paying rent in London. Now, at thirty-three, he's living in an enormous house overlooking the sea, less than an hour's commute from the office. There's no rent to pay, no mortgage to cover. We share the bills, he fills the car with petrol every so often, treats me to meals out and contributes towards the supermarket shop. He pays his way, but he's not putting down roots. Nothing belongs to him legally; he has no stake in our life here. It's not surprising that he feels vulnerable, but then so do I. There's nothing to link us together. He could walk out of my life at any moment and barely leave a trace.

I stare out of the car window at the grey expanse of sea, my thoughts washing over the past sixteen months. If I'd met Jack before my parents died, I wonder what difference it would have made. He never met the old me – I've no idea whether he would have liked her, or even preferred her. I used to be shiny and brittle, covered in a hard, reflective surface that everybody bounced off. Always up for a good time, getting pissed and having a laugh. I wasn't interested in serious relationships, declared I would put my career before any man. I was a journalist for a lifestyle magazine and lived off the freebies – meals in fancy restaurants, weekends away in expensive hotels, tickets for gigs, invites to gallery openings and nightclub launches. It was fun, fun, fun all the way, yet completely hollow.

Then Mum and Dad were killed in the hit-and-run and everything fell apart. There was a huge outpouring of grief in the village, tributes flowing in from colleagues at Social Services, not to mention cards and letters from previous foster kids – the success stories, that is, people who had grown up and gone on to lead happy lives thanks to my parents. But I couldn't cope; not with the funeral or the memorial service, nor with my judgemental aunts and uncles, certainly not with the police investigation. Everything I'd been hiding from all these years was suddenly right in my face. I had so much baggage weighing me down, I could hardly move.

My friends who knew me from university or work were sympathetic and supportive at first, but they couldn't understand why I had gone to pieces so completely. Of course it was a shocking tragedy to lose both parents in one go, but it was obvious my reaction was way over the top. Something else was going on, but I wouldn't tell anyone.

I threw in my job at the magazine and sank into depression. My friends stopped calling and texting to see how I was, stopped inviting me out – they felt helpless and didn't know what to do. Only Molly kept in touch, although I didn't see her often because she lived in my home town and was very involved in her wedding plans.

It had never occurred to me that Mum and Dad would leave everything to me in their will. I nearly gave it all away to charity, but Molly helped me see that I could use the inheritance in a positive way. I could escape from London and live a much healthier life, physically and spiritually. I would have time to take stock, rethink my career and maybe do something more worthwhile. In time, and with a bit of luck, I would fall in love, settle down and start a family. *Then* I'd be happy.

I was cynical about it at first. I wasn't sure I could transform, or that I was entitled to a second chance. But then I met Jack – on the Tube of all places. The train broke down between stations and we were stuck in the same carriage for two hours. We had to walk down the track through the filthy dark tunnel, and he held my hand all the way because I was scared. He invited me to go for a drink to recover and things moved quickly from there. He threw me the lifeline I needed. Changing my life was a daunting prospect, but if I could do it with somebody at my side, somebody who didn't know about my past, I reckoned there was more hope of success.

'I love you,' I say, squeezing his thigh. 'I'm really sorry about all this. I promise I won't let Lori stay for much longer. Then we'll get the house finished and everything will be all right.'

We get through the next week without too much problem. Jack leaves early for work each morning and Lori makes sure she's in her room by the time he gets home. She eats at about six, then goes upstairs and watches videos on YouTube, or calls her mum or whomever – I don't know what she does really, but the point is, she doesn't disturb us. In the daytime, she grafts for Alan: fetching and carrying, holding bits of plasterboard while he screws them in place, sweeping up, washing down, filling old cement bags with rubble. She won't put stuff in the skip, though, because that would involve going outside and stepping onto the driveway.

She hasn't mentioned Darren, but I know she's still scared of him. She behaves as if she knows he's out there, lying in wait. But how can he be, when he doesn't know where she is? Unless she told him, or told her mother, who was forced to reveal it. I should be able to ask her such questions, but it's embarrassing; she'll think I don't trust her. And I *do* trust her; it's just that sometimes what she says and what she does don't quite add up.

It's mid morning and I haven't got much to do. I find myself staring out of the large bay window of our bedroom, thoughts revolving in my brain. I can't see anyone watching the house. It would be possible, I suppose, to hide in the shelter on the other side of the road, next to the slope of grass and the benches where the old people sit. But it's too cold to stay there for long. Then there are the beach huts, but they're all boarded up for the winter. He'd have to break in, and surely somebody would notice. But then again, there's hardly anyone on the beach at this time of year.

Now that the possibility's in my head, I can't let it go. I pull on my coat and scarf, pick up my bag and slip out of the house. As soon as I step outside, the icy wind slaps me across the cheeks. I cross the road and walk down the steps to the lower promenade, where a row of beach huts faces the sea. They are packed together tightly, as if huddling from the cold, their summery paintwork – duck-egg blue, primrose yellow, baby pink and mint green – at odds with the dull greys and browns of winter.

I walk along the row, inspecting the padlocks and boarded windows. There's no sign of a break-in or anyone camping inside. No violent-looking man lurking in the shadows. Of course there isn't. I was scaring myself for nothing.

The breeze is sharp, but I carry on along the promenade, pulling my scarf up to just beneath my nose. I don't want to go back to the house yet. I'm sick of the noise and dust, the old seventies hits blaring out of Alan's radio. When I reach the pier, I head inland to the high street, which runs parallel with the Esplanade, and dive into a charity shop for the local hospice.

I run my fingers through the rail of women's clothing, looking for something in Lori's size. She desperately needs more things to wear. I feel bad that I haven't thought of it before. I quickly find a pink jumper that I know will suit her, then I see a patterned jersey top. I hold it up to the fluorescent strip lights, imagining the yellow and toffee-coloured swirly shapes hugging Lori's squat, round body. It's hard to choose for someone when you don't know their style. Not that it matters too much when she's still refusing to leave the house.

Why won't she go out? The question still nags at me. She's supposed to see her children once a fortnight, but she's been staying with us for nearly three weeks now, which means she must have missed a visit. Surely it's worth the risk of leaving the house to see her kids. I start flicking through a rail of jeans, trying to guess her size. Adding a pair of size 14s to my haul, I wander over to the till.

Perhaps Darren knows where the children are living and when Lori normally goes to see them. If so, that would definitely scare her off, but it seems such a shame that her kids are missing out. I remember that the foster kids my parents looked after often felt abandoned by their parents, not understanding that they'd been taken from them by force. I wish I could talk to Lori properly about it, but it feels awkward – too intrusive.

'Excuse me? I said, do you need a bag?' The assistant's voice lurches me out of my ruminations.

'Er, no, it's okay, I've got one.' I pull a crumpled plastic carrier out of my pocket.

When I arrive back at the house, I call out for Lori but she doesn't answer. She probably can't hear me above the noise of the building work. I take off my coat and scarf, then climb the stairs, eager to give her my small present.

Alan is taking up the floorboards in one of the front bedrooms. He says they're riddled with woodworm and all have to be replaced.

'Seen Lori?' I ask above the racket of some ancient pop song on the radio.

'In one of the back rooms,' he replies, putting down his claw hammer. 'I sent her to do some stripping; she was getting under my feet in here.'

I go back onto the landing and listen for the sounds of her scraping the walls, but I can't hear anything. No, that's not true, there's a faint sobbing coming from somewhere at the back of the house. I quickly walk down the dog-leg corridor and through a fire door, following the noise until I reach one of the smaller bedrooms.

She's sitting on the floor, on her knees, head bowed, hugging herself and crying. A bucket of soapy water and the scraper sit at her side. I crouch next to her, putting my hands around her shoulders.

'Lori? What's the matter?'

'Look,' she whispers, her voice choked with tears. 'Look at the wall.'

CHAPTER THIRTEEN

Stella

Now

I glance upwards at the half-stripped wall ahead of us and see several crude drawings made with coloured felt pen – thick, wobbly lines in black, red, green and blue.

My stomach sickens as I stare at the childishly drawn images – a series of cartoons featuring stick people, some big, some small, some wearing triangular skirts, with long hair flicked up at the ends. The men, who all have short hair sticking out of the top of their heads, are holding weapons, sticks or strange shapes that could be chairs or tables. One man is waving a large knife dripping with oversized drops of red blood.

'Oh God,' I whisper. 'This is awful.'

'Breaks your heart,' Lori says, finally lifting her head.

The stick women with the flicked-up hair and triangular skirts are cowering beneath the stick men, or lying on the floor with red scribbles around their heads. A smaller figure – presumably a child – is standing by herself to one side, looking on. Her black hair is long and wavy and her mouth is turned down to represent sadness. Blue tears are dotted on her face.

A tension inside me gives and I feel myself welling up. 'This must be what the kids witnessed happening to their mums before they came to the refuge,' I say.

'I guess so,' Lori murmurs, wiping her tears with her sleeve.

'It's so shocking, the violence of it … And it was under the wallpaper?'

'Yeah, a few layers down, so it must come from a good while back.'

I'm transfixed by the images, studying them one by one, trying to piece a narrative together. A little boy or girl must have drawn these pictures. But who were they and when did they do it? I feel myself gripped by their story. I want to know more.

'I can't work in here,' says Lori. 'It gives me the creeps.' She stands and picks up the bucket. Her hand is shaking. 'Sorry, I need a bit of a rest.'

'Of course – you've had a shock.' She leaves, and I hear her climbing the stairs to her attic room.

I sit down on the bare floorboards, with my back against the opposite wall, just gazing at the drawings, repulsed yet unable to tear myself away. I look again at the little girl with the jet-black hair. She's standing apart from the others, as if she's looking on. Somehow I have a really strong feeling that she drew the pictures, that it's *her* story being played out.

The room feels icy cold. I sense the ghosts of the house gathering in the doorway, slipping across the threshold one by one and sitting on the bare floorboards, resting their backs against the rough walls. Some of them are holding babies. Others beckon to toddlers to sit down. The murmurs quieten as everyone squeezes together and makes themselves comfortable. They stare up at me expectantly, as if it's my turn to begin proceedings. In the dim light, the ugly drawings start to flicker and animate. There are so many stories to tell here; who's going to start?

I find myself going back to my own childhood – I was an only child and yet grew up as one of many, a large, chaotic family of brothers and sisters who came and went, sometimes staying for months, sometimes only a couple of days. Our house was a refuge of sorts, although it never felt like a refuge to me. I was often standing on the edge, like the girl in the picture, feeling like my home was being invaded by unruly, troublesome strangers.

My mother's lap was never empty; there was always some baby being fed or a crying toddler being comforted. Dad worked during the day, but as soon as he came home, he'd be out in the garden kicking a ball with the boys, or in the kitchen cooking huge dinners. Some of the girls knew how to play nicely, but others were spiteful and rough with my toys. One tore the heads off all my Barbie dolls. After tea, they all squeezed together on the sofas and argued about which television programme to watch, or just bounced around the room, knocking things over and getting into pointless fights.

I had my own bedroom, the smallest one in the house. There were three other large bedrooms with sets of bunk beds, one for boys, one for girls, and another used for emergency cases. My room was supposed to be my private sanctuary, but the foster kids were always barging in. When I was a teenager, the older girls would ask to borrow my clothes and make-up – if I was out, which was often the case, they'd just take them anyway. Things would get ripped or lost. They got told off for that, but were never punished enough in my view.

'You have to understand, Stella,' Mum would say. 'You have a very privileged life. It's natural for them to want what you've got.'

The kids were treated extremely well, but almost every week somebody would run away and we'd have to call the police. The blue lights of the patrol car would flash through my window and there would be shouting matches in the street as the escapees were dragged back into the house. And then there was Kyle, of course, the boy who hit our house like a whirlwind. I don't want to think about him.

As a teenager, I spent as much time as I could at Molly's place. We'd do our homework together and often her mum would feed me and give me a lift home if it was dark. She was always going on about what saints my parents were, looking after all those poor kids, giving them so much love and patience. 'I couldn't do it,' she'd say. 'They're wonderful people, they deserve an OBE.' I found it odd that she never wondered why I was always round their house and couldn't wait to get away from my own.

I pull my arms across my chest and shiver. Remembering the past is difficult. If only more had been explained to me, I think, maybe I wouldn't have done what I did.

When Jack comes home several hours later, he finds me in bed, huddled beneath the duvet, still fully dressed.

'You okay?' he says. 'You look a bit flushed.' He puts the back of his hand against my forehead. 'You're hot. I hope it's not the flu.'

I throw the duvet off and stretch out my legs. 'No, don't think so. I just needed to lie down for a bit. Sorry, I haven't started cooking.' Recently I've been making proper food for him when he comes home, simple stuff I can cook on the hob. It's part of the unspoken bargain between us. He tolerates Lori's presence in return for no more ready meals.

'Don't worry,' he says. 'I'll order a delivery. Chinese?' He takes out his phone and calls the local takeaway, rattling off our usual list of dishes.

I get off the bed and try to plug my brain back into the real world, but I can't find the right sockets. I've been musing about the house's history for hours, trying to imagine what it must have been like all those years ago. This downstairs room must have been a communal space, I think. I see tatty sofas and stained coffee tables, posters on the walls, colourful rugs on painted floorboards. There are cardboard boxes of old clothes, broken toys, dirty mugs and baby bottles, magazines that have been flicked through a thousand times, ashtrays overflowing with cigarette stubs. Every object looks as if it had a troubled life somewhere else first.

'Half an hour,' says Jack, wrenching me out of my fantasies. I blink at him, not understanding at first. 'The Chinese.'

'Oh. Right.'

He frowns. 'You sure you're not ill?'

'Lori found something today.' He twitches slightly at the mention of her name. It's another clause in our silent contract – pretending she doesn't really exist. 'I think you should go and look.'

'Really? What is it? Woodworm? Dry rot?'

'No. Drawings. In one of the small back rooms, above the kitchen.'

'What sort of drawings?'

'You'll see.' He pulls a face. 'Please. It's important. I can't explain; you have to see them. I'll have a beer waiting for you when you come down.'

He sighs and slouches out of the door like a reluctant teenager. I slip my feet into my trainers and go into the kitchen. I take two bottles of lager out of the fridge and snap off the lids. Jack's footsteps in the room above make the ceiling quiver.

It's easy to imagine what this kitchen looked like a couple of decades ago, because nothing's changed. My eyes pass over the pine cladding, the orange and brown wall tiles, the chipped beige cabinets, the plastic worktop pocked with burn marks and scarred with scratches. I can see women slicing bread and chopping vegetables, stirring large pans of baked beans on the hob. I can hear them chatting and laughing while children run around their feet or tug at their skirts.

'Jesus, some of those images are horrific,' says Jack, re-entering. He picks up a bottle and swigs a large mouthful of beer.

'We think they're kids' drawings. They were underneath several layers of wallpaper so we reckon they're quite old.'

'They look pretty fresh to me; the colours are really sharp,' he replies, leaning against the worktop. 'I wish the food would hurry up. I'm starving.'

'It really upset Lori. Me too. I can't stop thinking about what the place must have been like when it was a refuge, what the women had to suffer before they came here, what the children had to witness. Those pictures bring it all home.'

He nods. 'Literally. We don't want that kind of violent stuff in our house. Ask Alan to paint over them.'

'Good idea,' I say, pleased that he said 'our' and not 'your', for a change.

The delivery arrives. We grab some plates and take our food into the front room. The sweet and sour chicken is rubbery and the salted squid is too salty, but neither of us comments. Jack tries to lighten the mood by telling me some funny story about a guy at work. I do my best to laugh in the right places, but my mind is still upstairs in the back room. We clear the plates and put the leftovers in the fridge, knowing full well that neither of us will eat them and in a few days' time they'll be thrown away. The atmosphere is too polite, too cautious. It's as if we are strangers being forced to share a bed.

In the morning, he gets up very early. I lie there, still half asleep, dimly conscious of his movements as he disappears to the bathroom, then comes back to dress in the morning dark.

'It's okay, I'm awake,' I say, switching on the bedside lamp. 'Didn't sleep very well.'

'No, you had a nightmare. You were talking in your sleep, I couldn't make it out. At one point I think you shouted, "Fire!"' He laughs. 'Any idea what that was about?'

'Not really.' I turn away from him so that he doesn't notice my pink cheeks. I remember the nightmare only faintly – a mishmash of the present and the past, of this house and the one I grew up in. My parents were in it, and so was the little girl in the wall drawing. She was a foster kid and she was staying in my room, which wasn't allowed. I think she was scribbling all over my walls and I was shouting at her to stop. The rest I don't want to think about …

Jack is buttoning up his shirt. 'I've been thinking about those drawings,' he says. 'They don't look old to me; they look freshly done. Are you sure Lori didn't do them herself?'

I ease myself onto my elbows. 'Of course she didn't. Why would she do such a thing?'

He tucks the shirt in. 'To get our sympathy? So we won't chuck her out?'

'That's ridiculous. They were under the wallpaper.'

'You've only got her word for that. Did she call you as soon as she found them or only once the wall was completely stripped?'

I sit up and fold my arms grumpily. 'I went upstairs and found her crying in front of them, if you must know. Don't be so horrible.'

'Do me a favour, ask Alan what happened.'

'Alan was in another room. I'm not checking up on her, there's no need.'

Jack sits on the edge of the bed with his back to me and pulls on his socks. 'Whoever did the drawings used marker pens; you know the type, they come in a set, black, red, blue, green. I happen to know that there's a packet in one of the boxes in the other room.'

'So now you're saying she stole our marker pens?'

'I'd just be interested to know if they're still there,' he says, lacing up his shoes.

I'm so astonished I don't know how to reply.

He stands up, then reaches for his jacket. 'I'm having lunch with some clients, so don't bother cooking for me tonight. See you later.' He blows me a kiss, then leaves the room. I hear the front door open and shut behind him. If Lori wasn't in the house, I'd scream.

It's still very early, not even seven a.m. Usually when Jack leaves, I snuggle back under the covers and try to catch another hour of sleep, but today I get up and throw on some clothes without washing first. I'm totally convinced that Lori *didn't* do those drawings – the hand is clearly that of a child, for a start, and why on earth would she do such an odd thing anyway? I know Jack's talking rubbish, but I want to be able to prove it to him.

I creep upstairs in my socks, trying not to make the floorboards creak, and tiptoe along the funny L-shaped corridor towards the back bedroom. The heating's been turned off on this floor, and it's freezing. I enter the dark room. Outside, dawn is breaking. Its cold greyness makes me tremble.

Switching on the light, I force myself to look at the drawings again. It's true that the colours are very vivid and the lines look fresh. But the pictures have been hidden beneath paper for years, so they wouldn't have faded. I trace the triangle of a woman's skirt with my finger, then press it hard against the wall. No ink comes off; it's completely dry.

Damp shreds of wallpaper lie at my feet. I crouch down and pick up a bunch at random, sifting through the tiny scraps, turning any larger pieces over to see if the pen left any marks on the underside, or stained the paste. But there's no conclusive evidence, no proof either way. I stand up and face the drawings again. The little girl with the black hair stares at me accusingly, the mouth that looked so sad yesterday set in a grim straight line.

Who are you? I whisper, holding my breath as I wait for a reply.

A shiver passes through me. I turn away from the wall, run out of the room and down the stairs.

CHAPTER FOURTEEN

Stella

Now

Alan's key turns in the lock an hour later and I walk into the hallway to greet him.

'Morning,' he says, stomping in. He's wearing a pair of new white overalls that make him look a bit like a snowman. 'It's like the Arctic out there; the wind off the sea's so sharp it could cut you in two.'

'Mmm, it's very biting sometimes.' I pause, feeling suddenly awkward. 'I, er, was wondering if you could do us a favour?'

'Oh yeah, what's that?'

'You know the drawings that Lori found in the bedroom?'

He looks downwards. 'Sickening stuff ... Makes you realise what those poor kiddies must have seen.'

'I know. It's shocking. We'd like you to paint over them. As soon as possible, if that's okay. It doesn't matter what colour; anything'll do.'

'I saw some old paint pots in the shed. I'll see if any of it's usable.'

'Thanks. Or just buy something cheap. I know it's going to be re-skimmed, but ... well, we'd like it covered up straight away.'

'Fair enough, you're the boss.'

Lori comes to the top of the first-floor stairs. 'You're late, Al!' she says. 'I'm up here, waiting for orders.' There's a false cheeriness in her voice.

'Cup of tea wouldn't go amiss,' he calls back.

'You and your cuppas ...' She thumps down to meet us. 'Morning, Stella. Sleep okay?'

'Not really,' I reply, wondering if she heard me walking around the bedroom at the crack of dawn.

Lori takes some bread out of the cupboard and pops a couple of slices in the toaster. As I watch her moving around the kitchen, as if she's quite at home, my thoughts drift to my earlier argument with Jack. I'm still furious with him and I can't leave it alone. I mustn't tell Lori what he said, of course; she'd be very upset. She seems in a strange mood this morning, as if her thoughts are far away. The discovery of the drawings seems to have affected all of us.

Alan comes in looking for his tea and I leave the two of them to chat. Instead of going back to my bedroom, I sneak into the second large reception room on the other side of the hallway, shutting the door with a quiet click.

I switch on the weak overhead light and go over to the cluster of cardboard boxes piled up in the corner. Some are large, some small, all sealed with brown sticky tape and labelled with their contents: *Oven dishes/jugs/Moroccan bowls*; *Posh glasses/blue vase/ Italian coffee set*. Jack moved into my flat in London a few months before I bought the house, so now our possessions are all muddled together. There are also a few boxes of memorabilia that I took from Mum and Dad's house. I didn't want any of the outdated, tatty furniture, so I got a charity to take it away.

I sort through the pile, looking for the box marked *Stationery*. As I kneel in front of it, I see that the sticky tape has been ripped off and then pressed back over the join. The tape has creased and lost its stickiness in parts. My pulse starts to race as I tear it free, open the flaps and look inside.

There's some coloured paper, a stapler, boxes of staples and paper clips, a tumbler of biros, a hole punch, plastic rulers, two reels of transparent tape. No marker pens.

But that doesn't necessarily mean anything. I have no positive memory of owning a set of marker pens. Even if Jack's right, they could easily have found their way into another box. He's a bit anal about these things, but we weren't *that* organised with our packing, surely?

I close the flaps again and sit back on my calves, thinking. I'd feel completely reassured if it wasn't for the fact that *this* box, clearly labelled with its contents, has definitely been disturbed. And that Lori slept in here that first night so she would have seen what's here. Which means that if she wanted to fake some drawings, she'd know exactly where to look for tools. But she wouldn't do something weird like that – would she?

I decide not to mention my findings – or lack of findings – to Jack unless he asks. It's late when he gets in, after eleven p.m. He makes a big show of being exhausted and not wanting to talk. I wonder if he's feeling embarrassed for accusing Lori but doesn't want to admit it. Either that, or he's simply forgotten about the drawings.

I can't forget, though.

The next day Alan obliterates the images with some smelly magnolia paint he found in the shed, but they are imprinted on my memory and won't go away. There's a bad atmosphere in the room and I'm starting to rethink my secret plans for it as a potential nursery. We could redecorate, lay a new carpet, put up new curtains and hang mobiles from the ceiling, but the drawings would still be there, dormant beneath the paint, plaster and paper.

Like time, food can be a great healer. So I head to Cathy's Café in the afternoon and buy some iced cupcakes in an attempt to jolly things up. Back home, I make three mugs of tea, put the box of cakes on a tray and carry it upstairs. To my surprise, Alan isn't around.

'He's gone to buy materials,' Lori tells me. She looks as if she's just come out of the shower. Her hair hangs like a thin wet curtain either side of her face and she's wearing the swirly patterned top and jeans I bought her the other day.

'You look great,' I say.

She smiles. 'It's nice to put some clean clothes on. The dust gets everywhere.'

'Tea and cake?'

'Yes please. Shall we have them in my room?'

My room. I like the way she says that. She takes the tray off me and climbs the stairs. I follow her, gasping in amazement as I enter the attic.

The room is barely recognisable, no longer bleak and damp but colourful and cosy. A string of paper lanterns glow above the bed. There's a knotted red rug on the floor, a paisley throw and several bright cushions on the mattress, a bedside table made out of an upturned crate, a shell lampshade overhead and a giant bean bag by the window. I had no idea all this was going on behind the scenes.

'Someone's been busy,' I say.

Lori puts the tray on the rug and gestures at me to sit on the bean bag. It's like sinking into a large bowl of Rice Krispies.

'Alan turns up with something virtually every day,' she admits. 'I keep telling him I'm only temporary, but he will insist. *You need home comforts*, he says … Daft bugger.' She opens the cake box. 'Ooh, muffins. Aren't they gorgeous! They look too good to eat.'

I let her have first pick and she chooses a cupcake iced with a large pink rose and silver balls. We peel the cases off and take large bites, giggling as spongy crumbs fall from the corners of our mouths and into our laps. I wash mine down with a large gulp of tea. Alan's mug sits there, reminding us of his absence.

'He's a lovely chap,' says Lori, obviously thinking the same thing. 'I wish my Darren was half as nice.'

'You haven't mentioned Darren for a while. How are things on that front? Any more texts?'

'No. He's ignoring me.' She licks her finger and picks the crumbs off her jeans, one by one. 'Don't want mice,' she says, catching my gaze.

'Is that a good or a bad sign? Him not being in touch.'

'Bad, I think.'

'Sounds like he's playing games,' I say. 'Don't be the one to crack first.'

'I know … It's weird, though, he's never been like this before.'

'You've never left him before.'

'True.' Her eyes glisten with tears. 'I don't want to go back yet. I don't feel ready.'

I reach over and grab her hands. 'Please, please don't go back to him.'

'It's easy for you to say,' she begins, but I wave her objections away.

'Look at you, you're so much happier and stronger without him. You don't need him, Lori, and nor do your children. Stay here for as long as you need. Then tell Social Services the marriage is over and you want your kids back. They'll protect you, I'm sure they will.'

She grunts. 'I doubt it.'

'Don't let him win. Let me help you. Please?'

'Thanks, love, you're a sweetheart.' She gently removes her hands from mine.

As the days pass, I sense Lori becoming increasingly anxious about Darren. Alan must be buying her cigarettes, because she keeps going into the back garden to smoke. She hasn't left the house since our disastrous visit to Citizens Advice. She must be going stir crazy.

The garden's very private. A brick wall, its top decorated with jagged pieces of glass, runs along the far end. There are high wooden fences on either side. It reminds me of a prison yard, although when Westhill House was a refuge, the garden would have had the opposite function. These were willing prisoners, and the object was to keep the perpetrators out.

Everything's totally overgrown, but it's just about possible to imagine what the garden was like back then. A large open space for little children to run around in, a vegetable patch at the bottom for women who wanted to grow things, and a paved terrace where everyone could sit out and breathe the sea air.

I stand in the conservatory watching Lori pace up and down, pulling on her cigarette and puffing smoke into the wintry sky. She stamps it out, then picks up the butt. I turn and hurry back into the kitchen – don't want her to catch me staring.

She comes back inside, shutting the door behind her. 'What are the plans for out there?' she asks. 'It's a huge space.'

I make a show of rummaging in the fridge. 'Well, some of it will be taken up by the kitchen-diner extension. Then we'll build a large terrace, re-lay the lawn and dig a pond at the bottom.'

'A pond?' She sounds surprised. 'What, for fish?'

I nod. 'I like fish. They're very soothing.'

She wrinkles her nose. 'Aren't ponds dangerous? For children, I mean … I guess you're planning to have kids.'

'Yes, eventually.' I feel my cheeks blooming. It's a sensitive subject between me and Jack. I'm thirty-one, and my biological clock is ticking. But our relationship has been going for less than a year; it's too early for him to make that kind of commitment. 'That's why I want the pond right at the bottom,' I say. 'So I can fence it off.'

'Oh, clever,' she says. 'Right. Better get back to work.' She puts the cigarette stub in the bin and walks out of the kitchen, heading for the stairs.

Our paths don't cross for the rest of the day. Strange that we can live in the same house and yet not be aware of each other's presence. What's it going to be like, I wonder, when Lori leaves and the building work is finished? It'll just be me and Jack. And the ghosts, of course. The violent drawings flash across my inner eye and I silently shout at them to go away.

Jack gets home at a reasonable time for once, and seems in a slightly better mood. I cook a hotchpotch meal of leftovers and we drink a bottle of wine. We don't talk about Lori, or the building work. Instead, we sit on the bed, legs outstretched, backs against the headboard, and watch a documentary on the laptop. If it wasn't for the grim surroundings, it would be no different from when we lived in the old flat.

I start to feel bad about being cross with Jack for his behaviour recently. He's clearly under a lot of strain. I even imagine we might make love, but when it comes to bedtime, he immediately rolls onto his side, facing away from me. Within minutes he's snoring lightly, so I turn off the bedside lamp and close my eyes, praying the nightmares don't come back.

It's half-two when I wake up, disturbed by a sound I can't identify or locate. I turn over to face Jack, but his side of the bed is empty. He must be in the loo, I think. But several minutes pass and he doesn't return.

I sit up, blinking into the dark, cavernous space.

'Jack? Are you there?'

I flick on the lamp, climb out of bed and put on my dressing gown. Leaving the room, I pad into the dark hallway, patting the wall as I try to find the light switch. The overhead candelabra flickers into life.

I pause for a few seconds, pulling the dressing gown across my body as my bare feet press into the ice-cold floor tiles. First I check the downstairs shower room, but it's dark and empty. The kitchen is dark too and there's no sign of light beyond. I open the door of the other front reception room, then the middle room, but meet only silent blackness. Where is he? I glance at the staircase. Surely he wouldn't go up there at this time of night?

A wave of panic rolls over me. Rushing back to the room, I pick up my phone to see if he's left me a message. But there's nothing. My heart starts to pound and I feel dizzy. He can't just have vanished into thin air. I sit on the edge of the bed and call his number, but his phone is switched off. The alarm clock on his side of the bed counts the minutes. My mind races through possibilities of where he might be, but none of them make sense.

Then I hear a familiar sound. The front door opening and closing, but very, very quietly. Standing up, I run out of the room and into the hallway. Jack is standing there, fully dressed and a little out of breath.

'Where the hell have you been?' I hiss. 'I've been worried sick.'

'You don't need to whisper. Lori won't hear you.' He unzips his jacket. 'She's not here.'

'What do you mean?'

'She left the house about twenty minutes ago.' He ushers me into the bedroom. 'It's so cold out there, I didn't have time to dress properly.'

'You followed her?'

'Yeah.' He climbs into bed fully clothed and pulls the duvet over himself. 'I couldn't sleep. Then I heard her coming down the stairs and leaving the house. So I threw some clothes on and went after her.'

'Why?'

'Because I wanted to know what she was up to, that's why.'

'She probably just needed some fresh air.'

'I followed her down the hill. She had no idea I was behind her. When she got to the pier, a car pulled up; she got in and it drove away.'

My heart sinks. 'What colour? What colour was the car?'

'Hard to tell. A dark colour.'

'Blue? Could it have been dark blue?'

'I don't know. Possibly. Why does it matter?'

I punch the headboard with my fist. 'It's Darren,' I say. 'She's gone back to him.'

Jack sighs with relief. 'Thank God for that.'

CHAPTER FIFTEEN

Kay

Then

Kay stood in the kitchen cutting off the ends of the flower stalks – at a sharp angle, the way her mother had taught her. It had been months since Foxy had bought her flowers, she reflected. These were from the girls at work. She filled the vase with tepid water and started arranging the blooms, unable to stop the wave of sadness that was breaking over her. Her colleagues had given her a card, too – *Sorry you're leaving!* it said, in bright pink loopy writing. They'd all signed it and left kind messages, wishing her luck for the future.

But there was no future. Not on the career front, anyway. Many Congratulations had never been her dream job, but she'd stuck it out for over two years and been promoted to assistant manager of the branch. Foxy had wanted her to leave soon after they'd married, but she'd reminded him that her money would help buy a few luxuries for the house. For example, they'd recently bought a snazzy music centre that combined a record deck, cassette player and radio all in one. And she'd been paying for Abigail's ballet lessons. She sighed. The little girl loved dancing, but she supposed all that would have to stop now.

She carried the vase into the lounge and placed it on the dining table. The chrysanthemums looked gorgeous but wouldn't last long in this heat. Everyone had assumed she'd left because she was pregnant, which sadly wasn't the case. She'd told them she simply wanted to devote more time to the family. Foxy never stopped moaning about the house being a mess, and he objected to her ironing in front of the television, even though they were usually his shirts. Also, he hated her working Saturdays and refused to look after Abigail. Instead, she had to get the child up extra early and take her on the bus to her parents' house. Then at the end of the day, she had to do it all in reverse. It was always nearly eight by the time she got home, too late to start cooking – he didn't like that either.

But the real reason he'd made her give up was his jealousy. True, they had met in the card shop, but that was the only time anything like that had happened to her. He refused to believe it. Flattering in a way, she supposed, standing back to assess the flowers, then rushing forward to rearrange them. A sign that he still found her attractive. Her colleagues thought it was ever so romantic when he turned up at the shop unexpectedly to 'say hello'. Kay knew he was actually trying to catch her out. One time he found her talking to a sales rep about a new range of greeting cards. When she got home that evening, he gave her a good hiding for 'flaunting your tits' at the chap. She couldn't go on like that. She gave her notice in the next day.

She instinctively rubbed a bruise on her upper arm – she could still see his finger marks from where he'd grabbed her a week ago after a row about something else, she'd forgotten exactly what. Something minor. His triggers were impossible to predict. There were more bruises on her back where he'd repeatedly knocked her against the wall. It was June. The weather was too warm to wear neck scarves and long-sleeved blouses. She was surprised the girls hadn't noticed her curious new fashion tastes, but it probably never occurred to them that he hit her. They thought he was lovely.

Everybody thought he was lovely – her parents, all her friends. Even *she* thought he was lovely – some of the time.

She went back to the kitchen to dispose of the foliage and cellophane. Maybe now that she'd left the shop, things would improve and the rows would stop. She would complete her chores while he was at work so that when he came home the house would be tidy and sparkling clean. And she'd make more of an effort with the cooking.

To be fair, Foxy had a lot on his plate right now. Micky was in trouble again and this time it was going to court. He'd been encouraged to join a local Sunday league football team, the idea being that sport would channel his aggression into something more positive. But there'd been a nasty incident on the pitch, during which Micky had managed to fracture an opposing player's jaw. He'd been charged with assault – much to his brother's fury and indignation.

Micky was pleading not guilty on the grounds of self-defence, but Kay didn't rate his chances. The Foxton brothers were too free with their fists. It seemed to be in their blood. She understood all the reasons – difficult childhood, alcoholic mother, growing up without a decent male role model – but even so. You'd think that if you'd been a victim of violence yourself, you'd be *less* likely to subject others to it, not more.

The following Wednesday, she collected Abigail from school as she always did. The skies were cloudy but the temperature was extremely warm. Muggy. She was trapped in a long-sleeved blouse and a pair of tight flares when she should have worn a summer dress. Her armpits were sticky with roll-on deodorant, but it hadn't stopped the sweat. She was sure she had damp patches and didn't dare raise her arms.

The bell had rung for the end of school. Within seconds the kids would start to stream out, like water from an overflowing bath. Kay stood in the playground trying not to catch the eyes of the other mums, who were standing in small groups, chatting. She was much younger than all of them and suspected they looked down on her for being a single parent. Not that she was single any more, but Foxy was refusing to adopt Abigail and wouldn't let her use his surname. School letters still came addressed to Miss Watson, even though Kay had told the office twice that she was married now. It was as if they didn't believe her.

She pasted a smile on her face and craned her neck, searching among the blue-and-white checked dresses for Abigail's jet-black hair bobbing between the blondes and mousy browns. Most of the boys and several girls she recognised from her daughter's class had already emerged and were being scooped up by their mothers, who were snatching reading bags and rescuing trailing cardigans. The corners of Kay's mouth turned from up to down as she waited. Where was she?

'Abigail's mother?' The teacher was walking towards her carrying a brown cardboard folder.

'Yes, that's me.' Kay felt her heart rate speed up. 'Where is she?'

'She's helping Mrs Evans tidy up the paint pots. I wanted to have a little word with you, if you don't mind. In private.' The teacher, Ms Gardiner – she was very particular about the Ms – gestured for Kay to follow her back into the building.

Kay scampered after her. 'What's happened? Is she in trouble?'

'No, she's fine. Shall we go in here?' Ms Gardiner led her into a small side room next to the office. It was known as the nit room, because it was where the school nurse inspected the children's heads. Inside, there was a narrow bed where sick pupils could lie down if their parents weren't available to take them home. There was also a small desk and two upright metal chairs with canvas seats. Ms Gardiner took one of them and nodded at Kay to sit in the other. She put the brown folder on the desk, but didn't open it.

'What's the problem?' Kay asked. Teachers always made her feel nervous, although to be fair, this one was young and very informal. She wore gathered skirts, long beads and hooped earrings. A hippy, and judging by the emphatic 'Ms', a women's libber. Today she was wearing a blue cotton top patterned with flocks of white birds. She probably didn't shave her underarms, Kay thought as she squirmed on her seat, waiting for Ms Gardiner to explain.

'We're a little concerned about Abigail,' the teacher began, leaning forward. 'She's become a bit withdrawn. She used to be so lively, so willing to join in, but recently …' She paused. 'I was wondering … is everything all right at home?'

Kay felt the woman's gaze burning into her face; it was as if she had X-ray vision and could see through the heavy foundation Kay had applied before leaving the house. There was the faintest remnant of a bruise on her upper cheek. Usually he left her face alone, but she'd got in the way of his fist, or so he'd claimed. Was Ms Gardiner looking at her long sleeves and putting two and two together?

'Everything's fine, thanks,' she replied firmly.

Ms Gardiner smiled weakly. 'I gather Abigail has a new daddy.'

'That's right. I got married last year … We're still sorting out the adoption,' she lied.

'I see. Does Abigail get on with your husband?'

'Yes!' Kay felt sick with nerves. If only she could lie down on that little bed.

'Only she drew this picture this afternoon and it worried me a little. It's not the first time either.' Ms Gardiner opened the brown folder and took out a sheet of paper. She handed it to Kay. 'I asked her to tell me about the drawing, but she refused. However, it, er … it kind of speaks for itself.'

Kay's hand started to tremble as she looked at the picture. It was clearly of the living room at home. She recognised the brown sofa and the vase of flowers on the dining table.

All three of them were there. A big stick figure with yellow flick-ups and a small one with curly black hair. Mummy and Abigail, both of them wearing blue triangle skirts and crying black tears. On the other side of the page, standing as far away as possible, was Daddy, tall and imposing. He had his mouth open as if he was shouting, and one arm was raised as if about to strike.

'It's just a drawing.' Kay sniffed. 'It doesn't mean anything.'

'Maybe not, but you can see how it could be interpreted.' Miss Gardiner took the picture off her and put it back in the folder. 'And given Abigail's changed behaviour ...'

'She gets ideas off the telly. I'll have to stop her watching *Doctor Who*.' Kay tried to laugh, but it came out as a frightened squawk.

There was a long pause. Kay wanted to run out of the room, but she was stuck to the chair. Her limbs had gone heavy and she was sweating profusely. She could feel her make-up melting and running off her face, exposing the truth that lay beneath. It was so shameful. She'd been hauled up before teachers before – for talking in class, bunking off games and once for smoking at the bus stop in uniform – but this was far worse. It was even more excruciating than admitting to her parents that she was pregnant.

'There are places you can go, you know,' said Ms Gardiner quietly. 'There's one recently opened in Nevansey; I volunteer there in the evenings and at weekends. It's a squat at the moment, but there's a group of us who are trying to get some funding from the council—'

'Sorry, I don't know what you're talking about.' Kay felt all her muscles stiffening.

'It's a refuge for women in danger. You can turn up any time of the day or night; nobody's ever turned away. And children are welcome too.'

Kay stood up. Her knees felt like bowls of jelly. 'I'd like to collect Abigail now. She'll be wondering where I've got to.'

Ms Gardiner scribbled something on a scrap of paper and put it in her hand. 'We're trying to keep the location a secret, for obvious reasons. Here's the address – just put it somewhere safe.'

CHAPTER SIXTEEN

Stella

Now

There's nothing else to do but go back to bed. Jack falls asleep instantly, but I toss and turn for another couple of hours. Why did Lori leave like that, without saying goodbye – without even saying thank you, more to the point? I feel defeated and upset. I'm cross with her for giving in to Darren, and even crosser with myself for not making her see sense.

I sink into sleep at last and am only woken by the sound of banging in the room above. Alan is already at work. Jack has left for London, feeling smug no doubt that he's been proved right about Lori. I dive under the duvet, trying to block out the noise. Alan's a nice guy, but today I wish I had the house to myself.

I get out of bed and pull on some clothes. My limbs feel heavy as I drag them around the room. I'm so tired. My skin itches, as if covered in a fine layer of dust. I need a cup of really strong coffee to get me started. Leaving my room, I go into the kitchen and put the kettle on. There's a strong draught coming from the back of the house. Irritated, I walk past the middle room and into the conservatory. The door is wide open, letting all the heat out.

Heaving a sigh, I go to shut it, then stop mid slam. Lori is out there. She's wearing the pink jumper I bought her from the charity shop, and the jogging bottoms she arrived in.

'Lori!' I shout. 'Hey! Lori!' She turns around and waves like nothing's amiss. I stomp onto the patio and pick my way down the overgrown path that runs to the bottom of the garden. 'Hey! What are you doing here?'

She takes a long drag of her cigarette. 'Just having a quick fag before I start work. Sorry, I know it's a filthy habit. I want to quit, but—'

'No, no, I mean, why did you come back?' She stares at me nonplussed. 'Last night. Jack saw you getting into a car and driving away.'

'What? I haven't been out of the house for weeks, you know that.'

'He heard you leave the house. He followed you.'

'He did *what*?'

'You got into a dark car. It sounded like Darren's.'

Her eyes widen. A chimney of ash forms on the tip of her cigarette. 'I don't know who Jack was stalking last night, but it wasn't me. I was in bed by eleven.'

'Right ... sorry. It was obviously a mistake ...'

'I wouldn't just leave like that.'

'That's what I thought. I was surprised, I couldn't understand—'

'So Jack's been spying on me, has he?'

'Not at all. He just thought he heard ...' I sigh. 'It doesn't matter.'

'It does to me. I've had enough of men watching my every move.' She stubs her cigarette out with an angry heel. 'He'll be reading my texts next.'

'Please, forget I ever mentioned it. My mistake, I must have misunderstood.'

We stand quietly for a few moments. I want to go but can't think of a good exit line.

'I'd love to help you clear all this, you know,' she says in a completely different tone. 'I'm a better gardener than a builder.'

'Feel free,' I reply.

Another pause.

'I was really upset when I thought you'd gone back to Darren,' I say. 'I'm scared that he'll attack you. You could be killed.'

She nods thoughtfully. 'Yes, I know that. You're a very special person, Stella. There aren't many in the world like you. Most of them look away, pretend not to hear, don't want to get involved. But you didn't hesitate.'

'It's how I was brought up.' My eyes well with tears. I feel such a fraud, piggybacking on the goodness of my parents.

'Don't forget to look after yourself too, okay?'

'Me? Oh, I'm fine.'

'Be careful of Jack. He likes to be in control.'

I force out a laugh. 'No he doesn't. We have a really equal relationship.'

She gives me an oblique glance. 'That's not how it looks to me. The house belongs to you, right? It's your money that's paying for the refurbishments. Jack is here on your terms and he doesn't like it. I know he doesn't want me here. He's jealous because you're giving me attention and he thinks you should only be focused on him.'

'You sound like you've read a book on the subject, Lori,' I say, surprised.

She blushes. 'No, no, I'm only going on what I see. My therapist used to talk to me like that, and at first I couldn't see what she was getting at.'

'Things have been a bit strained recently,' I admit. 'But really, we're good.'

'Glad to hear it,' she says, but I know she doesn't believe me. 'Right. Time I started work.' She walks back towards the house. I watch her tramping through the long grass, and my pulse quickens. What did she mean, *Be careful of Jack*?

I follow her indoors. She's already climbing the stairs, shouting out hello to Alan. I pick up my phone and call Jack, but it goes straight to voicemail. He always switches his mobile off when he goes into meetings, so it doesn't particularly surprise me. I leave a vague message asking him to call back when he gets a chance. But the hours go by and I don't hear from him.

It's impossible to concentrate on anything. The room is enormous and yet I feel confined, as if the walls are closing in on me while I'm not looking, centimetre by centimetre. I have a sudden urge to get out, not just out of the house, but away from the town altogether. I want to see Jack. I want him to hold me close and tell me everything's all right. That he made a stupid mistake thinking he heard Lori leaving the house. Perhaps it was a door banging in the wind. It must have taken him a few minutes to get dressed and go after her. He was half asleep; he probably saw somebody walking down the hill and thought it was her. As for the dark car; well, lots of cars are blue or black. It could easily have been a minicab. See? There's a logical explanation for all of it.

Why doesn't he call?

By the afternoon, I'm going crazy. We have to talk before he comes home. He'll be pissed off that Lori's still here, and I have to warn him. I don't want a scene.

I change into a grey shift dress, put on my red raincoat and a pair of smart ankle boots. London clothes. Thin and light, perfect for standing on the crowded, overheated Tube. It's a short walk to Nevansey station. There are two trains an hour and I just manage to catch the two forty-five p.m. It takes me directly into St Pancras and then it's just one stop on the Victoria line.

By four o'clock I'm standing in the foyer of his smart office block. Jack works for a design company, based on the fifth floor.

'Hi, I'm here to see Jack Lancing,' I say. The receptionist makes me sign in via a tablet. It takes a photo, the camera freezing on my startled gaze. There are dark rings beneath my eyes, reminding me of my terrible night's sleep. As she dials Jack's internal number, I suddenly feel like I'm doing the wrong thing. He's going to think I'm really weird, doorstepping him like this.

'Sorry, he's off sick today,' she says, replacing the handset. 'What's your name? I could try someone else.'

'That's okay, it was just a social call. I was passing by. On the off chance,' I bluster, then hurry out of the building, only stopping for breath when I reach the corner.

What are you playing at, Jack?

I immediately call him, and this time he picks up after two rings. 'Hi,' he says. 'Sorry I couldn't call earlier. Everything okay?'

'Where are you?' I demand.

There's the briefest of pauses. 'At work.'

'Don't lie to me, Jack. I've just been at your office. They told me you were off sick.'

'Ah … sorry. What are you doing in London?'

'Never mind that. What's going on?'

'Nothing much. I just fancied a day off. I'm at the V and A. There's a really interesting exhibition on—'

'Stay there. I'm on my way. Meet me in the tea rooms.'

'Don't be silly.' He sounds nervous. 'There's no need to do that. I'll come home.'

'No, I'm coming to you. We need to talk.'

He's waiting at a large round table, big enough to seat half a dozen people and covered in the detritus of several salad lunches. The place is horribly busy. I weave my way through the clusters of grey-haired ladies, who all remind me in some way of my mother, and sit down next to him. The smells of balsamic vinegar and cold coffee rise up my nostrils.

'It was the only free table,' he says apologetically. 'Would you rather go somewhere else?'

'No.' I unbutton my coat and ease it off my shoulders onto the back of the chair.

'What do you want? Tea or coffee? I think they do wine too.' He starts to rise, but I shake my head.

'I want to know what's going on.'

'Nothing's going on. I was in a funny mood this morning, that's all, couldn't face work. I do it about once every six weeks. Bunk off. Visit a museum or art gallery.'

'You never told me before.'

'I knew you'd disapprove, that's why. Sometimes I just need a bit of time to myself, you know? To do London things. There's fuck all happening in Nevansey.'

'Yes, you hate living there, you make it abundantly clear. Anyway, I'm not here to talk about Nevansey.' I start stacking the plates, scraping off the food remains and making a neat pile. I'm fizzing with irritation.

'They have staff to do that,' he says.

I put down somebody else's knife. 'It wasn't Lori you saw last night.'

He folds his arms. 'Yes it was.'

'You made a mistake.'

'I didn't.'

'Then how come she's still at the house? I spoke to her this morning and she insists she was in bed all night.'

He leans back in his chair and stares at the exquisitely tiled walls. 'She's lying.'

'I don't think so.'

'I know so.' I can't bear it when he goes all smug and know-it-all on me. 'I followed her and she got in the car and it drove off. My guess is the guy – this Darren, presumably – dropped her off later and she crept in.'

'She doesn't have a key.'

'There's a spare set in the kitchen drawer.'

'Why would she meet up with him? She hates him, she's terrified of him.'

'I expect they're on some kind of scam. They probably worked out you had thousands in your bank account for the building work. You should check your statements, change your passwords. Find a better hiding place for your book of codes.'

'That's a disgusting thing to say.'

'Why are you so naïve, Stella?'

'I'm not naïve. I just trust people.'

'Same thing.'

'It's not the same thing at all. Lori is a victim of domestic violence.'

'So you say.'

I scrape back my chair. 'Stop it!' I hiss. 'You're being vile. What's got into you, Jack? You never used to be like this. Ever since I bought the house you've basically been in a foul mood. Are you jealous? Do you wish your parents had died and left you a million pounds? Because if I could swap places with you, I'd do it like a shot.'

'Shut up,' he says in a low voice. 'Go back to your battered wife and leave me alone.' He looks down at the table and sets his jaw. A woman sitting by herself at a nearby table shoots me a curious look.

'Please, Jack, let's just talk. We can sort it out. I'll tell Lori she has to leave if you like. Just don't lie to me. I can't bear it.'

He closes his eyes, as if silently counting to ten. Then he looks up at me, his expression as serious as I've ever seen it. 'I'm pretty certain I saw her last night, but maybe I got it wrong. It was late and dark, I was tired. But if you're so trusting, then you have to trust me too. I'm trying to look after you, to save you from yourself.'

'I don't need looking after.'

'You do.' He leans forward. 'If Lori *did* sneak out to see her husband, for whatever reason, and he brought her back to the house, he now knows where she's living. Which means she's not safe, Stella. And nor are you.'

CHAPTER SEVENTEEN

Stella

Now

A week later, I get a call from the architect. The plans for the kitchen-diner extension have been approved with no amendments. A couple of months ago we would have celebrated with a bottle of champagne, but this morning I barely register a reaction.

'If you send me details of your contractor, I'll start the process with Building Control,' he says.

'Oh, um, yeah, okay,' I reply, pulling my mind away from other thoughts. 'I'll let you know.'

The phone call ends and I find myself drifting into the conservatory. It's a horrid narrow corridor and I'll be pleased to see it go. There's no doubt that the extension will make a dramatic impact, opening up the house and flooding it with light. But what's the point of creating a fantastic family space if you've no family to put in it?

I think of Molly, with her doting husband and gorgeous new baby. She still lives close to the commuter town where we both grew up, in a small but perfect house. For years I spurned the idea of a safe suburban life, but now I long for that kind of stability. Over the last few months I've found myself dreaming about wedding dresses and where we would have the reception. Maybe we could get married on the beach and then party in the garden.

Some hope of that, I think, staring through the windows at the wilderness that was once a lawn. It's not just the garden that's not ready, it's Jack. Everything was going brilliantly between us until we moved here, but recently I've felt as if our relationship has been slowly sinking into the mud. He's never properly engaged with the building plans, pretending to listen to my design ideas, agreeing because it's easier than arguing, always ending the discussion with 'It's up to you, it's your house.' Recently he hasn't even bothered to go upstairs to check on Alan's work. When I talk bathroom tiles or kitchen units his eyes glaze over and I can tell his mind is elsewhere. It's become *my* dream, not ours.

But it's not just about the bricks and mortar. Eventually the building work will be complete and there'll just be the two of us, living in our airy, light extension with its polished concrete floor and industrial lighting. Or maybe I'll be alone. Like a modern-day Miss Havisham, trapped in time, waiting for a future that can never be.

A lump hardens in my throat and I swallow it down. There's no point in feeling sorry for myself. I have to *do* something. Turning away from the garden, I walk back through the kitchen and into the hallway. A cacophony of banging, chatter and music is coming from upstairs. Alan has called in some extra guys to help put in the new ceilings. I think they're Romanian. Lori has been temporarily demoted to tea lady and seems to spend most of her time running up and downstairs with mugs. There's a cheerful mood up there, a camaraderie of dust and wet plaster. I'm not part of it. As far as the new guys are concerned, I'm the client. No, correction. I'm the wife of the client, who is a man of mystery, never seen. In their minds, I couldn't possibly know what I'm talking about, so my opinion is never sought. The new builders don't know how to react to me – whenever our paths cross, they lower their eyes.

I slip into our bedroom, closing the door behind me. The room looks as chaotic as ever, a mishmash of sleeping, working and eating.

I'm sick of the cardboard boxes, of not having my things around me. Sitting on the bed, I close my eyes. What to do? Of course, I could put the house back on the market tomorrow. I'd probably lose a lot of money, but if that's what it takes to save my relationship … Without Jack, there's really no point in having this place.

And yet I feel reluctant to go down that route. We made a joint decision to buy it; we knew it would be hellish living through the refurbishments but assured ourselves it would be worth it. He's not really giving it a try. He comes home from the office later and later each day, complaining about his workload or blaming the trains. Sometimes he doesn't even bother to text to let me know when to expect him. Last night I checked online and it said the trains were running on time, but when he turned up at half past ten, he claimed there'd been a signal failure.

'Really?' I said. 'It wasn't mentioned on the live updates.'

'Doesn't surprise me,' he answered gloomily. 'It's absolute chaos out there; nobody knows what's going on. I should never have moved out of London. It's taking years off my life.'

I know the travelling is difficult, but thousands of people commute every day and *their* relationships don't split up.

But not everyone has a stranger living in their house, I remind myself. Jack hates Lori living here. One minute he's telling me she's a fake, on a mission to scam me out of my savings, and the next he's warning me that her husband is about to storm the place, that my life's in danger too. He can't have it both ways. *Tell Lori to leave,* an inner voice says, *then he'll be happy and everything will be all right.* But another voice jumps into the conversation. *Why should you give in to him?*

When we argued at the museum, I offered to chuck Lori out, but I knew I wasn't going to. She's blossoming here, so much calmer and more confident, a completely different person to the one who knocked on our door six weeks ago. Like Alan said, she's a survivor, not a victim. This is the right place for her to be, better than some revolting bed and breakfast. I'm sure she'll eventually be strong enough to leave Darren for good and be reunited with her children, but until then, she needs to be here. I don't believe she went to meet him last week, I think either Jack was mistaken or – and it pains me to say it – he lied about seeing her get into the car.

It's the lies I can't take. Perhaps he's lying about all these evening meetings and cancelled trains. He definitely lied about being at work when he'd bunked off to the museum. What if he was meeting someone there? I remember the young woman sitting at the next table in the tea room. She couldn't take her eyes off us; I'm sure she was eavesdropping.

No, he wouldn't do that to me. I mustn't torture myself.

'I'm supposed to be seeing the kids tomorrow,' Lori says, finding me in the kitchen preparing a stir-fry. It's gone five. Alan and his crew have left for the day. She puts a tray of dirty mugs by the sink and turns on the tap.

I look up from the chopping board. 'Are you going to go?'

'Not sure. I haven't been outside the house for so long, I feel nervous.' She squirts washing-up liquid into the flow of hot water, then ruffles up the bubbles.

'I think you should go. It will cheer you up; you must be missing them so much. And they'll be missing you too.'

'Hmm, not sure about that. They blamed me for the rows, just wanted me to do what Daddy said so it would all stop.' She puts the mugs into the bowl and reaches for the cleaning brush.

I lay down the knife, wiping the onion tears from my eyes. 'They were too little to understand, that's all. It doesn't mean they don't love you.'

'No, I'm sure you're right … I just feel a bit anxious. In case Darren … you know …'

'I think we've established that he doesn't know where you are, Lori,' I say. 'And I'm assuming he doesn't know where the kids are living either?'

She scrubs away at a mug, then bangs it on the draining board. 'I hope not.'

'Anyway, I thought he was full of remorse for what he'd done.'

'Yeah, but he doesn't mean it. It's just a ploy to get me to come home.'

I move on to the carrots, slicing them into thin, even sticks. 'Well, it's good that you recognise that. You've taken a big step forward.'

She looks at me, puzzled. 'What do you mean?'

'You've realised there's no point in going back to him.'

'No, I *have* to go back to him. For the sake of the kids.'

'Uh-uh, you have to *leave* him for the sake of the kids!'

Her hands lift out of the bowl. 'You don't understand what it's like for women like …' She stops herself. 'Like me. You haven't got a bloody clue.' I go to answer, but she turns and walks out of the kitchen, water dripping from her fingers and splashing onto the floor.

Jack doesn't arrive home until gone eleven p.m. Friday-night drinks with work mates was tonight's excuse. In what I now think of as the old days, it wouldn't have been a problem. I would have met up with my own friends, or gone to join him in the pub. But this evening, his absence rankles. He knows I'm here on my own, with nobody to go out with and nothing much to do. I sense that he's punishing me, giving me a taste of what life would be like without him.

Two can play at that game, I think. The lights are out when he comes home, the heating long switched off. His portion of stir-fry has already gone into the freezer and there's no wine left. When he crawls into bed, I pretend to be fast asleep. But it doesn't seem to bother him. Within minutes, he's snoring peacefully. It's me who lies awake for the next two hours – thinking, thinking, thinking …

On Saturday morning I feel groggy, unable to stir myself. Jack's already up and about. I can hear him banging around. Maybe he's making breakfast as a peace offering? Glancing at the alarm clock, I'm shocked to see that it's gone ten o'clock. I get up and slouch into the kitchen, where he's standing in front of the counter eating a bowl of cereal.

'Hi,' I say.

He looks over his right shoulder. 'Hi.'

'How's things?'

'Good.' He puts another spoonful of muesli into his mouth. 'The rugby's on today. England v Wales. It's being shown at the Oyster Catch – the pub on the other side of the pier. Fancy coming along?'

Rugby's not my thing; usually I'm happy for him to watch it with his mates. But like me, he doesn't know anyone in Nevansey, so I smile and say, 'Yeah, why not?'

'Excellent.' He looks relieved. 'Best to get there early so we can nab a good table. We can have lunch.'

'Okay.'

I go back to the bedroom to get dressed, my spirits lifted slightly by his apparent eagerness to spend time with me, even though I know it's only because he doesn't want to watch the rugby on his own. But it's better than nothing. *Take the positives, Stella. Take them and build on them.*

As I pull on my jeans, my thoughts are briefly diverted to Lori. I push my head through the neck of my jumper and dig my arms into the sleeves. Now that we're going to be out all afternoon, she'll need a key to get back in. I go to the kitchen and take the spare key out of the cutlery drawer.

'What do you need that for?' Jack asks, taking a tea bag out of his mug and throwing it into the bin.

'It's for Lori. She's going to visit her kids today.'

'You mean she's actually going to leave the house?'

'That's the plan. It's an important step. I hope she manages it.'

'Me too,' he replies, but I can't work out whether he's being genuine or sarcastic. I leave the key on the worktop next to the kettle where I know she'll find it.

Jack seems impatient to get out. Instead of tramping down the Esplanade, we cross the road and take the path that runs behind the sea wall. The tide is out and the mud looks like a giant spillage of something nasty. A cold wind snaps at my ears, sharpening my nose to a point. I used to see a stark beauty in this landscape, but today it just looks ugly and grey.

As we walk past the beach huts, my eyes dart to their padlocked doors, checking they're all still intact. I don't know why, but I feel strangely vulnerable. As if someone's watching and noting our departure. This will be the first time in weeks that the house will be completely empty. Lori has become a live-in guardian, part of the tatty fabric of the place. In some ways, I feel that she has more right to be there than I do. *Don't be stupid*, I tell myself. *It's your home. Yours and Jack's.*

He's trying to engage me in rugby talk, wants a debate about our chances today against Wales and whether the England pack is strong enough. He knows I haven't a clue, let alone any interest, but he carries on regardless. I nod obligingly and make listening noises. The further away we get from the house, the more anxious I feel. Am I just being paranoid, or is something wrong?

CHAPTER EIGHTEEN

Stella

Now

There's fifteen minutes of the match left to go. The place is packed and incredibly noisy, as fans cheer and shout at the televisions. Our table, ideally close to the biggest screen, has become a dumping ground for dirty glasses and empty crisp packets. I feel uncomfortably hot. My head is pounding and my thick jumper is making my skin itch.

'Sorry, but I don't think I can take much more of this,' I shout above the din.

Jack squeezes my hand. 'That's okay. You need to get some fresh air. Take a nice long walk.'

'Yeah, I'll do that.'

'You could go as far as the boat sheds, see if you can pick up some fish for tonight.'

My heart lifts. It almost feels like the old days. I kiss him on the cheek and grab my things. 'See you back at the ranch. Won't be long.'

'Take as long as you like, clear your head.' He waves me off, then turns his attention back to the big screen.

Outside, the cold air acts like a compress on my forehead. I take deep breaths of it as I walk along the seafront, away from Westhill House and towards the older part of town. It's not an area

I know well. The tourist attractions, such as they are, give way to black wooden boat sheds, their concrete car parks fenced off with metal railings. But beyond those, and near the sailing club, is a row of huts that sell wet fish. Their opening times are somewhat unpredictable, and sometimes they have very little available, but it's always super fresh. When I have a proper kitchen, I tell myself, I'll come down here every week. I'll learn how to cook lobster and eat oysters like a local.

To my disappointment, all the sheds are closed. Maybe they don't operate at weekends. I turn around and retrace my steps along the promenade, before cutting inland to the high street. I guess it'll have to be pizzas instead tonight.

Arriving at the Co-op, I take a basket and throw in a bottle of Chianti, a couple of 'luxury' pepperoni pizzas and a bag of salad. Bananas, milk, some croissants for the morning. A few more ready meals to keep the freezer stocked. I'm contemplating the selection of chilled desserts when my phone rings. It's Jack.

'Stella? Where are you?' There's an odd urgency in his voice.

'At the supermarket. The fish sheds were closed. What's wrong?'

'We've been burgled,' he says.

My stomach turns over. 'Wha … what do you mean? How do you know?'

'I'm at home, aren't I? Just got back. I've called the police. They probably won't turn up for ages, but I didn't want you to worry if you saw their car outside.'

'Shit … What's been taken?'

He pauses. 'Just hurry up and get back, okay?'

I run to the tills, my hand shaking as I put the items on the conveyor belt. How could we have been burgled? Making a contactless payment, I stuff all the items into a bag and rush home, my mind racing ahead of me all the way. I already know what Jack will be thinking. That this is somehow connected to Lori.

As I put the key into the lock, he opens the front door. He looks nervous, as if he's about to break some very bad news.

'What's happened? Was Lori in? Is she hurt?'

He shakes his head. 'She's not here.'

'That's something,' I reply, putting the bag down and taking off my coat. 'What did they take?'

'A few bits. Don't touch anything,' he says. 'Not until the police have been. They might need to take fingerprints.'

Jack takes the shopping into the kitchen. My palm feels sweaty as I turn the door handle to the front room and enter.

Our plastic storage boxes have been emptied onto the bed. My bras, pants, socks and tights stare back at me, and I shudder at the thought of strange fingers picking over them. I look around, desperately trying to work out what's missing, but the obvious things are still here. Jack's guitar is leaning against the wall, my laptop sitting on the desk.

'I think I must have disturbed them,' Jack says from the doorway, as if answering my silent question. He comes up and gives me a hug. 'Are you okay?'

'I think so. Have they taken *anything*?'

He pulls away, looking uncomfortable. 'Hmm. Afraid so ...'

'What?'

'I'm not sure exactly ... but they've been through your mum and dad's stuff.'

'Oh my God.' I push past him and run into the room on the other side of the hallway. The place is a mess. Cardboard boxes containing my parents' personal effects have been ripped open. Some silverware has gone, as has my father's cut-glass whisky decanter. But most alarming of all, my mother's jewellery box – inlaid wood, lined with red velvet – is lying on its back, empty.

'No, noooo!' I wail, falling to my knees.

Jack is right behind me. 'What was in there?'

'Their wedding rings … Dad's gold watch … A necklace, earrings, I can't remember exactly.' A sob catches in my throat.

'I'm so sorry, Stella.' He crouches down beside me. 'Were they worth much?'

'No … hardly anything. But that's not the point, is it? They belonged to them. They're all I have left.'

'I know, it's so tough.' He squeezes my shoulder.

'How come they knew it was here? There are dozens of boxes they could have opened.'

'Maybe it was just bad luck. Or maybe they looked at the labels.' He reaches across and pulls one of the boxes towards him. On the outside, scrawled in felt pen, are the giveaway words: *M and D's stuff. Silver, glass, jewellery etc.*

'Oh God, how stupid of me!' I cover my face with my hands.

Jack stands up. 'The police will be here soon. The more information we can give them, the better our chances of getting the stuff back.'

'How the hell did they get in?' I say.

'I'm not sure. I had a scout around but I couldn't see any signs of forced entry. The back door was wide open, though, so either they got in some other way and left via the conservatory, or it was open from the start.'

I don't respond. Was it Lori's fault, then? She's always going into the garden to smoke. Did she accidentally leave the door open? It's a possibility, but I don't want to land her in it.

'And Lori's definitely not in the house?' I say.

'No. I don't know if that's a coincidence or …' He leaves the rest of his sentence for me to complete.

'Or what?' My tone is sharp. 'What are you trying to say, Jack?'

'I don't know. I just think it's a bit weird that she goes out for the first time in weeks and we get burgled.'

'This is nothing to do with Lori.'

He gives me a patronising smile. 'Well, you would say that.'

We leave the room as we found it. Jack opens the bottle of wine I bought for dinner and pours two glasses.

I secretly text Lori, asking how she is and when she's going to be home. I don't tell her about the burglary or that the police are on their way in case she's frightened off. She doesn't reply. I persuade myself that there's nothing suspicious about that. She's probably having fun with the kids and not looking at her phone.

Two male uniformed officers, PCs Brookes and Khan, turn up forty-five minutes later. They seem enormous in their winter padding, their dark clothes festooned with yellow fluorescent strips, reminding me of giant wasps. Their radios constantly bleep out unintelligible messages and they keep interrupting their sentences to listen to them.

We are standing in the conservatory, shivering by the still open door leading into the garden.

'Did you definitely close this door before you left the house today?' PC Khan asks.

'Yes,' I say quickly.

He points to the key still in the lock. 'Not very clever.'

'I know. But the fences are really high and there's a brick wall at the bottom. There's no way anyone could get in or out via the garden.'

'Oh, you'd be surprised,' says PC Brookes. 'I'll take a look.' He unclips a torch from his belt and steps outside.

'This used to be a women's refuge,' I explain to the other officer. 'They had a lot of security.'

'Yeah, I thought I remembered it. Westhill House, right? Closed down a few years ago. I've been called here a few times over disturbances in the street.'

'None of the cameras work any more,' says Jack. 'The alarm's defunct too.'

'But they weren't to know that. I'm surprised they risked it,' says PC Khan. 'Problem is, with no sign of forced entry, you're going to struggle with an insurance claim. Anyone else have a key?'

'Just the builder,' I say, reluctantly. 'But he wouldn't—'

'Can you give me his details?'

'And there's our guest,' Jack adds, giving me a meaningful look. 'Lori. What's her last name, Stella?'

'Er, I've forgotten,' I lie. She's never mentioned it and I've never thought to ask.

'She's one of Stella's waifs and strays. She turned up on our doorstep about six weeks ago and we can't seem to get rid of her.'

'Jack, that's not fair!' I turn to the officer. 'She needed somewhere to stay, that's all. We're helping her get back on her feet. I'm sure she wouldn't be involved in any burglary.'

PC Khan makes a note. 'You do have to be careful who you take in,' he says. 'A lot of homeless people have drug dependencies, which means they need a lot of money.'

'She's not a drug addict.'

'Or they have mental health problems. There was a case not long ago of a young man who killed an entire family.'

'I have pointed this out,' says Jack, 'but she won't listen.'

'Don't be so patronising,' I hiss. 'Lori's not mad and you know it.'

PC Khan breathes a sigh of relief as his colleague steps back inside the house. 'I can't find any obvious means of access.'

'Which means it was probably an inside job.' There's a slight tone of triumph in Jack's voice. I'm starting to feel really angry with him.

'Will you stop blaming Lori?'

The officers exchange embarrassed glances. I can tell they're not really interested in launching a major investigation. I'm wondering if they even believe us. No broken windows, no forced locks, nothing of great value taken … It's not making sense to them and it's not making sense to me either.

'What about fingerprinting?' asks Jack hopefully. 'Or DNA testing?'

'Lori slept in that room on her first night, so her DNA will be all over the place.' I glare at him. 'And a professional burglar would wear gloves.'

'Thank you, Sherlock,' he quips.

There's an awkward pause.

'Let's start with the builder's details,' says PC Brookes. 'We can at least run him through the database.' I hurry out, going into the bedroom and rummaging in the desk drawer for Alan's business card. There's a bad feeling growing in my stomach. I'm sure he's not involved in this, and I don't think the Romanian plasterers are either. If we start accusing them of theft, they could walk off site.

The officers are on their way out when I come back into the hallway with the business card. PC Khan scribbles down Alan's details, then snaps his notebook shut.

'Right then. We'll be in touch.'

'Thanks for coming over so promptly,' says Jack, showing them out.

My gaze lingers on the closing door. 'So what was that all about?' I say.

'What do you mean?' He puts his hands in his pockets. 'I'm sorry you got all offended about your friend, but I had to say something. I mean, it *is* a bit suspicious …'

I take a deep breath, letting the words that have to be said rise into my mouth. 'Did you stage it?'

He lets out an incredulous puff of laughter. 'What? Don't be stupid. You think I'd call the police—'

'Yes, I do. As soon as you heard that Lori was going out for the day, you came up with this disgusting plan. You probably knew the fish sheds would be closed. You sent me all the way down there to give yourself enough time to get home.'

'That's absolute rubbish. Why would I do that? What are you talking about?'

'I reckon you had just enough time to mess the place up a bit, hide my parents' things—'

'This is ridiculous,' he splutters. 'Why would I do that?'

'To get at Lori.'

'Oh right, so you'd rather accuse *me* than a complete stranger … Jesus, you don't even know her full name!' He lifts his hands in a despairing gesture. 'You heard what the policeman said. Foolish, gullible people end up dead.'

'I'm not so gullible that I can't see what you're doing,' I say. 'Lori warned me about you and now I see what she was getting at. First you tried to make me think she'd done those drawings, then you pretended she'd gone to see her husband. You've been lying to me about work and now you do this. You're gaslighting me. And what's worse, you're exploiting my grief for my parents. Where have you hidden their things?'

He takes a couple of steps back. 'Gaslighting? Honestly, Stella, you've got it badly wrong. You need your head examining – you're letting this woman get right under your skin. She's manipulating you; she's got you exactly where she wants you. This is serious. She's got to go. Like tonight. As soon as she comes back, that's it, she's out. And if she refuses to leave, I'll call the police again.'

But I'm not going to let him distract me. 'What was the final score, Jack? In the rugby.'

He hesitates. 'I'm not answering that.'

'Tut, tut. You should have googled it. But you didn't have time. You probably ran all the way back from the pub. You had so much to do before I came home – mess the place up, hide the stuff, call the cops—'

'Shut up, will you? You're making me really angry.'

'All you have to do is tell me the score.'

He glowers at me. 'For fuck's sake, it was 12–3, now stop this.'

'Yes, that was the score when I left. But there was still five minutes on the clock. Shall we check?' I reach down for my bag and take out my phone.

'I mean it, Stella,' he says. 'Stop this right now or you're going to regret it.'

'Are you threatening me?' He snatches at the phone but I whisk my hand away.

'Look! I can't remember the final score, I was too upset about the burglary. I felt really sorry for you because I knew how upset you'd be about losing your parents' belongings. I did know it, but it's gone out of my head.'

My fingers are shaking as I type in: *Rugby England v Wales final score*. I feel the air being sucked out of my body as the result comes up on the screen.

CHAPTER NINETEEN

Kay

Then

As Kay walked home with Abigail, the piece of paper burned in her palm. She wanted to let it go, to drop it into the gutter, but her fingers refused to loosen their grip. *Just put it somewhere safe*, Ms Gardiner had said, leaning into her. She was wearing patchouli oil and smelt of exotic secrets.

'What did Miss say?' asked Abigail.

'Oh, nothing much. We were talking about the summer fete. She asked me to make a cake.' It was only half a lie. A note had been sent out asking for contributions. Abigail looked up at her doubtfully. She was a bright kid, not easily fooled, but she didn't question further. Maybe she'd seen the look of shock on her teacher's face when she drew the picture. Maybe, in her own little way, she'd been trying to help.

Kay unlocked the front door and they stepped into the house. Seeing the brown sofa and the wilting flowers on the dining table made her stomach lurch. The drawing had been realistic in so many ways.

You can turn up any time of the day or night.

'Why don't you go outside and play on your space hopper?' she said.

Once Abigail was safely installed in the garden, Kay ran upstairs to her bedroom. She uncurled her fingers and the scrap of paper sprang open. *Westhill House. The Esplanade, Nevansey.* There was a phone number too, and a name next to it. *Franny. CALL ME ANY TIME*, it said in capital letters. She folded the paper into a tiny square, then hid it in a packet of sanitary towels.

She tried to imagine Westhill House. If it was on the Esplanade, then it probably faced the sea. Kay had been to Nevansey several times. It was about forty-five minutes away by bus. She used to go there with her mates when they were teenagers and do the amusement arcades, or hang around the pier hoping to get chatting to boys. That was before she fell pregnant and lost her childhood. Westhill House sounded like it was beyond the pier and up the hill. But it didn't matter; it was extremely unlikely she'd ever go there. A squat? That was illegal, wasn't it? The last thing Kay wanted to do was get in trouble with the police.

Nobody's ever turned away.

That couldn't be true. What happened if there weren't enough beds? And what about the kids? How would Abigail get to school?

Besides, things weren't *that* bad. Ms Gardiner – Franny – had put two and two together and come up with twenty-six. She was probably one of those man-haters who went around trying to prise women away from their husbands. Kay didn't want to be a divorcee, a single mum again. She didn't want another failure on her record. Her parents would be furious if she walked out on her comfortable life on the Fairmead estate and took Abigail to live in a squat. Weren't they filthy dirty and full of people on drugs? It was out of the question. Ridiculous. Things really, really weren't that bad.

But she couldn't bring herself to destroy the piece of paper.

She went over to the window and looked down into the garden. Abigail was bouncing around on the orange ball with her black curls flying, looking like a witch on a new-fangled broomstick. Was Ms Gardiner right about her being withdrawn at school?

She looked happy enough at the moment, but then Daddy wasn't home yet. It was true, when Foxy was around, Abigail hid in her bedroom. There was very little communication between them. In the beginning Kay had tried so hard to make them love each other, but she'd all but given up now.

She still believed that having a child of their own would make all the difference. Foxy was incredibly committed to his brother; she was sure he'd love a child just as fiercely if he or she were his own flesh and blood. And he wouldn't dare to strike Kay while she was pregnant.

She opened the drawer of her bedside cabinet and took out her packet of contraceptive pills. He'd said several times recently that he didn't want another kid, but that was only because he couldn't imagine how amazing it would feel. A lot of men didn't think about becoming fathers until it happened, then the moment they held the baby in their arms they were besotted. She pushed today's tiny pill out of its foil case and balanced it on the tip of her finger. He wouldn't have to know. When she fell pregnant, she would blame the contraceptive failure on an upset stomach. The same thing had happened to her friend Ruth, and her husband had been thrilled.

Before she could change her mind, she walked into the bathroom and flicked the pill into the toilet bowl, flushing it immediately. She felt dizzy with excitement, almost as if she'd just conceived. The squat was not for her; that was just running away, it was defeatism, somewhere women went when there was no other choice. But having a baby was a positive move. It would bring her and Foxy together, turn them into a proper little family. Kay felt herself growing stronger by the second. She would turn this marriage around. Whatever it was she was doing wrong, she would put it right.

*

A month had passed. A whole month of letting him see her take her pill and then spitting it out when she went to the bathroom. Her period hadn't come, but that didn't necessarily mean anything. Sometimes it took months for your natural cycle to return; she wasn't going to get her hopes up. Anyway, they had enough to worry about at the moment.

It was the first day of Micky's trial, and Foxy was insisting she came with him to sit in the public gallery. He'd taken a precious week's holiday so that he could be there every day. 'We have to put on a good show for the jury,' he told her. 'Wear something decent; we don't want any tits on display.' She didn't remind him that he'd made her throw out all her low-cut tops ages ago.

Micky had scrubbed up well – his hair was cut short and he was wearing his brother's wedding suit, even his silver tie. He was almost unrecognisable from the scruffy layabout who hung around their house every weekend. When the judge came in and everyone stood, Kay did a double take. It was like seeing her own husband in the dock.

She didn't want to be here; it was embarrassing to be in the camp of the accused. Please God the case wouldn't make the local paper and her parents find out. Micky waved up at the gallery and Foxy nudged her until she waved back. She didn't dislike her brother-in-law, but she thought he was a fool. There was no doubt in her mind that he'd walloped the other player as hard as he could, but he was pleading self-defence.

'It was just a punch-up,' Foxy had said when Micky was charged. 'A waste of public money taking it to trial.'

'But the bloke's jaw was broken in two places,' Kay had pointed out, instantly regretting her bravery.

'If you're not careful, you'll end up worse,' he'd snapped, but he'd spared her that time. You never knew with him. Sometimes she'd say something completely innocent and she'd get a nasty slap. Other times they'd have a blazing row and he wouldn't touch her. It was the unpredictability that kept her on her toes, ever watchful, ever waiting.

The trial began with the case for the prosecution. Every time the barrister said something negative about Micky, Foxy tutted and shook his head gravely. Kay twisted her fingers nervously in her lap as she listened to various witnesses describe Micky's professional foul in forensic detail, as if that were the crime that was being tried. She found it tiresome and stupid. In one way, Foxy was right. It was six of one and half a dozen of the other. Why should this case come to court when husbands were beating their wives on a regular basis and getting away with it? She adjusted her scarf, making sure last night's bite wasn't on show. It was knotted so tightly around her neck, it made her look like an air stewardess. If only, she thought. She liked the idea of flying around the world.

Just as it seemed they were making progress, the judge stopped proceedings for the day. It was only three p.m. 'He wants to get a game of golf in while the weather's nice,' whispered Foxy. 'What a bastard.'

The following day, Micky took the stand. He'd been well coached, Foxy had seen to that. He looked so clean and smart, like butter wouldn't melt in his mouth. When he was asked to describe what had happened, he gave an Oscar-winning performance. 'I went for the ball and I won it, no way was it a foul. I'd made him look a fool, see, and he lost his temper, just started punching me. I was really scared. I put my hands up to protect myself and accidentally caught him on the cheek.'

They went to the cafeteria while they waited for the jury to decide. Foxy was agitated. 'What's taking them so long?' he moaned. 'Anyone would think it was a bloody murder trial.'

'I expect they're arguing about whether it was self-defence or not,' Kay ventured.

'It's clear, isn't it? If a bloke hits you, you hit him back.'

'But that's retaliation. The judge said in his summing-up that you can only use reasonable force—'

'Yeah, yeah, I know, I was there, right? But it doesn't make sense. A man's not a man if he doesn't fight back.'

And what about when a woman fights back? Kay sighed and drank her tea. There was no point arguing with him, not when he was so worked up.

The jury took two hours to come to a decision, and in the end, the judge had to accept a majority verdict. Micky was found guilty of assault and given a six-month sentence, suspended for two years. Foxy nearly exploded with fury, and she had to grab his hand to stop him making a scene and getting arrested himself.

'At least it's suspended,' she said as the three of them left the court.

'Yeah, but it's still a conviction, it goes on his record. He'll lose his job and he'll never get another one. He'll be on the dole for the rest of his life.' Foxy marched on ahead to the bus stop, Kay and Micky running to catch up. She felt sorry for the boy. Unemployment was at a record high and there was no sign of the situation improving. The Queen's Silver Jubilee had cheered the country up a few months ago, but doom and gloom had descended again and the winter ahead looked bleak.

'Don't worry! I'll sort it out,' Micky called after him.

They sat on the bus in silence all the way home. As soon as they arrived, Kay rushed off to pick Abigail up from school. When she got back, she found the brothers sitting in the lounge demolishing cans of lager. The atmosphere between them was strange – she couldn't describe it exactly, but it smelt bad.

'Go upstairs and play,' she told Abigail. The girl didn't need any encouragement.

'I tried my best to help you, but you let me down, mate,' Foxy said, snapping open another can. 'Got to learn to keep your fists to yourself.'

Kay couldn't bear the hypocrisy of it. 'You can talk,' she blurted out.

He looked up at her coldly. 'What's that supposed to mean?'

'You use your fists when you feel like it.'

'Shut up! Shut up!'

There was silence. Micky's eyes flickered between them; he sniffed the air for the truth.

'You saying he punches you?'

'Punches, slaps, bites. He stubbed out his cigarette on my arm last week. Want to see?' She began to roll up her sleeve. It was crazy, provoking him like this, but in the moment she didn't care. She'd had enough of covering up for him, letting everyone believe he was a saint – the charming husband, loyal brother, respectful son-in-law, amusing friend.

'Go to your room,' Foxy barked. 'I'll deal with you later.' He glared at her, waiting for her to move, but she couldn't. Couldn't, wouldn't, shouldn't. 'I said go!'

'That's your wife you're talking to,' said Micky. 'Show some respect.'

'Keep out of it, all right?'

Micky put down his can and stood up. 'No, I won't keep out of it. Kay's been good to me and she's good to you too. You should treat her right.'

'Oh, I see, that's what this is all about.' Foxy rose and squared up to Micky. 'You've been screwing each other behind my back.'

'Don't be silly, Foxy,' she interrupted. 'Course we haven't.'

Micky looked at his brother, disgusted. 'You're losing the plot, mate.'

'Did she throw herself at you? The slag.'

'Don't call her that.'

Kay turned to her brother-in-law. 'I think you should go.'

He shook his head. 'I'm not leaving you with him, not like this.'

'It's okay. I'll be okay.'

'No you won't! He's gone mental.'

Foxy gave Micky a shove. 'Get out. This is my business, nothing to do with you.'

'Please, just go,' Kay said, shaking all over. 'It'll be all right.'

Micky took off the suit jacket; she thought he was getting ready for a fight, but he put on his donkey jacket instead. She heard her daughter's footsteps running down the stairs and her stomach jolted.

'Get. Out. Now.' Foxy jabbed at Micky's chest.

'Why are you shouting?' Abigail asked, poking her dark curls around the door frame.

Micky shot his brother a look of withering contempt. 'I used to look up to you, Alan, but you're out of order. Way out of order.'

'Who's Alan?' asked Abigail innocently. Kay put her finger to her lips, gesturing at her to keep out of it. Micky always used his brother's proper name, refused to call him Foxy. She didn't know why exactly – maybe he thought it was childish, or maybe he didn't like him taking sole ownership of their surname.

'You lay another finger on her and you'll have me to reckon with. Got that?' And with a shake of his fist, he stormed out, slamming the door.

Foxy didn't move, didn't say a word, but she could feel his temper building, like a pot rising to the boil. Now what? she thought. As if she didn't already know …

CHAPTER TWENTY

Stella

Now

'The final score was 12–6,' I say. 'Wales had a penalty in the seventy-seventh minute.'

He grips the sides of his skull. 'Jesus Christ, what does it matter? The game was already over. Wales couldn't win, I'd stopped paying attention.'

'I don't believe you, Jack.'

'Leave me alone! You're doing my head in.'

'I know you too well. I can tell you're lying to me.'

'I'm not. I'm not! Stop being such a bitch!'

His insult sends an electric charge through the room. I feel a fissure cracking between us, pushing us apart. We are on either side of the fault line, alone and unable to reach each other. I never thought I'd ever feel so distant, so alienated from the man I love. We stare at each other, reeling from the aftershocks. He's shaking – I can't tell whether it's with anger or fear.

My voice is strained, the air stuck in my lungs. 'Please stop denying it. You're insulting my intelligence.'

He throws a look at me, his eyes flickering with contempt. 'Okay, okay, I did it, I faked it.'

Even though I already knew, his words still punch me in the guts, making me gasp. 'My God, Jack … Why?'

'Why do you think?'

'I don't know. To hurt me, I guess. You were pissed off because I let Lori stay and didn't tell you. You wanted revenge.'

'No, that wasn't it. I *was* pissed off, yeah, but only because you weren't listening to me.' His voice ratchets up a notch. 'The thing about you, Stella, is you always have to be in the right, you're never in the wrong. Your motto is all women are good, all men are evil bastards.'

'That's not at all what I think.'

He starts to pace around his side of the room, flinging his arms up. 'You go on and on about your gut instinct, but when it comes to *my* instinct, you're not interested. Men aren't allowed to have instinct; that's a woman's thing. You see, I knew Lori was trouble, I clocked it right from the beginning. I tried to warn you, but no, no, you knew better.'

'But you *don't* know that Lori's trouble,' I say firmly. 'You've got no evidence, other than the stuff you've made up. She's an innocent victim, not a criminal. When I think of the hell she's been through … and then you try to set her up as a thief! That's completely unforgivable.'

'I wanted the police to check her out, that's all,' he says, not giving in. 'I was sure they'd already know her. I bet you anything Lori's not her real name and she's got previous. That's why she's refusing help. She's a con artist, it's obvious. All I needed was for them to take fingerprints and DNA. I was sure she'd come up on their database and then we'd know her true identity.'

'That's really twisted, Jack.'

He looks at me pleadingly. 'You don't understand. I was trying to protect you.'

'Seems like *you're* the only person I need protecting from,' I say slowly.

He doesn't respond. The silence between us crackles like static. I fold my arms closely across my chest as the chasm between us widens.

'Now can I have my parents' things back? Please don't make me search for them. Spare me that at least.'

He closes his eyes and takes a deep breath, then opens them again and leaves the room.

I sit down heavily on the bed. My chest is tight; it feels as if somebody's gripping my heart, squeezing with all their might. How could Jack have done this? I knew things weren't great between us, but this is way beyond anything I could have imagined.

He re-enters a couple of minutes later carrying a plastic Co-op bag, which he empties onto the bed. My parents' possessions lie there in a small heap – the whisky decanter, the silver sugar bowl, the napkin rings engraved with their initials, personal items and pieces of jewellery, some gold or silver, the rest worthless tat, but all of it priceless to me. It glints in the light of the overhead bulb like paltry treasure.

'I would have given them back eventually,' he says petulantly. 'I'm not that much of a shit.'

I decide not to reply to that. Instead I pick up Dad's watch and study it for a few moments, feeling the worn leather strap, running my fingers around the face with its Roman numerals. He wore it every day for as long as I can remember; it was part of him, almost as familiar to me as his voice and his pale hazel eyes. Resting the watch in my lap, I lift up a gold chain of Mum's and hold it against my neck. The cold metal sends a shiver through me.

Jack sits on the edge of the bed, half turned away from me. He looks down at his hands, weaving his fingers into knots. 'I'm sorry,' he says. I sense a 'but' coming, and sure enough … 'But you were being impossible. I couldn't think of any other way to get through to you.'

'Other than by stealing my dead parents' valuables and accusing some poor woman who's already suffered appalling abuse from her husband and lost custody of her kids … That was the only way, was it?' I sigh. 'This is really dark, Jack. This is ... I don't know ... unspeakable.'

'Lori definitely met up with someone; that wasn't a lie,' he says after a few moments. 'I saw her get into a car.'

'Well she denies it, so who do you think I'm going to believe?' I snap.

'Just because she didn't steal the stuff doesn't mean she's on the level.'

'I don't want to talk about Lori.'

'I'm just saying ...'

'Well don't.'

There's another long pause, pregnant with thoughts. I stare at the tangle of jewellery, and memories from the past tumble around my mind.

'I think we need some space from each other,' I say, lifting my head and talking to his back. He makes a small movement, something like a flinch. 'It's impossible for you to stay here while Lori's still around, and I'm not prepared to chuck her out.'

'Okay,' he says in his smallest voice. I know that tone; it's melted my heart in the past, but not today. Not any more. 'For how long?'

'I don't know. Until we know how we feel, I guess.'

He turns to face me. 'I already know. I love you, Stella.'

'You've got a funny way of showing it.'

'Honestly, I've only got your interests at heart.' He registers the disbelief on my face. 'But whatever you say, I'll piss off, leave you alone to think things over.'

'I think it's for the best ... Where will you go?'

'Dunno. I'll make some calls.' I know he won't stay with his parents – they'll demand to know what happened and he won't want to tell them. But he has plenty of friends, most of them pre-dating our relationship. They'll get a carefully edited version of the story and he won't be short of shoulders to cry on. Everyone loves Jack.

I stand up and walk around the bed to face him. 'And you need to call the police and tell them you made a mistake. Say you found the missing stuff.' He grimaces. 'If you don't do it, I will, and I'll tell them the truth. Wasting police time is a criminal offence.'

'Okay. Leave it with me.'

'No. Do it now.' I give him PC Khan's business card. He reaches into his back pocket and takes out his phone. I listen to him leaving a message, his voice shaky and embarrassed. 'We found the stuff; you don't have to check out Alan Foxton, or the woman who's been staying with us. It was a mistake. Sorry for the inconvenience,' he mutters, ending the call.

We both turn our heads as we hear the front door opening and then closing. I immediately leave the room, shutting Jack in and crossing the hallway. Lori is easing off her boots – or rather, my boots. Her cheeks are flushed, her badly dyed hair frizzing with evening mist.

'How did it go?' I ask.

'Good, thanks,' she replies, unbuttoning the red jacket. She must have lost some weight these past few weeks, because it fits her better now. 'We went to the park. They wanted to go to McDonald's, but I didn't have enough cash.' She hangs the jacket on a peg. 'Still, we had a nice time on the swings, then we went back to the foster carer's and they let me stay while they had their tea.'

'Sounds good. And they're all right, Casey and …'

'Jamie. Yes, thanks. Better than last time. Said they missed me.' Tears well up in her eyes. 'That meant a lot.'

'Of course.' I hesitate. 'Have you eaten?'

'Just a couple of biscuits.'

'I've got some pizzas if you're interested. And a bottle of red.'

Confusion flashes across her face. 'Won't you be eating with Jack? I don't want to intrude.'

'Jack's going away for a bit.'

'Oh.' She peers at me, trying to read my expression. 'Well, um, yeah, that'd be great, if you don't mind.'

'I'll call you down in about an hour.'

She takes the hint and climbs the stairs to her room, clutching the brown handbag she took with her when she escaped. I imagine its contents – purse, phone, mirror, lipstick, passport, a few photos perhaps. What would I take if I only had a few minutes to decide? When it comes down to it, so few objects are absolutely essential. But one's sanity is a must.

I go into the other reception room, frowning at Jack's deliberate disarray of packing cases and cartons. Bending down, I pick up the jewellery box and take it back to the bedroom.

Jack is packing a holdall. His eyes are red and he looks as if he's been crying. I don't feel a flicker of sympathy. My heart sits like a stone in my chest – as hard and cold as any pebble on Nevansey beach.

'I'm going to stay with Dom,' he says. Dominic is a university friend who lives in Hackney.

'That'll cut down your commute,' I comment tartly, sitting down and putting my treasure back in its box.

He glances at me. 'I don't want to go, you know. I'd much rather stay.'

'We both need the space. There's a lot to think about.' I gesture at the four walls. 'I know it's not worked for you, living here.'

He stuffs a jumper into the bag and zips it up. 'I'm sorry, Stella.'

'Yes, so you should be,' I say through tight lips.

'I'll call you tomorrow.'

'Maybe give it a few days? I'll call you.'

'Whatever.' He picks his jacket off the chair and slips it on, then takes his beanie out of a pocket and pulls it over his head. We stare at each other for a few seconds, not saying anything, both of us thinking that maybe it's all over, maybe he'll never set foot in the house again. Unless it's to collect the rest of his belongings and return his key. The thought shudders through me.

'Right. I'm off now.'

I nod. Tears are blurring my vision, making the jewellery look like globules of light under water. I shut the lid and swallow hard.

Jack goes to the door, pausing with his fingers around the handle. 'I know you don't want to hear this, but … be careful about Lori,' he says.

A small laugh escapes from my mouth. 'Funny. She said exactly the same thing about you.'

CHAPTER TWENTY-ONE

Stella

Now

Lori leans across to top up my glass with Chianti. I gesture at her to stop, but she shakes her head and fills it to the brim.

'Medicinal,' she says, putting the bottle down and settling back into the creaky deckchair. I dragged her into the conservatory to eat because I couldn't face sitting in the front room. It's freezing in here, and although the pizza warmed me at first, my body is slowly turning to ice, the cold creeping up from my extremities, working its way towards my heart. I stare at my watery reflection in the dark windows, wondering how it has come to this.

Jack will be well ensconced at his friend's place by now, curled up on the sofa in the cosy sitting room, full of beer and indignation, ranting about how badly I treated him, no doubt. Rewriting the narrative to make himself the victim and me the perpetrator. That thought doesn't make me feel angry, or even particularly upset. I feel numb, knocked into neutral. In the past, I'd have worked my way through a whole box of tissues, but tonight I haven't cried once.

Lori picks up her packet of cigarettes and takes out her lighter. 'Do you mind?'

'No. Go ahead.' Jack would have had a fit, but I no longer care about the smell or even the passive smoking. Nothing seems to matter any more.

She lights up and draws the nicotine into her lungs. 'If you ask me, you're well out of it.'

'Maybe … I dunno …' I sigh. 'I always thought we had a really good relationship.'

'Not from where I was standing.'

I look at her sharply. 'What do you mean?'

'Well, you spent all your time trying to please him, worrying about what he'd think, wanting his approval …' She puffs out smoke. 'It was like you were scared of him.'

'No, not scared … I just wanted him to be happy, that's all.'

'What about *your* happiness? Doesn't that count for anything?' I chew my lip, giving Lori's words my full consideration. 'Well?' she urges.

My brain scrambles for an answer. 'When you're a couple, it's about being happy together, isn't it? If he's happy, that makes me happy, and vice versa.' I drink and the wine seeps into the fabric of my brain.

'I don't think Jack gives a shit about you being happy. It's all about him.'

'That's not entirely true. He didn't want to leave London but he moved here to please me. When we met, I was really struggling with some issues over my parents' death and he helped me massively. He's actually a very loving, supportive person.'

'There you go again defending him.'

'But—'

'If he's so supportive, why did he pretend your parents' things had been stolen?' She flicks ash onto her dirty plate. 'I mean, I understand he was trying to turn you against me, but why be so hurtful? It was just cruel.'

'He was angry with me for letting you stay and not telling him.'

'But you only did that because you were scared of him.'

'I suppose so.' I let out a long, regretful sigh. 'We both made mistakes.'

'It's not your fault, Stella. That's what you kept telling me when I first arrived, remember? I didn't get it at first, but now I understand. I see your messed-up relationship and it makes me realise—'

'It's not messed up.'

'Isn't it?' She turns her head towards me and looks deeply into my eyes. 'He may not hit you, but that doesn't mean he's not abusive. We're both victims – just in different ways.'

'I don't want to talk about it any more. Too tired, too pissed.'

'Fair enough,' she says, heaving herself off the deckchair. 'It's late. We need to go to bed.'

I reach out and grab her hand. 'Thanks for keeping me company tonight.'

'It's the least I can do.' She squeezes my cold fingers. 'You're a good girl. You deserve better than Jack.'

'Hmm …' I say. 'I'm not so sure about that.'

I manage to spend most of Sunday in bed – sleeping, dozing, drifting in and out of dreams, or starkly awake, staring at the cracks in the ceiling. I can move my limbs, but they feel as if they don't belong to me. My stomach is churning and my head feels stuffed with fur. Maybe I'm sickening for something, or maybe it's just grief. The air is thick with Jack's absence. I close my eyes and touch the cold space next to me, conjuring up his body, smelling his scent, hearing his breathing. It feels like I'll never see him again, although I know that's unlikely. He's not dead, just somewhere else.

Lori knocks on the bedroom door just after eleven, offering tea and toast. I murmur thanks, but send her away. Some of the things she said last night about Jack were harsh, and I feel too bruised to listen to more of the same. She may well be right, but I need to come to my own conclusions, not feel pushed along by the tide of her opinions. I was the same when she first arrived on my doorstep. How articulate we are about other people's problems, I think, pummelling air into my pillow and lying down again.

The hours are long and viscous; it feels as if I'm pushing them through a sieve. I finally get up at six p.m., but never make it out of my pyjamas. My phone is constantly at my side as I wait for Jack to call or text, even though I told him not to contact me. I said we needed space from each other, but right now I'm lost in it, wandering around in the void.

I don't know where to go. All the rooms are either cold, piled up with stuff or choking with plaster dust. I trail listlessly through the ground floor, opening doors and sniffing the air for a few seconds, then retreating. The house seems larger than ever, everything raw and exposed, no safe corners to hide in. I can't go into the turret room because it's next to where Lori's sleeping – that's her territory now.

To make matters worse, Alan doesn't turn up for work on Monday morning. The Romanians are here at eight on the dot, but they refuse to start until they've seen 'the boss'. Apparently he owes them money for last week. I call his mobile but he doesn't pick up. Nor does he respond to my messages.

'I think he must be ill,' I say.

'So now *you* pay us,' replies their ringleader, a tall, thin man with a bald head.

'Sorry, that's not how it works. I pay Alan, he pays you.'

Miffed, they march into my kitchen and help themselves to coffee, leaning against the units and chatting in their own language. Somehow I know they're talking about me. *Where's her husband? Why doesn't he take charge?* Lori tries to persuade them to carry on with the plastering, but they just shrug and dip biscuits into their mugs. I look on powerlessly from the doorway, wondering whether dunking is a Romanian habit or whether they've picked it up from the Brits.

'If you don't want to work, go home,' she says, making the sort of shooing gesture I'd use to chase cats away. 'Alan will call you.'

'Need our money,' the tall guy repeats.

'I know, but you have to talk to him about that, not us.'

We try Alan again, but there's still no answer. I'm starting to worry. He's usually so reliable. In all the weeks he's been working here, he's hardly ever taken a day off, and even then, he told me about it in advance. This behaviour is very unlike him.

'Do you know where he lives?' asks Lori, once the Romanians have been persuaded to leave. 'Maybe we should go round to his house and check. He might have had a heart attack or something.'

'No, he never gave me his address.'

'It must be on the building contract.'

I shake my head. 'We never got round to doing one.'

My mind shoots back to the first time I met Alan. I can see him now in his navy overalls, standing on the doorstep with a notebook in his hand, sucking on the end of his pencil.

'I understand you need a builder,' he said, whipping out a card from his top pocket and handing it to me.

'Oh. Um, yes … Did you see my advert?'

'That's right.' He peered beyond me into the hallway. 'This is a job and a half.'

I let him in and we walked from room to room as I tried to explain our vision for the ground floor.

'Sounds lovely,' he replied, 'but you need to sort your basics out first.'

'I know there's a lot to do … How many guys do you have on your team?'

He laughed. 'I'm a one-man band, me. I can do most things myself, but if I need to, I bring in specialists. I'm a lot cheaper than your big outfits with their VAT invoices and stuff.'

We carried on with the tour, coming back downstairs and going into the garden. He walked to the end and paced about for a few moments, looking up at the house and even peering into the shed.

'I can see why you bought it,' he said, tramping back through the overgrown grass. 'It's a beautiful house. I mean, it *will* be once you've done it up.'

'Are you interested?'

'Oh yeah, for sure. I love these kinds of projects. Much more interesting than a new-build. Only thing is, I can't give you a fixed price. How long is a piece of string, eh? Tell you what. You pay me a weekly rate plus materials at cost. Seven hundred and fifty a week. Cash.'

'Right, er, I don't know, sounds good,' I said, as waves of relief washed over me. 'I'll talk to my partner and be in touch.'

He grinned. 'I can start as soon as you like. Just had a job cancel on me, so I've got a gap.'

Finally I had a solution. But when I told Jack over our takeaway that evening, he was less than convinced. 'Cash only? The guy sounds like a crook. But that's who you're going to get if you put an ad in the Co-op. For God's sake, what were you thinking?'

'Look, I'm not saying he's the world's best builder, but he's a really nice guy.'

He narrowed his gaze. 'How old is he?'

'I don't know, in his fifties.' I put down my fork. 'Don't be silly. I don't *fancy* him! He's old enough to be my dad.' Jack huffed in disbelief. 'Why are you being so snarky? I thought you'd be pleased. At least we can get started. Let's give him a trial. One week. Please.'

He tutted. 'Okay, but if it goes wrong, it's your fault.'

'He's probably got the flu,' says Lori, breaking into my thoughts. 'He's been looking very tired recently. Working too hard. Bit old for this lark.'

'Has he ever mentioned a wife or a partner?'

Lori thinks for a few seconds. 'Not that I can remember. I got the impression he's divorced. Or a widower.'

'I hope he's okay.' I look around at the vile kitchen, the sickly colours enough to turn my stomach. 'The extension's supposed to be starting soon. I can't do without him.'

She knits her eyebrows at me. 'Yes you can. Or rather, *we* can.'

I laugh. 'We're not builders, Lori.'

'I know, but there's plenty of general labouring stuff we can do while he's off sick. The work doesn't need to grind to a halt.'

Her words spark a small flame inside me. She's right. We don't have to hang around waiting for some man to lead the way. And it's not as if I'm overburdened with other work. Doing some hard grafting on the house will take my mind off my troubles *and* be really useful and cost-saving. God knows how the budget is going; all I've done is take money out of the cashpoint and I've not kept proper track. If I can save a few pounds, so much the better.

'I'm up for it, if you are,' I say.

She nods eagerly. 'That's the spirit, love. Fuck men, eh? Who needs 'em?'

CHAPTER TWENTY-TWO

Stella

Now

'Jack? It's me.'

'Just a sec,' he replies. I hear his footsteps crossing the room, a door closing, shutting me out from his new life. 'What is it? Only I'm on my way out.'

The coldness in his voice shivers down the line. I lean against the headboard and pull the duvet over my legs. This is the first time we've spoken since he left, almost a week ago. It took all my courage to make this call and I can't believe he's already trying to end the conversation.

'I'm just ringing to see how you are,' I say limply.

'I'm fine.'

And how are you, *Stella?* I silently reply on his behalf. *I'm feeling really awful, actually. Missing you but also still furious. Lost. Disorientated. Dismayed. Confused.*

But instead I say, 'I was thinking, we should talk.'

He sighs. 'What's there to talk about?'

'Everything!'

'Everything?' He laughs.

'What's so funny about that?'

I can hear him walking around, opening a drawer, the sounds muffled as he tucks the phone under his chin to heave on his coat.

He's behaving exactly as he does when his mother rings – refusing to stop and listen properly, multitasking because he's not interested in what she has to say.

'Please, Jack …'

'Look, it's simple. Get rid of that woman and then maybe—'

'You're hardly in a position to make demands,' I cut in. 'Anyway, this has nothing to do with Lori. Things were going wrong before that and you know it; she was just the spark that set things alight.'

He makes a noise in his throat. 'Granted. But she hasn't exactly helped.'

'She's not going anywhere for now.'

'Okay. Then I'm not coming back.'

'I don't *want* you back,' I snap. 'Not at the moment, anyway. What you did was utterly appalling.'

He grunts again. 'Whereas you, my darling, are perfect in every single way.'

'Oh piss off, I didn't say that. You're deliberately misunderstanding.' My pitch ratchets up a notch. 'We're not a couple of teenagers who've had a bit of a tiff. We need to talk things through, work out what we want to do. I'm happy to try couple counselling if you think—'

'We don't need counselling. Get rid of Lori, sell the house and come back to London. We should be able to afford a two-bedroom flat in Stokie.'

'I don't want a two-bedroom flat. I want to be here.'

Stalemate. Silence.

'This is not about where we live, or the money; it's about our relationship,' I say, my voice trembling with anger.

'Yeah, yeah, I know.' Another pause. 'Look, I've got to go, I'm meeting the guys. It's comedy night at the Brakspear, remember?'

Yes, I remember. It was a regular haunt of ours – loads of our mates would turn up and we always had a laugh, regardless of the quality of the acts.

'Enjoy the show,' I say, lacing my words with sarcasm, and end the call.

Swinging my legs over the edge of the bed, I put my boots on and stand up. I'm shaking with fury. I reach for my coat and check that my keys are in the pocket. As I leave the room, Lori is coming down the stairs with a tray of dirty mugs from our day's work.

'Going out?' she says.

'Yup, need some fresh air.' I fasten my coat, cursing as the zipper catches.

Her eyes scan my face. Even in this dim light she can see that I've been crying. 'Everything all right?'

'Not really. Just spoken to Jack. He's being such a knob.'

'That's men for you.' She rolls her eyes. 'Darren, Jack ... even Alan has let us down.'

'Yeah ...' I agree uneasily. I've never been one to make sweeping statements about the inadequacies of the male species, although the men in our lives do seem to be behaving spectacularly badly. 'What's the latest with Darren? You haven't mentioned him for ages.'

'Er ... nothing to report. Same old, same old.' She makes to move towards the kitchen.

'What does that mean?' I pull on a woolly hat. 'Is he in calling-you-a-slag mode or begging you to come home?'

'A bit of both.'

She edges past me with the tray and my gaze follows her into the kitchen. She's been very vague about Darren recently. She no longer seems convinced that he's lying in wait outside, or driving around Nevansey hoping to find her, and yet she still refuses to leave the house. Maybe she's agoraphobic, I think, as I open the front door and breathe in the cool, briny air. I couldn't stand being cooped up for weeks on end; it would drive me crazy.

A light, cold rain is falling. Droplets of icy water spatter my cheeks as I cross the road and walk towards the beach, stuffing my hands into my pockets, my fingers curled into tense fists.

The steps down to the promenade are slippery with algae. I walk a few yards, then stop by the huts, turning to stare out to sea, but it's too dark to see anything. A swathe of blackness stretches before me. The tide is so far out, I can barely hear the waves slapping against the mud. To my right, the distant lights of the pier twinkle like a diamond necklace thrown into the sea. The land on my left rises to a peak and then stops abruptly. There's nobody around, not even a dog walker. I can sense the darkness creeping up behind me, placing its hand on my shoulder.

Would I miss all this bleak nothingness if I sold Westhill House and moved back to London? I transplant myself for a moment – standing on the Tube, sweaty in my winter coat, negotiating busy pavements with an umbrella, always nearly late or unsure where I'm heading, checking Google Maps and trying not to get my phone nicked by some kid on a moped. Or driving down congested roads looking for parking spaces that don't require a permit, reversing into blind spots, edging into streams of traffic, dodging reckless pedestrians and mad lane-changers, being beeped because I'm a second late responding to a green light. And that's just getting around, let alone the unaffordable cost of living, dealing with people trying to rip you off left, right and centre. Just thinking about it makes my head pound.

I didn't realise how much I hated all that stress until we came here; I couldn't return to the city now. But Jack never wanted to move in the first place; he only did it to please me. I could tell that he was really happy to be back in familiar surroundings, with the regular crowd, doing the things he used to do – that *we* used to do. He didn't seem to be missing me at all.

Surely our relationship is more important than where we live? He's made his position very clear, and yet I feel unable to leave this place. There's a story that hasn't been fully told, secrets yet to be revealed. I didn't choose to live here – the house chose me. It won't let me leave until the job is finished, and maybe not even then.

There's been no word from Alan all week, despite my leaving countless messages on his voicemail and bombarding him with texts. I nearly called the police to report him missing, but after the recent embarrassment over the fake burglary, I decided not to bother them. How do you know if somebody's missing if you don't know where they're supposed to be?

'We have to face it, he's done a bunk,' Lori says as we begin our second week without him. 'How much did you pay up front?'

'Nothing. I paid him weekly. Plus materials, of course.'

She fills a large bucket with soapy water. 'Did he give you receipts?'

'Um … a few. He was really good at first, but I haven't had any for weeks. I assumed he was just saving them up.' I blush, realising how stupid that makes me sound.

'Hmm … So you don't know if he actually bought the stuff.'

'Well he obviously bought *some* stuff – plasterboard and electric cable, that sort of thing. But he seemed more interested in demolition than building.' I reach for the plastic box of scrubbing brushes and old cloths, thinking of the thousands I've paid out in small denominations over the past few months. Fifty quid for this, a hundred for that … It all adds up.

Lori twists her mouth. 'And you paid him cash in advance to give to the Romanians?'

I nod, chewing my lip. I don't want to believe that Alan was cheating me, but it's looking more and more likely. The plasterers came knocking last Friday, having failed to find him themselves. They almost frogmarched me to the bank and made me hand over the cash they claimed they were owed.

'There must be some explanation,' I say. 'Perhaps he decided it was too big a job and was embarrassed to admit it. Or maybe his mother's been taken ill suddenly—'

'He told me his mother had died,' she interrupts, tying her hair back and covering her head with one of my scarves. We're working on the floorboards today. They're coated in ancient lino glue and bits of dried plaster, full of holes and spiky with old nails. I want to sand and seal them eventually, but they might not be in good enough condition to save.

'I don't understand it,' I sigh. 'I liked Alan; so did you, Lori. He was sweet. He made you sandwiches every day and gave you all those things for your room. I'm not giving up on him yet.'

'Sounds like how I used to be with Darren,' she says. 'Always making excuses for him.'

I give her a piercing look. 'But not any more?'

She shrugs. 'It doesn't matter. I'll never escape from him. He'll get me in the end.'

'Don't say that.'

'It's true, Stella. Sad to say, but true.' A dark cloud crosses her face for a moment, then she picks up the heavy bucket and goes upstairs.

We work hard every day, on our hands and knees, digging out nails, scraping away gunge, chipping off the plaster. It feels odd not to hear the strains of Alan's seventies chart music reverberating through the empty rooms, his voice singing slightly out of tune. I put my phone on maximum volume, but Lori doesn't appreciate my playlist – either the music's too dreary or it gives her a head-ache. Instead we work in companionable silence, broken every so often by Lori's questions about my childhood, my parents, how I met Jack, what I want to do with my life. Sometimes it feels like she's interviewing me for a job, or I'm talking to a counsellor. She never offers her own experiences in return, or expresses an opinion. I feel as if she's siphoning me off, piece by piece, and storing me in her brain. There are moments when I want to unburden myself, tell her the shameful truth that not even Jack knows, but the story is buried so deep, I'm unable to dig it out.

Since Jack left, we've taken to eating together in the evenings. We're still on the ready meals and takeaways – after a hard day's grafting, neither of us is interested in cooking. We eat in my room, using the desk as a dining table. It's warmer than sitting in the conservatory and I quite like the company. Last night I invited her to watch a film on the laptop, and we sat on my bed groaning, laughing and weeping at *Mamma Mia!*

Jack would never have agreed to watch such 'dross', as he would have called it. I miss him, and yet I don't miss him. Life's simpler now I'm no longer creeping around trying to keep him happy. But the space next to me in the bed feels bigger with every passing night. Sometimes I forget that he's not there and reach out to touch him. I've turned the alarm clock off, but still wake up at half six, expecting to hear him moving around the bedroom as he gets dressed in the dark.

It's Thursday, early evening, when we hear the knock at the door. We're in my room – Lori's halfway through a shepherd's pie and I'm tackling a rather slippery lasagne.

'Who could that be?' I say, putting down my fork.

'Amazon?' she hazards.

'No.' I stand up. 'Maybe it's Alan.'

'I doubt it,' Lori replies. 'You won't see him for dust.'

I go into the hallway and she follows, but hangs back at the threshold. There's a dark shape behind the reinforced glass and I immediately think of Lori's arrival all those weeks ago. Surely it's not another abuse victim seeking shelter?

'What if it's Darren?' I whisper.

She shakes her head. 'Too small.'

Taking a breath, I turn the handle and open the door. A small cry escapes from Lori's mouth as we stare at the woman standing before us. She looks to be in her mid forties, her wavy black hair flecked with silver grey. Her features are heavy – brown eyes, thick straight brows, olive skin, full lips.

'Abigail!' Lori says, springing forward, a look of panic on her face. 'For Christ's sake, what are you doing here?'

CHAPTER TWENTY-THREE

Kay

Then

There was a pattern to their lives, thought Kay as she squirted window cleaner on the glass. Not the normal kind of pattern that most married couples followed – work during the week, Friday night at the pub, the supermarket shop on Saturday morning, Sunday lunch with family … All that happened too, of course, but it was underscored by a darker tune.

Three weeks would go by quite happily, with barely a cross word between them. He would insult and criticise her for sure – she was lazy, she cared for Abigail more than him, she overspent his hard-earned wages, she was too friendly with the neighbours – but if she managed to stick to her promise to herself not to retaliate, it wouldn't go any further. Sometimes she bit her tongue so hard she thought her teeth would cut right through it.

Then some little thing would go wrong – she would run out of sugar for his tea, or a stain on his shirt would refuse to come out – or he'd accuse her of 'carrying on' with the postman or the mobile fishmonger. She'd stupidly defend herself, and once his voice was raised, the flying fists were not far behind. It was always her fault. He didn't want to beat her but she *made* him lose his temper. Why couldn't she behave herself like other wives?

Immediately after each attack, he went into a lighter key. He tended her wounds, rubbing in arnica for the bruises, cleaning any cuts or bites so they wouldn't become infected. When he broke her arm, he took her straight to hospital, claiming she'd slipped on the wet kitchen floor. She didn't dare to contradict him. Sometimes her injuries were so bad she could hardly walk.

She squeezed out the cloth and wiped the glass. The windows had become so dirty over the winter months, the water was almost black. But now it was March, almost spring. Feeling oddly tired, she paused to stare into their neat rectangular garden. The forsythia had just come out – she loved its sunny yellow flowers; they were so cheering. And there was pink blossom on the cherry tree. The lawn could have its first cut of the year soon, and Abigail would be able to play on the grass again without getting covered in mud.

But the warmer weather would bring complications as she tried to cover up the marks on her flesh. 'You mustn't let anyone see,' he'd warned her the last time. 'Just think what your parents would say if they knew how badly you treated me. They would be so angry with you, Kay. After all I've done – making an honest woman of you, giving you a lovely home, looking after your bastard kid …'

Honest woman. It was ridiculous, talking like that, as if she was some nineteenth-century tragic heroine. This was 1978, the era of punk. Some people of her age were walking around with spiky dog collars on and safety pins in their ears; they took the mickey out of the royal family and didn't give a shit about marriage. In some circles, being a single parent was a badge of honour.

Just not the circles she moved in, Kay reflected as she emptied the bucket and refilled it with clean water. What you saw on the telly or read about in the papers didn't bear much relation to most people's lives. In this town, change moved at a snail's pace. Her parents had lived through the privations of the war, and their narrow views had been passed down to their children. But Kay had always felt that urge to be part of the new, more liberal generation, as she'd proved that night in Torremolinos. Some would say she'd simply been a naïve fool, but she preferred to think of it as an act of rebellion, albeit not a conscious one.

She took the bucket back to the living room and began to rinse the suds off the patio doors. If only she'd been able to follow through – left home barefoot and pregnant, travelled around Europe, joined a commune, shacked up with some bloke who believed in free love, given birth under the stars. Instead, she'd allowed herself to feel ashamed and unworthy and had ended up with a deeply traditional man whose views were bloody Victorian.

'You made your bed, now you have to lie in it,' her mother had said when she fell pregnant. It was the same now – she'd made a new bed when she married Foxy and there was no getting out of it. So when he hit her, she accepted his perverted logic and took the blame; tried to hide her injuries, especially from him. At bedtime, she got undressed and put on her nightie in the bathroom, so as not to remind him of what he'd done.

'Look at the state of you,' he'd say if he walked in on her naked. 'You're disgusting. If you're not careful, you're going to end up dead. Do you want me to have a criminal record like Micky and not be able to get a decent job? Am I going to end up in jail for the rest of my life just because you're such a crappy wife?'

Poor Micky was no longer invited to the house, and Foxy refused to take his calls. Kay was blamed for the family split. 'If you hadn't been giving him the come-on every time my back was turned, none of this would have happened,' she was told. Not that she'd flirted with him for one single second. All she'd done was smile when he praised her apple crumble.

She sighed to herself. She'd never thought she'd say it, but she missed Micky. He wasn't the sharpest knife in the drawer – too easily led – but last summer he'd stood up for her, and shown himself to be a man, whatever that meant. Since then, they hadn't had any visitors for Sunday lunch, not even her parents. Foxy had refused the dinner invitations they'd received when they first moved to Fairmead and nobody had asked a second time. Kay's job was a distant memory, and she hardly ever saw any of her old friends. Foxy refused to babysit and she could hardly ask her parents to come over when he was in the house. Even if he had let her go out with the girls, he'd have accused her of getting off with men and given her a hiding. It simply wasn't worth it.

She stood back from the glass, changing her position and angling her head to check for smears. Her mother swore by newspaper for the final polish, but it made no sense to her. Why rub dirty newsprint over nice clean glass? She pulled off her pink Marigolds and flung them into the plastic box of cloths, brushes, creams and sprays, where they hung like dead hands. She was sick of cleaning. Nobody ever came over to admire her efforts. She only did it because he'd moan if there was fluff on the carpet or a dirty ring around the bath.

Exhausted, she sat down on the sofa, kicked off her slippers and put her legs up. He was such a different man to the charming Foxy she'd married eighteen months ago. She picked a feather off the cushion and put it in her apron pocket. It was only half nine, far too early for elevenses, but she had an empty feeling in her stomach and craved a dry biscuit. Her breasts were tender too. The curse must be on its way, she thought, although it was hard to know because her cycle was all messed up since she'd stopped taking her contraception. She'd thought she'd fallen at first, but the test was negative. Dr Davison said it was something called 'amenorrhoea' – apparently some women stopped having periods altogether when they came off the pill. It had sounded very serious. She'd panicked and started taking it again, but then she'd missed a few and now she didn't know where she was. She was no longer sure she wanted another baby anyway.

She hugged her breasts. Her nipples were stinging and she had a strange taste in her mouth. It was like when a filling fell out, or you accidentally bit on Kit Kat foil. Metallic. She'd tasted it before, exactly the same, years ago. The sensation had only lasted a couple of days and she'd forgotten about it.

Her stomach flipped. Sore, heavy breasts, unusual tiredness, no curse, slight sick feeling and now this peculiar taste. Jesus wept ... Was she pregnant? Was there already a new little person growing inside her? A flutter of excitement instantly spread through her body and she sat up straight, eyes wide open.

What had she done?

She leapt off the sofa and her legs almost buckled beneath her. How many weeks gone was she? It was impossible to tell. But first, it had to be confirmed. Running into the hallway, she picked up the phone and dialled the surgery. Luckily there'd been a cancellation – could she get down there in twenty minutes? She said she could.

She threw on the first jacket that came to hand, pushed her feet into some shoes and picked up her bag. She left the house in a fluster, forgetting to check that the taps had been turned off and the back door had been locked. Her heart was beating a gallop, struggling to keep up with the sudden change of pace. Just a few minutes ago she was cleaning the windows and feeling a bit grotty; now she was about to find out something that might change the entire direction of her life.

It would be all right, wouldn't it, if she were pregnant? Her mother had said countless times that what Foxy needed was a child of his own, to complete the family and cement the marriage. He'd said that he didn't want children, but she didn't believe him. How could you *not* want to be a parent? She couldn't think of anything more satisfying than to love and care for a child. And Foxy was so full of his own importance, she thought he'd want to leave something of himself behind after he died.

Her footsteps quickened as she approached the parade of shops that served the new estate – a butcher's, a newsagent, a small budget supermarket, launderette, hairdresser, chemist and post office. Everything you needed, close at hand. The doctor's surgery was on the corner of the next block, where rambling Edwardian terraces met the new, compact semi-detached houses. She'd been there several times before, mostly for Abigail, but also for the previous pregnancy test that had been a false alarm. But this wasn't a false alarm, she knew it. As she pounded along the pavement, she felt her breasts bouncing and imagined them full of milk.

Enormous thoughts tumbled around her, making her breathless. She felt simultaneously joyous and terrified. It would be all right. Hard work, of course, but in the end, it would make life easier. He wouldn't strike a pregnant woman, for a start. The kind, loving Foxy would emerge and the cycle of violence would be broken; she would protect the baby and it would protect her. And once it was born, she would have more freedom – he could hardly refuse to babysit his own flesh and blood. He would have someone else to love and lavish attention on, lifting some of the pressure off her shoulders.

It would be good for Abigail, too. Only children were often high achievers, but it was just as important for children to learn to share. She was sure the little girl would be thrilled to have a baby brother or sister.

She paused at the door of the surgery, placing her hand on her tummy, as yet as flat as an ironing board. Was it a girl or a boy? she wondered. She'd always known Abigail was female, but her instincts weren't telling her anything with this one. Presuming, of course, that she was actually pregnant. Well, there was only one way to find out. She inhaled deeply and pushed open the door.

'You're WHAT?!' he screamed when she told him that evening after they'd eaten. She'd cooked smoked haddock, one of his favourites. 'How's that even possible? You're on the pill!'

'It's not a hundred per cent reliable, everyone knows that,' she answered, having already rehearsed her defence. 'And I had a stomach upset a while ago, remember? I think it must have passed straight through.'

He looked at her keenly. 'How far gone are you?'

'About six weeks, the doctor thinks. Due late November.'

'Not too late then.'

Her blood ran cold. 'What do you mean?' she said, although she knew full well.

'Not too late to get rid of it.'

'But why would we want to get rid of it? We've created a new life, Foxy, that's a beautiful thing.'

He snorted dismissively. 'How do I know it's mine?'

'Of course it's yours,' she answered, wringing her hands. 'Don't say that, it's hurtful.'

'You're on your own here, hours on end, day after day. You could be entertaining all sorts.'

'For God's sake, you make me sound like a prostitute. I'm your wife. We're going to have a baby.'

He shoved his empty dinner plate away. 'Nothing to do with me. You told me you were on the pill.'

'I was, you know I was – I mean, I still am, only obviously I've got to stop taking it now, the doctor said.' The lies were making her burble. It had been so easy at the time, popping the pill into her mouth in front of him, then keeping it on her tongue until she could spit it into the toilet bowl. She'd convinced herself that she was doing the right thing, that he would be delighted once he'd got over the initial shock. But now his eyes were blazing with anger and she could feel the steam rising inside him, like a pressure cooker about to explode.

'I love you,' she said, trying to control the fear in her voice. 'This is your baby, our baby. We can have a fresh start, be a proper family.'

He stood up, pushing over the chair. 'Well I don't want it, so get rid of it.'

She clutched at her stomach. 'I can't … I won't.'

'Jesus Christ, woman,' he shouted, coming towards her with a raised fist. 'Why won't you ever do as you're bloody told?'

CHAPTER TWENTY-FOUR

Stella

Now

'What's going on?' I say, my eyes flicking between Lori and the woman standing in my hallway. 'I thought nobody knew where you were.'

Lori reddens, 'They don't ... I mean, Darren doesn't know. Just ... just ...' she fixes the woman with a look, 'Abigail.'

'Call me Abi. I'm Lori's friend, her *best* friend,' Abigail says, extending her hand. 'I was so worried, I made her tell me where she was hiding.' Ours eyes meet as we shake – her grip is firm and she holds onto my fingers for a second longer than feels comfortable. 'But please don't worry, her secret's safe with me.'

'I'm sorry, Stella,' Lori begins, twisting the edge of her jumper as she always does when she's stressed. 'I wanted to ask you if she could visit, only I never got the chance.'

Never got the chance? We've been working side by side all week. I quickly scan my memory. I'm sure Lori's never mentioned Abigail. She's only ever talked about Darren, her kids and her mother. No siblings, no friends by name – best or otherwise.

'You should have told me you were coming, Abi,' Lori says ruefully.

'I got sick of waiting for an invite. I was frantic, I wanted to make sure you were okay.'

The three of us stand there awkwardly, unsure of what to say next. Our visitor glances from left to right and up and down, soaking in her surroundings. Looking at it from her perspective, I realise what a terrible mess we're in. Bags of plaster are stacked up by the door next to lengths of plastic trunking and metal edging strips. Small lumps of rubble, splinters of wood and torn pieces of packaging litter the floor. Everything is covered in a thick film of dust. Large dirty boot prints have been pressed into the stair carpet, and the floor tiles are streaked with mud.

'You weren't joking when you said it was a building site,' she remarks.

'I don't mind,' Lori says stiffly. 'It's better than being on the streets.'

'True.' Abi reaches into her bag and pulls out a bottle of wine. 'I haven't come empty-handed,' she grins. 'Do you have glasses, or is it paper cups around here?'

'Glasses.' I gesture towards the kitchen, but she's already heading there, seeming to know her way.

'Sorry, she's always like this,' says Lori, before running after her. I remain in the hallway, feeling like I've just let a tornado into the house.

Abi pours out the wine and, feeling uneasy about letting her into my private space, I suggest we sit in the chilly conservatory. She and Lori plant themselves in the musty deckchairs while I pop to my room in search of blankets and something for me to sit on. As soon as I exit, they start to whisper. I linger in the kitchen, straining to hear, but I can't make out any words, just their tone. Lori sounds a bit pissed off, Abi is being placatory, but firm. I tuck two blankets under my arm and push the office chair into the corridor. The squeaky wheels herald my approach and they stop talking.

'Marvellous,' says Abi, taking a blanket off me and smoothing it over her woollen skirt. 'Brrr ... So, here we all are ... It's lovely to meet you at last, Stella. I've heard so much about you. I have to say, I think you're amazing.'

'No, I'm not.'

'You are, you are. Poor Lori turns up on your doorstep, battered and bleeding, and you just take her in, no questions asked. Not many people would have done that.'

'I only did what seemed right,' I say. 'She was in a bad way and she thought we were a refuge.'

'Yes, I know. It's outrageous that the place was closed down. The government says it cares about abuse victims and then cuts most of the funding—'

'Get off your soapbox, Abi.' Lori gives her a warning look.

'I'm sorry. It just makes me so angry. Women are getting murdered every week and nobody helps them. Only kind, decent people like you.' There are tears in her eyes as she raises her glass. 'A toast. To Queen Stella, long may she reign.'

'Honestly,' I say, 'it was nothing.'

'It wasn't – you saved her bloody life.'

'The story's not over yet,' Lori says quietly, topping up our glasses.

'I know, but I'm still going to thank Stella for everything she's done, okay?'

'Yes, yes, of course. I didn't mean—'

'Please, it's fine. I really don't need any more thanks,' I say.

There's a pause, during which I consider these two women, who seem to be the unlikeliest of friends. Not just their personalities, which couldn't be more different, but their social status and even the way they talk. Abi speaks clipped RP, whereas Lori has the local estuary twang.

Sipping at my wine, I ask, 'So, how did you two meet?'

'At school.' Abi reaches out and squeezes Lori's hand. 'We've known each other as long as we can remember, haven't we, hon?'

Lori nods. 'She was the brainbox, always at the top of the class. I was the thicko.'

'That's not true.'

'Is too and you know it.'

'She always puts herself down,' Abi says, releasing Lori's fingers. 'The things she could have achieved if only—'

'Not now, eh? Stella's not interested.'

Abi leans back into the saggy deckchair and crosses her ankles. 'You can see how close we are; we tear each other to shreds.'

I observe her silky black tights and expensive leather ankle boots, a far cry from the baggy jogging bottoms and stained mules that Lori turned up in weeks ago. She catches me staring and I look away, pretending to study some leaves brushing the window in the wind instead.

'Well,' she says, after a pause. 'As pleasant as it is sitting in this ice box of a summer house, what I'd really like is a tour.' Leaving Lori to do the honours, I retreat to my room, feeling ever so slightly pissed off. Maybe it's simply because Lori lied to me. She insisted she hadn't told anyone where she was living, but she obviously gave Abi this address. No wonder she was cross with her for turning up unexpectedly. Who is Abi, anyway? How come I've never heard of her?

Never mind, I think. I shouldn't be so grudging. It's nice for Lori to see a friend; she's been isolated for too long. And Abi seems like a no-nonsense type, very pro-women; she's unlikely to tell Lori to go back to Darren and put up with the beatings. Maybe she'll talk some sense into her, shatter this stupid dream that he'll change and the family will be reunited. If she really is Lori's best friend, perhaps she'll invite her and the children to come and live with her.

Twenty minutes later, there's a tap on my door. 'Come in,' I say.

Lori enters with Abi at her shoulder. 'Sorry to disturb you.'

'That's okay. What do you think of Westhill House?' I ask Abi.

'Big,' she replies, looking around, her gaze landing briefly on the enormous marble fireplace. 'Loads of potential.'

'That's what everybody says.'

She smiles. 'I gather you've been let down by your builder.'

'So it seems …'

'*And* your husband.'

'He's my partner,' I correct, wondering whether that's even true any more.

Lori winces. 'Abi, please …'

'He's, er, staying in London for the time being,' I continue, flustered. 'For his job. It wasn't working out, commuting and trying to manage the, er …' My words die away and I cast my eyes downwards. I'm sure Lori's told her everything.

'Basically, you've been left in the lurch,' says Abi. 'When the going gets tough, the women get going but the men run for the hills, right?' She laughs wryly.

Lori edges forward. 'Abi wants to help.'

'Sorry?'

Abi grins. 'With the project management. I hear you're snowed under, have lost control of the budget.'

'Well, not exactly …'

'Look, I'm between contracts, on gardening leave for a couple of months – that's what they call it, only I don't have a garden,' she laughs. 'I'm moving to a rival competitor and I'm not allowed to start my new job until there's been a gap. Anyway, I'm bored out of my skull and looking for something to get my teeth into.' She waves her arms expansively. 'This is the perfect solution.'

I consider her smart clothes and expensive haircut. 'What kind of work do you do?'

'Management consultancy.'

'Oh, right,' I say, none the wiser. 'Do you live locally?'

'No, no, I moved away years ago. I'm in Bath now.'

'Why would you want to spend your time doing building work?'

'It's obvious, isn't it?' She smiles. 'I'm really grateful for what you've done for my dear old friend and I want to pay you back in some small way.'

'That's very kind, but it's really not necessary.'

'I know, but I *want* to do it,' she presses. 'I was going to volunteer at the hospital, but I thought, actually, this is more worthwhile. I could really make an impact here, move things forward, get you back on track.'

'She's so organised, she could run the country,' says Lori proudly.

Abi casts an affectionate glance in her friend's direction. 'Well I wouldn't go *that* far, but I do have a lot of experience. And I'm a great believer in women taking control and doing it for themselves.'

I glance down at her left hand. No wedding ring, I note. It doesn't surprise me. She's way too scary for your average guy. That's not to say she isn't attractive: those dark, sultry looks are very alluring – thick wavy hair, jet-black with lightning streaks of silver, unblemished olive skin, amazing brown eyes. She might be in her forties, but she'd still turn any man's head.

'Well?' she says. 'Will you let me help you out for a couple of weeks at least? Just to be clear, I don't need paying. I'm still collecting my salary.'

'Er, to be honest, I don't know what's going on. Lori and I have been doing our best, but ... Maybe I should just quit, put the house back on the market and walk away.'

'But you don't want to, do you? You want to see this through, just as you planned. Am I right or am I right?'

Her gaze burns into me as she waits for my answer. 'I suppose that is what I want,' I mumble eventually.

'Then let us help you.'

'But I don't know if it's the *right* thing to do. It's so complicated. There are things I need to sort out with Jack.' I press my fingers against my temples, trying to subdue the raging thoughts that are threatening to burst out of my brain.

Abi looks at me kindly. 'We won't discuss it now. Sleep on it and we'll talk again in the morning.'

Lori steps in. 'Is it okay if she stays over tonight?'

'I'm happy to share the airbed, don't mind roughing it,' Abi adds. 'It'll be like old times, won't it?' She breaks off suddenly. 'Of course, if you'd rather I found a hotel …'

'No, it's fine,' I say, recovering myself. 'Please stay. And thanks, your offer is incredibly generous. We'll discuss it over breakfast.'

'Great. I don't want to force you,' she says. 'Although given the mess you're in, you'll be an idiot if you turn me down.'

I get into bed and lie there for a few moments, staring at the familiar cracks in the ceiling, reluctant to turn off the lights and plunge myself into darkness. The atmosphere has subtly changed since the arrival of our new guest; it's as if the house itself is shifting about uneasily, disturbed by her presence. Something about this Abigail person isn't quite right, but I can't put my finger on it. Why is she here?

As I drift off to sleep, the empty rooms above me start to fill with ghosts. I can hear footsteps running across the floor, children play-fighting, babies crying, the chatter of female voices, the drone of a vacuum cleaner. Cigarette smoke is wafting down the stairs; there's the sharp smell of bleach and the sweet stench of dirty nappies, aromas of different dinners being cooked all at the same time. Chaos in the kitchen, laughter in the lounge. A silly argument kicking off in the hall. I see women pegging out washing in the garden – getting on with the stuff of life. Or curled up in armchairs staring blankly into space, wondering what's become of them and what future lies ahead. It's there in full colour, playing like a movie – only I'm not watching, I'm in it.

The sense of the past is overwhelming. I can feel the house's heart beating. It feels so real I could switch on the light and there would be women sleeping on makeshift beds all around me. But I stay in the darkness, feeling their emotions break over me like waves.

CHAPTER TWENTY-FIVE

Stella

Now

I stare at the laptop screen, my vision blurring with stupid tears I can't hold back. The last few months of bank statements make for grim reading – the 'out' column packed with almost daily cash withdrawals and contactless payments and no income set against it. I click on 'make a transfer' and top up the current account from my savings yet again. There are still thousands left, but the pot is dwindling, my inheritance running through my fingers like sand. Worst of all, I've no idea where all the money's been spent.

Leaving the room, I go upstairs. It's still early, the dawn barely broken, and neither of my guests seems to be awake yet. I stand at the large bay windows of the so-called master bedroom and look out. The sky is grey but strangely luminous, the clouds edged with a pink glow. There's a silvery sheen on the sea and the mud is shiny, as if it's been polished in the night. It's not conventionally beautiful but it still takes my breath away.

The room, however, is a total wreck. It looks as if Alan kept starting jobs then gave up and moved on to other things. Several floorboards are missing and there's a tangle of wiring between the joists. A partition wall has been taken down and the bath suite removed. There are holes in the saggy ceiling and cracks in the cornice; the radiator has been wrenched from its moorings. I shiver, folding my arms across my chest. The place couldn't be further away from the beautiful mood boards I created, which now feel like a sick joke.

Moving on, I go to the back of the house, where the Romanians were working. The earthy smell of new plaster fills my nostrils as I enter the room where the violent drawings were. They're still here, of course, just hidden. I run my fingers over the flesh-coloured walls, tracing the pictures that are etched on my brain – the stick women with the triangular skirts and flicked-up hair, the man holding a weapon dripping with blood.

'There you are,' says a voice. I nearly jump out of my skin and turn around to see Abi. She's fully dressed, hair brushed, make-up applied, as if about to leave for work. 'Sorry, didn't mean to scare you.' She hovers at the threshold.

'Didn't hear you coming,' I reply.

She enters cautiously, looking around the empty room as if searching for something. 'Why are you in here?'

'Just checking what's been done and what hasn't.'

'Hmm …' She goes to the window and stares out, transfixed for a few moments by the view. 'Have you made lots of changes in here?'

'Yes. There used to be a shower room in the corner. The house was divided into tiny bedsits, you see, so the women and their children had a space of their own.' She nods, still gazing down into the garden. 'There were some drawings on the wall that I had covered up.'

She swings around on her heel, her eyes wide. 'What sort of drawings?'

'Scenes of domestic violence. They looked like a child had done them; they were very … vivid. Explicit.'

'Which wall? Show me.'

'This one,' I say, pointing to the clear expanse of drying plaster. 'Lori found them when she stripped the wallpaper. It was very upsetting.'

'Not as upsetting as witnessing the real thing,' she replies, staring at the wall.

'No, of course not. I didn't mean to imply—'

'Children are often the most badly affected. Even if they're not physically beaten themselves, the impact on them can be devastating and can affect the rest of their lives,' she continues all in one breath. She gulps in air, holding her hand to her throat, the smart, glossy facade cast aside for a second to reveal somebody younger, more vulnerable. 'Sorry, can we get out of here? I'm feeling a bit claustrophobic.'

'Of course,' I say. 'I know what you mean, there's a creepy atmosphere. I thought once it had been replastered it would be okay, but obviously not.'

We go downstairs together, and by the time we reach the ground floor, Abi has composed herself. 'Sorry about that,' she says, glancing behind her, then lowering her voice. 'I was thinking about Lori. Those poor kids. I don't know exactly what they saw, but it must have been really bad for them to be taken into care.'

'Yeah, I've been wondering about that.' We go into the kitchen and I reach for the kettle. When in doubt, make a cup of tea, I think. 'My mother was a foster carer; we had troubled kids in the house all the time. I'm sure some of them came from violent homes. When I was little, I had no idea, I mean, nobody told me what they'd been through. I was just told their mummies and daddies couldn't look after them, I didn't understand.'

'Why would you?'

'There was this boy called Kyle …' I bite my tongue, wondering why I'm telling her all this. I've never even spoken about it to Jack.

'And?' she prompts.

I feel myself colouring up. 'Nothing … it doesn't matter … He was very damaged, that's all … Tea? Toast?'

'Please.' Abi opens the cupboards, looking for mugs. 'Domestic violence is damaging to everyone involved. Usually the victims blame themselves.'

'You mean Lori.' I take four slices of bread out and pop them into the toaster. 'I don't mean to interfere, but I don't understand why she wants to save the marriage. Darren's never going to change, is he?'

Abi puts a finger to her lips and closes the kitchen door. 'I've been telling her to leave him for years,' she says quietly. 'But she's got this idea fixed in her head that all children need their fathers, which simply isn't true.'

'If she's not careful, she'll lose the kids altogether.' The kettle comes to the boil and I pour water into our mugs.

'Or worse.' Abi screws up her mouth. 'Thank you for keeping her safe. One of the main reasons I wanted to come here was so I could work on her. Get her to see sense.'

'You sound like a very good friend. I wonder why she didn't come to you in the first place.'

'Darren knows where I live.' She pours milk into her mug and puts the carton back in the fridge. 'Anyway, enough about that. Have you decided about my offer of help?'

'Er, yes. I'd like to accept, if that's okay.' The toast pops up and I grab the hot slices, dropping them onto a plate.

'Excellent,' smiles Abi as I put on the spread. 'We'll make a list of what still needs doing and pull together a schedule. Then I can start contacting builders for quotes.'

'I went through all that last time and it wasn't very successful. They were all way too high.'

'Hmm, going with the cheapest quote is often a false economy.' She sips her tea, then puts the mug down on the counter, leaving a red lipstick mark on the rim. 'I'm happy to take a look at your budget.'

I laugh grimly. 'There isn't one really. Just a pot of money in the bank that keeps going down.'

'Oh dear. We'd better get it under control before there's nothing left.'

As I go to agree, my phone starts to play a familiar ringtone from my jeans pocket. 'Sorry, I need to take this.' She smiles assent and I open the kitchen door. 'Hi, Jack,' I say, moving rapidly down the hallway and into the bedroom.

'How's it going?' His gruff accent chokes me up.

'So-so, not too bad. How about you?'

'I'm good, thanks, yeah.' He sounds certain, not like he's pretending. 'Look, we need to talk.'

'Yeah, I've been saying that.'

'I know, I know, I've been avoiding you, but you're right. We can't go on like this.'

'What do you mean, being apart?'

'We need to resolve things. And I'm running out of underwear.' He emits a small chuckle but I don't join in.

'Okay. Shall I come to Dom's or do you want to come down here?'

'I'm really busy at work and … I presume Lori's still there?'

'Yes.' *There are two of them now*, I add silently. *Double trouble.*

'Would you mind packing some of my stuff up and meeting me at St Pancras?'

I feel a spark of irritation. 'I'm not Deliveroo, Jack. I'm completely cool with having a proper conversation about our relationship, but if all you want is a few more shirts and your guitar—'

'I couldn't care less about any of that,' he interrupts. 'I just thought, if you're coming to London anyway …' His sentence tails off. 'Look, forget it.'

There's a very long pause. I pull at a loose thread on the duvet cover, determined not to be the first one to speak. The silence aches between us and my stomach twists itself into knots. Why does he want more of his things?

'Look, I'm really sorry your parents died,' he says finally.

'Sorry, I don't understand. What's that got to do with it?'

'Everything! When we met, I knew you were grieving, but I didn't realise just how badly it had affected you. I was a shoulder to cry on, nothing more.'

'That's so not true,' I say hotly. 'We fell in love.'

'It all happened too fast. I moved into your flat after a month—'

'Your lease was up, it made sense.'

'It was too soon. The next thing I know, we're moving out of London, buying a mansion by the sea. I felt like you were just going down your own track, like it didn't matter what I thought. Then Lori turned up and you ignored me, like I was the old toy you no longer wanted to play with.'

His words sting. 'That's unfair,' I protest, getting off the bed and pacing around the room. 'Lori's a victim of domestic violence; we had to help her. My parents would have taken her in without a second thought.'

He pauses and I hear a faint sigh. 'See what I mean? It all goes back to your mum and dad. You spend your whole life trying to be like them. But this is about *us*.'

'I know that. Why do you think I bought this house? I want it to be our forever home. I want to get married and have children.' I stop by the window and stare at the distant view of the sea. 'I'm over thirty now, I can't afford to hang around.'

'Yes, your body clock's ticking away and you need a sperm donor.'

'Don't say that, it's horrible. It's not like that. How many more times do I have to tell you: I love you, Jack.' Emotion wells up in my throat and I swallow it down.

'Really, Stella? I'm not sure you know what love is,' he replies, his tone hard and cold.

'I'm not sure *you* do,' I retaliate. This is all sounding so wrong. It's as if we've let go of a beautiful balloon and we're watching it float away, helpless to catch it and bring it back safely to earth.

'The thing is …' He hesitates. 'I've not been completely honest with you.'

'Oh?' My stomach flips over and I put a hand on the mantelpiece to steady myself.

'I've, er … not been staying with Dom. I'm sorry, I wanted to tell you the truth, but the timing wasn't right.'

'Where are you then?'

'With, um …' He takes a breath. 'With a girl called Pansy. She's a designer, works on my team.' *Pansy, Pansy …* Jack used to talk about everyone at work, but I don't think he ever mentioned a Pansy.

'What are you saying?'

'We've been, um … We, er, got together at the Christmas party. Neither of us meant it to happen; it was just a one-off, a drunken moment. I said I didn't want to carry on … then in the new year, with all the problems with the house and the travelling … and then Lori turning up … it kind of started again, and then …' He pauses for a breath. 'Well, if I'm honest, I feel happier than I've been for years.'

'You bastard,' I mutter. 'You bastard.'

'It wasn't deliberate, really it wasn't. I've never been unfaithful before. Dom says it was an accident waiting to happen. I felt neglected, like you didn't care. You shut me out …' He carries on emptying his shit down the line. I can't listen any more, my head already bursting with his cruel, heartless words.

'You're leaving me for this, this Pansy person, is that what you're saying?' My mouth tastes of bile. 'We've been together a year and you're dumping me over the phone?'

'I didn't mean—'

'Why didn't you just text me? Or post it on Instagram?'

'I only faked the burglary to make you come to your senses and get rid of Lori, but then you chucked me out. What was I to do?'

'Oh, I see. So *I* pushed you into her bed, *I* forced you to have an affair? Don't give me that bollocks.'

'You know things weren't good between us. We were already in trouble.'

'Bullshit. We were building a future together, making a home for our family—'

'I don't want children,' he says quickly.

'That's a horrible thing to say.'

'I've tried to tell you countless times, but you refuse to listen.'

'Liar!' I shout. 'You're such a liar! You never said that. Whenever I talked about wanting kids, you smiled and nodded. If I'd known that—'

He inhales as if to bite back, then stops himself. 'Look,' he says after a few seconds. 'I'm not proud of what I've done, but it's not *all* my fault.'

'Oh just piss off, go back to your little Pansy. I couldn't care less. I don't want you, I don't need you. You can fuck right off!' I punch the red telephone symbol and hurl the handset across the room. It smashes against the leg of the desk like a ball hitting a wicket and falls to the floor. Throwing myself onto the bed, I bury my face in the duvet and scream.

CHAPTER TWENTY-SIX

Stella

Now

'Stella? Are you okay? Can we come in?'

I lift my head from the pillow as the door opens and Lori pokes her head around the frame. Abi is hovering behind her, her dark eyes full of questions.

'Er, yeah … okay …' I wipe the tears away with my sleeve and sit up. They enter and stand either side of the bed like two administering angels.

Lori puts her hands to her mouth. 'My God, what's happened? Abigail heard you crying.'

'Jack's left me,' I croak. Lori looks confused – after all, it's old news. 'No, I mean, it's not just temporary, it's properly over. He's found someone else.'

Abi makes a contemptuous noise. 'This is why I don't have relationships with men.'

'You poor thing,' says Lori, sitting on the edge of the bed and putting a hand on my shoulder. 'How did you find out?'

'He rang and told me. Didn't even have the guts to tell me to my face. She's some girl from work, they've been having an affair. Apparently it's *my* fault, I drove him to it.'

'Jesus Christ,' says Abi. 'They never take responsibility, do they? I can't bear it.' She moves away and paces around the room. 'As soon as there's a problem, either they punish us or piss off, find some new idiot to prey on. You know what it is, Stella – he couldn't bear you controlling the purse strings.' She waves at the walls. 'All this was bought with your inheritance, right?'

'Let's not talk about that now, Abi,' says Lori. 'She's upset enough as it is.'

'I'm just saying, Stella is the one with the money, which gives her power, and men don't like it when women have the power.'

'Abi! Calm down, will you?' Lori fixes her with a glare. 'Make Stella a coffee or something.' Abi goes to answer, then marches out of the room. 'Sorry about that. She's got a real thing against men.'

'It's okay,' I say. 'I'm sorry, this is really embarrassing.'

'Don't be silly. You saw me in a far worse state.'

'But Abi's only just met me …'

'So what? It doesn't matter, and anyway, you can see how much she's on your side.' She laughs slightly. '*Too* much, almost.'

'I can't believe it,' I say. 'There were no clues.' I stop. No, that's not true. After Christmas, there were a lot of late nights and excuses about cancelled trains. We only had sex twice in the last few months, which I put down to the airbed and the fact that we were living on a building site. He was distracting me, like a close-quarters magician, making me focus on the wrong issues while he engineered his tricks. And then he had the cheek to say it was all my fault. *An accident waiting to happen* – how dare he?

'You're in shock. You need to take some deep breaths.'

'I know.' I push air down into my lungs. My chest is hurting, like somebody's standing on it.

'It's horrible when you feel out of control, it's the worst thing.'

I reach for a tissue and blow my nose. 'I didn't *want* to inherit the money – I was only trying to do the right thing, something Mum and Dad would have approved of. For me and Jack, for our future. But now he's saying he never wanted children. He doesn't want to be with me at all, he wants this Pansy woman. I don't understand, what did I do wrong?'

'You didn't do anything wrong,' Lori soothes. 'You're a really good, strong person.'

'No I'm not. I'm awful. This is all a punishment.'

'A punishment? No, no, that's not true.' She pushes a stray hair off my wet cheek. 'I'm really sorry, you don't deserve all this, but you'll pull through. We're here to help you. Neither of us will leave you in the lurch. You can rely on us totally.'

The next few days pass almost imperceptibly. It's as if a fog has drifted across from the sea and enveloped the entire house, clouding my vision so that I have no idea when day turns to night and then becomes day again. I largely stay in my room, only venturing out to use the bathroom. I've never felt so weak and tired, and I've got a permanent headache, like I'm sickening for the flu. I keep expecting to wake up with a fever and a streaming nose, but the illness doesn't develop, just lurks at the edges of my system, threatening me. It's very similar to how I felt after my parents died, which suggests what I'm experiencing is grief. Only it's something far more nebulous that has died – a vision of the future that can never be.

I don't want to go into the rest of the house – the terrible mess mocks me, emphasising my stupidity. I've had plenty of time to think about all that's happened since Mum and Dad died, and I realise now that I was wandering around in a fog even then. I knew deep in my heart that Jack wasn't completely on board, but I chose not to confront the truth. And if I'm honest – and it really hurts to admit this – I almost felt entitled to have my own way because I was grieving. My pain cancelled out his feelings. He was trying to please me because he knew how much I was hurting. But that never works, not in the long term.

Abi doesn't see it that way. She thinks I've nothing to feel sorry for, that he's totally in the wrong and his behaviour has been appalling from the beginning. To her, he's a predator who latched onto me when I was feeling vulnerable. She thinks he was probably after my money. But she doesn't know Jack like I do; she's never even met him. It's easy to stand on the outside looking in and make judgements about other people's lives.

Lori doesn't judge. She brings me drinks and food, sits on the bed and waits patiently for me to say something. I have a very short playlist, going over the same things again and again, but she doesn't complain or contradict me. The tables have definitely turned – now I'm the survivor and she's the Good Samaritan.

It must be lunchtime, or thereabouts, because Lori has just entered with a bowl of soup on a tray. Abi went out to fetch some shopping and has been busily cooking proper meals to tempt my waning appetite.

'Grub's up,' Lori says. 'Carrot and coriander, home-made.' She rests the tray on the mattress and the soup slops around the bowl.

'Thanks.' I scramble to sit up. 'Um … what day is it?'

'Sunday,' she smiles. 'Shall I draw the curtains? It's so dark in here, no wonder you've lost track.' She crosses to the window.

'Weren't you supposed to be seeing your kids this weekend? It's every other week, isn't it?'

'That's better. Look, the sun's shining.' She turns around. 'Yes, it was a visit weekend, but I decided I was needed here.'

'What? That's silly, I'm not ill.'

'You've been crying almost constantly, you won't eat and you haven't left the room for three days. This isn't just about Jack; this is because of everything you've been through –it's been building up like a volcano, and now it's erupted.'

'I feel really bad,' I say, staring into the orange soup speckled with herbs. 'You should have gone, Lori. Your kids needed to see you.'

'They're fine, they're being well looked after,' she says. 'Anyway, my visits make things worse, stir everything up again.'

'But you're their mum. You don't want them to think you've abandoned them.'

'It's okay, Stella, don't worry about it.' Her tone is brittle. 'Eat your soup before it gets cold.' She leaves the room.

I pick up the spoon and stir the liquid thoughtfully. I clearly touched a nerve, but I can't work out what upset her. Lori has been wonderfully kind to me, but she's been on edge recently, particularly since Abi turned up. Maybe she's had enough of living here; maybe she wants to leave and get on with the rest of her life but now feels obliged to stay. I don't understand what's happening about Darren, or why she isn't fighting for her kids. I'd be desperate; I'd do anything to get them back. But I'm not Lori, am I? I don't know what's going on inside her head.

Deciding to buck up my ideas, I get out of bed and shower, then get dressed. As I brush my hair, I give myself a talking-to in the mirror. *Stop being so selfish*, I say. *Your injuries are nothing compared to what Lori has had to endure.* My pale, tired face stares back at me, looking disgruntled.

I take my tray back to the kitchen and pour the soup down the sink. I feel guilty about not eating it, but I don't seem to have any appetite at the moment. Just at that moment, Abi enters from the back of the house. I quickly turn on the tap to swirl the remains down the drain.

'You're out of your pyjamas,' she says approvingly. 'Excellent.'

'Life goes on, I guess.'

'Yup.' She pauses. 'I've been doing an appraisal of the current situation. Hope you don't mind, but I've set myself up in the office.'

'Office?'

'The little room next to the conservatory.'

'Oh, right. Yes, I suppose it *was* an office at one time. All those shelves.'

'Exactly.' She gives me a fixed grin. 'Anyway, I've made lots of lists and I've contacted some local builders, asking them to come over next week to quote for the job. We need to prepare a proper brief for them to put costs against, otherwise we won't be able to compare like for like.'

'Okay … sounds good …'

'Don't worry, I'll handle them when they turn up. I won't let them pull the wool over your eyes.'

'Thanks, that'd be really helpful.'

'We just need to talk about your budget,' she continues. 'I don't know how much you've got to spend.'

'There's just over a hundred thousand left in the savings account.' Her eyebrows rise in surprise. 'It sounds a lot, but there's so much to do. I've no idea if it'll be enough.'

'We'll make it enough,' she says. 'Cut our coat. Lori says you were planning an extension?'

'Yeah, a big kitchen diner with bifold doors leading onto the patio.' I look around at all the pine cladding and sigh. 'I had such grand plans. It was going to look amazing.'

'We'll get there,' she replies. 'Just leave it to me.'

The first builder turns up on Monday morning. Abi introduces me as 'the client', and then I retreat to my room and busy myself at the desk, acting as if I'm far too important to be bothered. I hear them standing in the hallway talking about time frames and guarantees.

'She was badly let down before,' she says, 'but I'm project-managing now and I'll be keeping a very close eye on things.' Their voices fade as they go upstairs. It's such a relief not to be doing this myself. I must offer Abi a fee, I think. She's been so efficient and helpful. Last night we went through the accounts together and added up the expenditure so far.

'Where are the receipts?' she asked. I gave her a plastic wallet stuffed with grubby bits of paper. 'This can't be all of them. Hmm … I think he was skimming off the top.'

I think of Alan. Is he a crook? Maybe I'm a fool, but I'm still reluctant to believe it. I open the desk drawer and take out his flimsy business card. I tried so many times to contact him and left dozens of messages. I've given up on the idea of him coming back, but I feel I deserve an explanation at least. It would help me draw a line under it.

Before, his phone has gone straight to voicemail, but this time the number rings out several times. I stare at the screen, listening to the bleeps, silently begging him to pick up. But the call is rejected and I'm invited – yet again – to leave a message.

'It's Stella here,' I say, trying to keep my voice steady. 'I hope you're okay. Please call or send me a text. I'm worried about you. I just want an explanation. If I've offended or upset you, I'm really sorry. Hope to speak to you soon.'

Abi knocks on the door twenty minutes later. She comes in and stands by the desk. 'One down, three to go,' she says, clearly pleased with herself. 'I quite liked him, seemed to know what he was doing. He's got references, said we could go and visit some other jobs he's done, which is reassuring.'

'Good,' I say. 'I never asked Alan for references, stupid really. He was old school, didn't have a website or anything.'

'How did you find him in the first place?' she says.

'He just turned up on the doorstep. I put an advert on the community noticeboard in the Co-op. I think that's how he found out about it.'

'Hmm …' she says. 'So you don't really know anything about him.'

'No. All I have is his card.' I pick it up. '"Alan Foxton, Builder. No job too big or too small." No address, just his mobile number.'

'What did you say? Give me that.' She snatches the card from my fingers and stares at it. 'Oh my God … oh my God …'

'What's wrong? Do you know him?'

Abi starts to sway; her hand is shaking, the card flapping in her hand like a tiny white bird.

'What is it? You okay? Abi … Abi? What's the matter?'

Her eyes roll towards the back of her head and she opens her mouth wide, gasping for breath. I leap up to catch her and she falls heavily into my arms.

CHAPTER TWENTY-SEVEN

Kay

Then

Kay ran upstairs and into the bathroom, shutting the door and sliding across the bolt with trembling fingers. He bounded up the stairs behind her.

'What are you doing in there?' he shouted, pounding his fist against the door.

'Just leave me alone, Foxy,' she begged. 'I'm going to throw up.'

'Mummy?' Abigail's high-pitched voice, full of concern.

'Go back to your room. Now!' Foxy barked. 'Keep out of it.'

'But I want Mummy!'

'A hiding is what you'll get if you don't do as you're told.' Abigail squealed and Kay imagined him slapping her daughter around the face, pushing her back to her bedroom.

'Leave her be, Foxy!' she shouted as the sound of scuffling and screaming continued on the other side of the door. What was he doing to her? It was no good, she would have to come out. But before she could slip the bolt, she heard Foxy cry out in pain and swear.

'You little tyke!' he shouted. 'You wait till I get hold of you!'

She flung open the door just in time to see Abigail hurtling down the stairs in her pink pyjamas.

'The cow bit me!' He was rubbing his hand and sucking on the wound.

Kay tried to get across the landing, but he was blocking her way. In the hallway below, Abigail was standing on tiptoes, reaching up to the door latch. The door shuddered open and she ran out in her bare feet.

'Abigail! Come back!' Kay cried, then turned to Foxy. 'Let me pass. She can't go out, she'll get run over!'

'It'll be her own stupid fault if she does,' he snarled.

'You can't say that; she's only seven. I need to go after her.'

'You need to do as I tell you.' Foxy was burning up, his ears and cheeks flushed red. 'You're making me very angry, Kay,' he added, dragging her by the hair into the bedroom and flinging her onto the mattress. He took the key from the door and locked her in from outside.

She felt truly sick now; her heart was racing uncontrollably and she was sweating. This was far worse than all the blows he'd ever struck. Her little girl was out in the street, in the dark, and she couldn't reach her. She lifted herself off the bed and staggered to the window, opening it and leaning out.

'Abigail! Where are you, love?'

The front garden was empty, the gate swinging open. Kay blinked into the evening gloom, searching for her daughter's silhouette in the pool of light coming from the lamp post on the other side of the street. But there was no sign of her. How could she have disappeared in such a short space of time?

'Abigail! Abigail! Please – talk to Mummy!' she shouted, her voice dipping with hopelessness.

She tasted fear in the back of her throat. Why wasn't her daughter answering? Had something happened to her? It would be easy for a driver to hit a child darting out from between the parked cars. But there'd been no screeching of brakes, no sound of a crash.

The air was still and silent, the pavements empty. If she called for help, nobody would hear her and it would only make things worse with Foxy. Perhaps Abigail was hiding. It would be the sensible thing to do – to crawl under a bush or crouch behind a dustbin. She was such a smart kid, not eight until next month, and yet so grown up compared to how Kay had been at that age.

'Abigail? Are you there, love?' she said in a loud stage whisper, pausing with her mouth open, waiting for a sign – a word, a rustle, a white arm waving out of the darkness. But nothing came. 'Just wait there, sausage. Mummy will be down as soon as she can.'

She drew her head back inside and stood with her back against the wardrobe, trying to steady her racing heartbeat. Her ears were pricked, but all she could hear was the blood rushing through her head. Where was Foxy? What was he doing? He must have gone downstairs.

She moved forward and rattled the door, knowing it wouldn't open but still feeling the need to try. She'd once seen someone slide a sheet of paper under a door, shake the handle until the key fell onto the paper, then pull it back into the room. But that had been on some television programme; it probably didn't work in real life. Besides, she had no paper to hand, and the door was so tightly fitted it scraped the carpet.

Jumping out of the window was impossible – she was too high up and there was nothing below to break her fall. She would have to wait until Foxy opened the door, but who knew what kind of mood he'd be in? He was so unpredictable. He could be working himself into a frenzy, clicking his knuckles, boxing the air; or drinking himself into a slump of self-pity. This wasn't the first time she'd been locked in. It usually took about half an hour for him to come back, and then he'd either beat her or they'd have sex – sometimes both. He seemed to think that forcing himself inside her was an act of forgiveness on his part, proof that he still loved her despite the fact that she drove him to violence. His logic was crazy but she'd fallen for it all this time. Not any more, though.

She put her hand on her stomach, pressing it slightly as if trying to touch her unborn child. What had she been thinking? She'd been living in a foolish fantasy world, believing that another baby would wave a magic wand over their relationship and put everything right; that fatherhood would transform this monster into a loving, caring, gentle man. Getting pregnant had only made things worse. She couldn't have an abortion, she just couldn't, but …

She heard a car pull up outside the house. Blue lights flashed into the room for a few seconds, then stopped. Police? Ambulance? Why were they here? *Oh please God, let it not be about Abigail.* Before she could run to the window, the bedroom door opened and Foxy marched in, grabbing her roughly by the arm and pulling her onto the landing.

'You say one word against me and you're dead,' he said, pushing her down the stairs as the bell rang. He opened the door keeping one arm tightly gripped around her waist.

'Mr and Mrs Foxton?' said a uniformed officer. There were two of them standing there, both men, both terrifyingly tall. She stared down at their large black boots.

Foxy smiled politely. 'Yes. What's this about?'

'Is it my dau—' Kay started, but Foxy tightened his hold, trapping her voice.

'Abigail is with a neighbour, she's quite safe. Mind if we come in for a few moments?'

'Please do.' Foxy stepped back to let the policemen in. They walked into the living room, observing the surroundings – the telly playing some sitcom, the remains of the evening meal congealing on the plates. Their large frames seemed to take up the entire space. 'I can't imagine why you're here,' he continued evenly. 'Not bad news, I hope?'

The officer took out his black notebook and flipped it open. 'We had a 999 call from a neighbour. Your daughter knocked on her door in her pyjamas and said "Foxy is killing my Mummy". Foxy – is that you?'

'Yes, everyone calls me that.' He let out a small, nervous laugh. 'I'm very sorry that our neighbour was fooled into thinking there was some kind of drama going on. As you can see, it's pretty quiet.'

There was no evidence of their argument: no upturned chairs, no smashed windows or food thrown against the walls. The bruises on her body were old, and he'd given her no fresh marks this evening, not yet anyway. But now that Abigail had caused this fuss – God bless her, she'd only been trying to help – there would be hell to pay once the police had gone.

'The neighbour said she heard shouting earlier,' said the other officer.

'That was me telling Abigail off, I'm afraid. She's a difficult child, very aggressive. She bit me – look!' Foxy proffered his hand; the tiny teeth marks were still visible. 'When I tried to discipline her, she ran out of the house. I knew she hadn't gone far, but I was teaching her a lesson, letting her sweat it out for a bit. I'm very sorry, I had no idea she would go telling such awful lies; she really is the limit.'

The policemen exchanged a glance. The one with the notebook scribbled something down while the other one stared at Kay closely. She could feel his eyes burning her face, searching for answers. She so wanted to tell him the truth, but she didn't dare. They wouldn't believe her anyway. Foxy was being his usual charming public self.

Officer number two lowered his eyebrows. 'I hope you don't mind my saying, Mrs Foxton, but you look like you've been crying.'

'She finds Abigail's behaviour very upsetting, don't you, love?' Foxy interjected, squeezing her waist until it hurt.

Kay nodded. 'I'd like her to come home now,' she whispered. 'Can I go and get her, please? Who's she with?'

'We'll bring her to you.' The second policeman walked out of the room. 'The neighbour would prefer to remain anonymous,' his partner added.

Foxy huffed. 'I bet she would. Interfering busybody. Abigail's got a lot to answer for too. What a dreadful waste of time.'

'That's kids for you, I'm afraid.' The officer shut his notebook and returned it to his top pocket. 'Best of luck.'

Foxy showed him out while Kay ran to the front window to look for Abigail. She wondered which neighbour she'd gone to. There was an older lady next door, recently widowed; Abigail chatted to her sometimes when she was playing in the garden. On the other side was a family with three boys who were wearing the lawn away with their football. Kay didn't know any of them by name, just smiled and murmured hello if they happened to meet in the street. The people opposite had only just moved in; she didn't know much about them. Foxy would always give a cheery wave to the neighbours and make the obligatory remark about the day's weather, but that was as far as it went. Privately he slagged them off and forbade her to have anything to do with them.

'Mummy, Mummy!' Abigail ran through the house and wrapped her arms around Kay's legs.

'There, there, it's okay, you're home now …' She bent down and hugged her daughter as tightly as she could without squashing her tiny ribs. Foxy stood behind her, arms folded, a disapproving expression on his face.

'Right, we'll be getting off,' said the officer.

'Of course. I'm sure you've got plenty more important things to attend to,' Foxy replied, walking him back to the front door. It opened and closed again, and Kay heard her husband release a heavy, angry sigh. He came straight back into the room and ripped Abigail out of her arms, grabbing her by the shoulders and spitting words into her face.

'You pull a number like that again, and I *will* kill your mother!'

That night, Kay lay in the darkness, unable to settle. Abigail had been sent to her room and had eventually sobbed herself to sleep. Foxy had taken all her toys and dolls, saying he was going to send them to the children's hospital. He even went into the garden and slashed her space hopper with a kitchen knife. Now it was lying on the patio like a dead thing. Kay imagined him tearing at her flesh in the same way. Who knew what he'd do next?

He was lying next to her in the matrimonial bed, snoring loudly. Putting on such a show for the police had exhausted him and he'd sunk three cans of Special Brew after they'd gone. For some reason he hadn't given her a hiding this time, and for that she was grateful. Maybe it was because she was pregnant, God help her, or maybe the police visit had rattled him. He wouldn't want to end up in prison like Micky. Oh no, Alan Foxton was the opposite of his little brother – responsible, hard-working, as straight as a die. It was as if it hadn't even occurred to him until tonight that wife-beating was a crime.

But she wasn't stupid enough to believe that one visit from the cops would change him. This couldn't go on; she and Abigail had to leave. Why, oh why had she deliberately got herself pregnant? It was madness. They couldn't go to her parents, not after all the bother she'd put them to in the past. Besides, they really liked Foxy and wouldn't believe her. Falling on friends wasn't an option either – he'd complained about all of them and she'd been forced to break contact. She didn't have a job any more and wouldn't get a new one now she was expecting. Where could she go? How would she afford to live?

She felt tears rolling down her cheeks and onto the pillow. What an almighty mess she'd made of her life, starting with those Bacardi and cokes in Torremolinos, although that sounded like she considered Abigail a mistake, which wasn't the case. She loved her daughter to bits and would fight to the death to protect her. Marrying Foxy was the stupidest thing she'd ever done, although nobody else could see it – nobody *wanted* to see it. If she stayed with him, the situation was only going to get worse. *I will* kill your mother, that was what he'd said tonight. Abigail could end up an orphan; the new baby might die in the womb. She couldn't do that to her children. She had to escape.

Her eyes had adjusted to the lack of light and she could make out the chest of drawers quite easily. Inside, hidden amongst the sanitary towels she no longer had need for, was the slip of paper Abigail's teacher had given her. She remembered some of the details of the refuge – Westhill House, Nevansey. A squat, Ms Gardiner had said. Kay dreaded to imagine what the place was like; it was probably filthy and didn't even have gas or electricity. But it had to be better than begging on the streets, and there'd be other women there too, who'd seen violence themselves and would understand what she was escaping from.

Tomorrow morning, after Foxy left for work, she would keep Abigail off school, pack a suitcase and make her way to Nevansey. She didn't want to leave her lovely house or give up her status as a respectable married woman, but she had to act now, before it was too late.

CHAPTER TWENTY-EIGHT

Stella

Now

Abigail lies on my bed, curled up foetus-like, her fist in her mouth. Lori is sitting at her side, stroking her back gently and murmuring words of comfort.

'I've brought you some water,' I say, putting the glass on the table.

'Thanks,' whispers Lori. She gives me a slight smile, as if expecting me to leave the room. But it's *my* room, *my* bed Abi's resting on. I feel like I need an explanation, at least.

'Why did she faint?'

'Oh, er, she gets dizzy spells,' Lori says. 'They happen out of the blue. Blood sugar or something, I think.'

'Really?' I can't keep the doubt out of my voice. 'It seemed to have something to do with Alan's business card. She said "oh my God" several times, then collapsed.'

'She meant "oh my God, I'm going to faint", I expect. It's embarrassing, yeah? She'll pull round in a few minutes. Actually, if she could have a biscuit or something sweet, that might help.'

Lori wants me out of the room, I know it – the air is thick with their secrets. I have an urge to stand my ground, but if Abi is genuinely ill, it will seem unkind. So reluctantly I go into the kitchen in search of chocolate digestives.

My thoughts, however, refuse to leave the room. I replay what I saw. Abi fainted in shock, not because she had a sugar dip, and it had something to do with Alan. She must know him. Know him and hate him – maybe even fear him. I can't think why anyone would be scared of sweet old Alan, but there has to be a reason for such a dramatic reaction.

I slice open the packet of biscuits and the smell of sweet chocolate fills my nostrils. I pop one into my mouth, then assemble half a dozen or so on a plate and carry it back to the front room.

Abi is sitting up now, sipping the water and looking rather shame-faced. I proffer the biscuits and she takes one gratefully. I should offer to make some tea, really, but that would keep me out the room for longer, and I need to be here. I need to know what's going on.

'What's wrong?' I ask.

The two women exchange a look. 'Nothing's wrong,' says Lori.

'Nothing at all,' echoes Abi, her mouth full of crumbs. 'I'm fine now.' But I don't believe them.

'You can trust me, you know,' I say awkwardly. 'I think I've already proved that, several times over.'

'It's a medical thing,' Lori insists.

Abi nods in agreement. 'I'm fine, really I am. I'm sorry, it's my own fault, I didn't have any lunch. I've been trying to lose weight and … well, I obviously went too far.'

'I warned you,' adds Lori for good measure. 'You do everything to excess.'

Abi swings her legs over the edge of the bed. 'Thanks for coming to the rescue, Stella,' she says, 'but I'd like to go upstairs and rest.'

This is not good enough. I set my mouth in a stubborn line. 'If you know Alan – if there's some problem with him – please tell me. I have a right to know.'

'There's no problem,' says Lori firmly. She helps Abi to her feet. 'Come on, let's leave Stella in peace.'

They exit arm in arm, leaving me stranded, feeling stupid. Did I get the wrong end of the stick? Perhaps it was just coincidence that Abi fainted while she was reading Alan's business card. And yet … I bend down and pick up the card from where it fell from her shaking fingers. If she won't tell me what the connection between them is, perhaps he will.

As before, the number rings out several times before going to voicemail. I leave what feels like the twentieth message, only this time my tone is different.

'Alan, it's Stella here. From Westhill House. Look, I don't expect you to turn up any more or even give me an explanation about why you walked out on the job. This is something different. Do you by any chance know an Abigail?' I pause. Abigail *what*? I don't know her surname. Don't know a thing about her, for that matter. 'She's a friend of Lori's, mid to late forties, very dark looks, sort of Mediterranean. I'm certain she knows you. Anyway, if she means anything to you, please give me a ring. Thanks.'

I end the call with a sigh. He won't respond; I don't know why I even tried. For some reason, he doesn't want to have anything more to do with me, or with the house. Just like Jack. I turn to the invisible spirits of all the women who used to live here. *What is it about this place that makes men run away?*

Abi and Lori have disappeared upstairs and there's been no sight or sound of them for hours. I wonder what they're doing up there. Is Abi really resting, Lori nursing her? Or are they concocting a story to put me off the scent? The atmosphere in the house is charged; the walls are sucking the energy out of me. I badly need some fresh air – a quick walk on the beach at least – and yet for some inexplicable reason, I can't leave.

Something else is tugging at my brain, demanding my attention. It feels important, but I can't work out what it is. Not to do with Lori or Abi, or even Jack … Some appointment, perhaps? I reach for my phone and look at the screen. Today's date stares back at me. Ah, that's it. How could I possibly have forgotten?

It's the anniversary of my parents' death tomorrow. So much has happened recently, the day has crept up on me unawares. Last year it was like having a mental countdown clock flashing in my brain. The nearer I got to the anniversary, the more my stomach twisted with anxiety about how I would cope. But this year I've only been dimly aware that the dreaded day was coming.

Tears spring into my eyes and my vision blurs. Two years without Mum and Dad. They were so respected in their community, left a hole in so many people's lives. They remembered every child who ever came to them, even if they only stayed for a couple of weeks. Dad took photos of new arrivals and stuck them on the fridge to make everyone feel part of the family. After they moved on, the photos were transferred to scrapbooks. Mum wrote the children's names underneath, together with the date of their arrival and a few comments – *Leah loved fish fingers* or *Tyrone drew amazing pictures*. I still have those books in one of the boxes in the other room. I don't know what to do with them, can't bear to throw them away.

Last year, Molly came with me to the cemetery to see the rose bush and the commemorative plaque. It rained solidly all day and we huddled beneath my tiny handbag umbrella, heads touching, water dripping onto our shoulders. She didn't complain when I said I wanted to stay for a few more minutes, just patiently let the rain soak her back and turn her fingers to ice as I stared at the small plaque, reading their names over and over. Afterwards, we went to a nearby pub and had lunch. We talked about the tragedy of their deaths and the savage injustice that their killer had never been found. Molly had always suspected they were deliberately mown down, perhaps by some former foster kid out for revenge.

'But you don't understand, everybody loved them,' I said. 'There was nothing to get revenge for.'

'What about that fire?'

'The police asked me about that.'

'Where's that boy now? He'll be grown up, of course.'

'The police checked him out. He's in prison for drugs offences. The perfect alibi.'

'Hmm … I suppose he could have paid someone else to do it.'

I felt suddenly sick. The idea hadn't occurred to me until that moment. Images from that terrible night came flooding back. The choking smoke, the alarm blaring, kids screaming, my parents carrying them down the stairs in their arms and laying them on the front lawn, then running back into the smoking house to get the others.

I'll go to the garden of rest tomorrow, I decide. Face it on my own. I'll tell Mum and Dad everything that's happened and see what answers come to me. It's been a long time since we had any kind of conversation.

The day passes without my being aware of the light fading, and suddenly it's dark again. Still not a squeak from Lori and Abi. They must be starving hungry up there. So much for Abi's blood-sugar issues. I leave my room and wander around the ground floor, half expecting to find them cooking in the kitchen, or eating in the freezing conservatory, or chatting in the room Abi has commandeered for her office. But they're not there. Nor are they in the other reception room, hiding behind the storage boxes.

I climb the stairs to the first floor to check the bedrooms and bathrooms, picking my way carefully over gaps in the floorboards, trying not to brush against the dusty walls or catch myself on protruding nails, avoiding the ragged splinters where the door frames have been wrenched off. The place has been torn limb from limb, ransacked and then abandoned. There's so much to do here and I know I'll never face it on my own. I need Abi and Lori's help just as much as Lori needs me. But there should be complete honesty between us – no secrets. I'm not going to be fobbed off with excuses. Abi collapsed because she recognised Alan's name, and I have to know why.

I walk up the next flight to the very top of the house. There's a small landing and three doors. One leads to the room overlooking the garden, the second to the tiny turret room on the corner, and the third, with the sea views, Is where Lori – and now Abi – sleep. A sliver of light is escaping from under their door. I can hear talking. Moving closer, I press my ear against the wood and listen.

It's Lori's voice I hear first. 'If you want to leave, that's fine by me.'

'No, no way,' says Abi. Her voice is deeper, older, scratching against the inside of her throat.

'But this changes everything, surely. If it *is* him, it means she told you the truth.'

'I still have to find out for sure.'

'Foxton's not that unusual a name. It could be a coincidence, you know.'

'No, there's got to be an explanation.'

'Well, he's not coming back. He's taken Stella's money and done a runner.'

Abi's voice. 'But what if he *is* Foxy? Why did he come here in the first place? That's what's scaring me. There's got to be a reason, but I can't work it out.'

Foxy? I lift my ear from the door and step back. The floorboards creak and I freeze.

'Did you hear a noise just then?' Abi sounds anxious.

'It's nothing,' Lori soothes. 'Just the house settling. Come on, calm down … It's going to be all right, I promise.'

CHAPTER TWENTY-NINE

Stella

Now

As I turn off the M25 at the usual junction, I find my thoughts constantly straying to the situation back home. The conversation I overheard last night continues to play in my head, as if my brain recorded it and set it on a loop. Now I know for sure that Abi *was* reacting to the name on the business card, and that she had a bad experience with somebody called Foxy. Such a creepy nickname. It makes me think of foxes in children's fairy tales. They're always sly and untrustworthy, constantly working some scam. But whether Abi's Foxy and Alan Foxton the builder are the same person, we don't know.

What did she say, exactly? *Why did he come here in the first place? That's what's scaring me.* She meant Westhill House. And that makes me think that maybe there's a reason she's here too; that it's not just to pay back the favour I did for her friend. Could it be connected to the house's past life?

I pull away from the traffic lights, cross with myself for going over it yet again. I don't want to keep thinking about all that. This is Mum and Dad's day.

Turning off at the Old Stag roundabout, I drive past the garage where Dad always bought his petrol and the parade of shops where Mum made her everyday purchases. The shops are so small they can only stock a limited range of goods, but that never mattered to my parents. I can hear Mum's voice telling me for the hundredth time that *we have to support the local shopkeepers or they won't survive.* Unfortunately, not many other people followed their example. Most of the shops I remember from my childhood are still there, but they're looking starved and weary, on their last legs. A few have closed down completely, giving Springfield Parade a desolate air.

I drive under the dark bridge that used to scare me when I was little, and head away from the village. Within a couple of minutes I'm in open countryside – flat grassy fields, the odd horse and a smattering of low trees. Old farms have been turned into gated developments and barn conversions. It's typical Essex commuter belt. The price of property has leapt up since the announcement of an even faster line with direct connections to the West End.

The garden of rest is part of the new cemetery and crematorium, built in the middle of nowhere. It's busy today. A funeral must be going on in the main chapel, because there's another cortege lurking by the front gates. I overtake at a slow, respectful speed and park in the overflow car park, away from the gathering mourners.

As I turn off the engine, a message comes through on my phone. For a second, I think it might be from Jack, wondering how I'm feeling, but no, it's from Molly.

How are you, hon? Thinking of you today, hope you're okay xxx

I quickly tap a reply, telling her I'm in Larkswood and asking if she fancies meeting up for lunch. She replies instantly.

Bit tricky with Zara in tow! Want to come to me instead? Soup and sarnies?

Yes, that would be great, I type. And I mean it. Molly is exactly the person I'd like to spend time with today.

It's not raining like it was a year ago. The sun is sharp and bright, but there's a cold wind, which has free rein to blow across the gravestones. I remember how there was nowhere to take shelter last year, how the rain formed shallow puddles in the gravel paths, how Molly and I had to pick our way around the edges, muddying our shoes on the sodden grass. It's an easy walk today, on my own.

The garden of rest is empty and I'm glad I'm alone; it means I can have a private conversation. One way, of course, but better than nothing.

'So, another year has gone by,' I say, standing in front of the rose bush. In summer the blooms are a peachy pink. The bush has grown a few inches and is looking a bit straggly. It probably needs pruning, but I don't know how to do it. 'Things have changed a lot,' I continue in a low voice. 'I bought a house with the inheritance money. It's right by the sea, you'd love it. Used to be women's refuge. Ironic, eh? Needs a lot of work, but that's another story ... Anyway, this woman knocked on the door late one night, she'd escaped from her violent husband and she was all bruised and bleeding. I took her in, looked after her, just as you would have done. I think – I *hope* – you'd have been proud of me ... of how much I've changed.'

I crouch down in front of the commemorative plaque. The engraved letters look darker, the grooves full of dirt, and the brass has lost its sheen. I read the words in my head. *Elaine and Peter Johnson. They shared their lives until the very end.* Their deaths suddenly feel like a long time ago.

The ground is damp and soft. I close my eyes and try to breathe in their spirits, to feel their familiar touch and hear the sound of their voices. But the ashes I buried are just ashes, nothing more.

'It didn't work out with Jack,' I whisper, my voice breaking as a lump hardens in my throat. 'I tried really hard. The house was supposed to be a forever home, for the family we would have one day. My dream was so strong, it was like a boat and I was at the helm steering. But he wasn't even on board; he was still in the water, being pulled along on the end of a rope that broke before we reached dry land.'

I swallow hard. My thighs are aching and I stand up, wobbling before I regain my balance. My heels sink into the springy earth and I unstick them, one at a time.

'He's left me,' I continue. 'Somebody called Pansy. A silly name for a grown woman ... Yes, Mum, I know that's a mean thing to say. He hurt me really badly, but you probably think I deserved it, after everything I've done. When you left me your money, I thought it meant you'd forgiven me, but maybe it was a punishment. Maybe the universe thought I'd got off too lightly and decided I still needed to pay.'

The cold wind is making me shiver. I kiss my fingers and place them on their engraved names, leaving a damp mark that instantly disappears, then button my coat to the chin and go back to the car.

Before setting off, I text Molly. *Be with you in about ten mins. Okay?* I hope she has a hot cup of coffee waiting for me.

'Well this is a nice surprise,' she says, standing in the doorway, her baby daughter hoisted onto one hip. Zara is ten months old, which means there's only two months of Molly's maternity leave left. 'You should have told me you were coming over today.'

I step inside and we hug, then I follow her down the hallway to the kitchen. I'm so used to the vast expanses of Westhill House that everything feels cramped and narrow, making me squeeze my shoulders together. It's a lot warmer, though. Cosier, too. I've almost forgotten what proper central heating feels like.

The kitchen diner, about an eighth the size of the one I'm planning, is cheerfully messy. A saucepan of congealed porridge sits on the hob. There are plates and mugs waiting to be loaded into the dishwasher. I smile at the fridge door, which is covered in brightly coloured magnets – an apple, a banana, a balloon, a flower, the numbers one to five.

'Watch out for little plastic balls,' says Molly, plonking Zara into her high chair. 'She's started throwing them out of the pool. We're going to have to lose that toy before somebody breaks their neck.' I laugh, bending down to pick up a few and toss them back into their proper place. 'You look frozen,' she adds. 'Soup now or coffee first?'

'Coffee, please. I haven't had one yet today and I'm feeling a bit shaky.'

'Not surprising.' She plugs a little sachet into the machine. 'How was the garden of rest?'

'Restful. I had a little chat to Mum and Dad, got a few things off my chest.'

Molly gives me one of her deep, searching looks. 'How are things?'

'Not great.'

'Still got your guest?'

'Lori? Oh yes.'

Her eyebrows rise beneath her glossy fringe. 'What's Jack got to say about that?'

I shake my head and plunge in. 'He's gone. Dumped me for a girl in the office.'

'Fucking hell …' Molly covers her mouth. 'Oops, got to watch what I say, she'll be talking soon.' She peels a banana and cuts it up, puts a few pieces on Zara's high-chair tray. I watch her poke them with her chubby little finger, then push them off the edge and onto the floor. 'So … what happened?'

I tell her about Jack faking the burglary, about how he was convinced that Lori was some kind of con artist. 'He was so jealous of this poor abused woman who had nothing, it was pathetic. The more he tried to get rid of her, the more I dug my heels in,' I say.

'Hmm … Doesn't that sound a bit familiar?'

My cheeks colour up. 'I don't know what you mean.'

She shrugs, deciding not to press further, and adds a few florets of cooked broccoli to the mush on Zara's tray. 'So Lori's not moving out any time soon. You okay with that?'

'Yeah, she's been really kind to me. And her friend's there too.'

'Her friend? What's the deal? Are they paying rent?'

'No. They're camping in the attic and I feed them in return for them working on the house. Loads of people do it these days, especially on building projects. We're part of the sharing economy.'

Molly looks confused. 'And this friend, is she a domestic violence victim too?'

'No, she's just helping out. Abi's really good at project management, which is great because I've lost my builder, who walked off with a load of cash, and now it seems there's some weird connection …' I tail off, realising how odd this is all sounding. I'd better not tell her about the latest development and the mysterious Foxy.

Molly picks up the discarded banana and broccoli and puts them in the little compost bin on the windowsill. 'Not interested, sweetie? How about an oatcake?' Zara, who has cleared her tray without putting a single thing in her mouth, looks unenthusiastic.

Molly pauses with her hand on the biscuit tin. 'Is that why Jack left? Because you wouldn't tell these women to go?'

'Basically, yes. He doesn't know about Abi, but he had a real thing against Lori; he was so mean to her. Then again, he'd already slept with this girl at work, so maybe he was using Lori as an excuse to split up. You know, so he could put the blame on me. He lied, Molly. He lied and cheated; he's been appalling.' I look through my bag for a tissue.

'That's really bad, and obviously I'm not condoning it.' She breaks an oatcake into pieces and passes one to Zara. 'But surely you of all people should understand his position.'

'What? What are you saying, Molly?' My mouth tightens.

'Come on, Stel ... it's me you're talking to. Surely I don't have to spell it out. There's a pattern here, isn't there?'

'This has nothing to do with Mum and Dad,' I say quickly, feeling my heart starting to race. I look away, studying little Zara, who is crumbling the oatcake and making a miniature sand pie. But there's no deceiving Molly; she knows me better than anyone.

'You're doing to Jack what your parents did to you,' she says slowly. 'You felt you were ignored for your whole childhood. You were jealous of the foster kids, you despised your folks for giving them so much attention—'

'I loved my parents,' I protest. 'They were amazing people.'

She gives me a stern look. 'You say that *now*, but when they were alive, you hated them.' I gasp, as if she's just struck me. 'Don't deny it, you know it's true. I know you never told Jack the truth about that relationship. As far as he knew, they were saints and you adored them, but it's me you're talking to now, remember? I was there.'

Molly has always been on my side. She remembers only too well how I was always hanging around her house when we were teenagers, complaining about the situation back home. My parents were never interested in my problems – they were always considered insignificant compared to the troubles of the foster kids, and looking back now, I realise they were right. I hadn't been physically or sexually abused, my parents weren't drug addicts or criminals, I'd never been starved or left to wander the streets at night. But I couldn't see it back then; I just felt jealous and neglected.

'And you know something,' Molly continues. 'I don't blame you for hating them. They cared more about that revolting boy who tried to burn your house down than they did about you. It broke their hearts.' She sighs. 'What was he called?'

'Kyle.' Just saying his name out loud makes my blood run cold.

'Yes, that's right, Kyle. He nearly killed the lot of you. I'm not surprised he ended up in prison. I still think he could have had your parents murdered.'

'Don't say that. I can't bear it.' I stare into my coffee mug, thinking, *Please, please, don't let that be true.* Tears well in my eyes and I pluck a tissue out of the box on the table. 'Sorry.'

Molly sits down and takes my hands in hers. 'I know you don't want to hear me say this, Stella, but you need help. There's a hell of a lot going on for you emotionally: issues with your parents you haven't even begun to work through, the building project, and now this split with Jack. I'm really worried. You need to talk to someone, a grief counsellor maybe.'

I quickly shake myself out of the past. 'No, no, honest, I'm okay. I don't need therapy.'

'Well I think you could find it really useful. You're very vulnerable, and people are taking advantage. I don't understand why there's another woman staying with you now; it all sounds weird.'

'I'm fine, honest.'

'No you're not, it's obvious you're struggling. I know you extremely well, remember?' She lets go of my hands and stands up. 'I know *everything*.'

Not quite everything, I think. Almost, but not quite.

She lifts Zara out of the high chair and wipes her face with a cloth. 'If you want my advice, you need to take control of the situation at home. It's not good. I'm frightened for you. I think it's about time you told your guests to leave.'

CHAPTER THIRTY

Kay

Then

'Excuse me, I'm looking for Westhill House,' Kay said to the tall woman with tightly permed hair. 'Have I come to the right place?'

'I should think so. In you both come.' She smiled, showing a gap in her front teeth. Her face was gaunt and pale, even ghost-like, but her eyes were kind.

'Thank you.' Kay picked up her suitcase. 'I'm Kay, and this is Abigail.' She gestured towards her daughter, who was still standing on the steps, looking out to sea. 'We'll go on the beach later,' she told the little girl, placing a hand on her shoulder. 'But first we've got to find our bedroom and unpack. Exciting, eh?'

Abigail turned around, frowning. She clearly hadn't bought the story Kay had tried to sell her on the bus journey – a surprise holiday at the seaside with swimming, buckets and spades, ice cream and a stick of rock if she was good. It didn't make sense to be going away when school had only just started again after the Easter break. But at least she had brightened up at the news that her stepfather would definitely not be joining them on the trip.

It was too chilly for paddling, and the sea looked brown. Two seagulls swooped across the front garden, one of them landing on a pillar. Their cries seemed to chorus 'Welcome!' Kay clasped Abigail's icy hand and pulled her into the house.

She'd told her daughter they would be staying in a hotel, but this was anything but. The hallway was a chaotic mess of coats, scarves and woolly hats, thrown onto hooks, slung over the banisters or just dumped on the floor. Chunky boots, scuffed trainers and tiny wellingtons caked in mud made a teetering pile in the corner; there was sand everywhere, and the musty smell of dry earth.

The wallpaper was dark green vinyl, the painted woodwork yellowed and chipped. Kay had a brief flashback to Hotel Cascada in Torremolinos – the last time she'd had a proper holiday and the only time she'd been abroad. How she'd marvelled at the dazzling white walls and shiny marble floors, being mopped almost constantly by cleaners. Of course, she'd known the refuge wouldn't be like *that*, but even so …

'I'll take you to see Verity first,' said the woman with the perm – Kay had found out she was called Pat. 'She's our house mother, she'll sort you out.'

As Kay followed Pat down the hallway, she tried to glance into the reception rooms on either side. There were women lounging on sofas in one, and some noisy vacuuming going on in the other. She could smell baby poo, Johnson's talcum powder and buttered toast all mixed up. The sounds of lively female chatter and pop music drifted towards them from the back of the house, where she guessed the kitchen was.

'Verity's in charge,' said Pat. 'She's staff; the other workers are volunteers. Everyone adores her, but don't mess her around or she'll have your guts for garters.'

She knocked on a door, pushing it open without waiting for a response. A large older woman – in her sixties, Kay guessed – was sitting behind a desk. She had long grey hair and was wearing an embroidered caftan that had gone out of fashion about ten years ago.

'This is Kay,' Pat said. 'She's come to join us.'

'You made it here. Well done!' Verity said, as if she'd been expecting her. She stood up and enveloped Kay in her capacious bosom. Her voice was deep and her accent quite posh. 'I want you to know that you are among friends, people who understand and care. We'll look after you. Nobody can harm you here. You're safe.'

'Thank you,' Kay replied, realising that she was starting to shake all over. She reached for a chair. 'Sorry, I've come over a bit funny.'

'It's the shock, that's all; everyone feels a bit wobbly at first. You'll soon settle down.' Verity turned to Abigail. 'What lovely brown eyes you've got. What's your name, dear?'

'Abigail,' Kay intervened. 'She's only seven; she doesn't understand what's going on.'

'She'll be fine. We have about a dozen kids here at the moment. It's like having a jolly sleepover party every day.' As if on cue, there was a loud rumbling sound overhead, like a small train running back and forth.

'Aren't they at school?' Kay asked. The worst thing about this whole business had been taking Abigail out of her primary.

'Some are, yes, it depends on how long they stay and whether they're up to it. It's not a big problem. We have volunteers who come in to teach the children so they don't fall behind.'

Kay nodded. 'Like Ms Gardiner? She's Abigail's teacher, she volunteers here. She was the one who told me about the place.'

'Yes, exactly like Franny! She's marvellous, you'll see her at the weekend. Now then, let's find you somewhere to sleep.'

It was strange, Kay thought as she followed Pat upstairs, that she hadn't had to explain why she'd come. Verity hadn't asked to see proof of her injuries, or even her identity. They simply believed her, accepted that she needed to be here. Their trust and generosity made her feel weak at the knees. Or maybe it was morning sickness. She hadn't mentioned she was pregnant yet – she hoped that wouldn't be a problem.

She was taken to a small room on the first floor. She had prepared herself for the possibility of having to share a bedroom, but she was shocked by the sleeping arrangements. There were two sets of bunk beds, a double mattress on the carpet between them and a grubby single in front of the door, which meant everyone had to tread on it to get in or out of the room.

'Sorry, it's all we've got at the moment,' Pat said, pointing at the single mattress. It was covered in pale brown stains. 'Hope you don't mind sharing with your little girl.'

'She'll want to be with me anyway,' Kay replied, trying to keep her expression cheery, although her spirits were dropping fast. She squeezed Abigail's hand. 'It'll be fun, won't it? Like camping, only indoors.' She'd never been camping; it didn't appeal. Hard ground, creepy-crawlies and peeing in a bucket. Which made her wonder how many bathrooms there were and whether they had hot water. There was a distinct smell of unwashed bodies. If this room was anything like the others, there must be about thirty women living here, maybe more.

Pat grinned. 'I'll get you a clean sheet. If you need any more clothes, there are boxes of jumble downstairs in the communal lounge, all donations. Just take what you need, but remember, there's nowhere to keep anything.' It was true. There was no space for any other furniture, not so much as a drawer to put her things in or a hanger for her clothes. She would have to live out of the suitcase, although God knows where she would put that.

It's a squat, she reminded herself silently, *not Hotel bloody Cascada. What did you expect?* It was all a bit ghastly, but it would do for now.

She rested the case on the mattress. 'How long do people stay?' she asked.

'For as long as they need. We don't push anyone out – not unless they break the rules – and we never turn anyone away. That's why we're full to bursting.'

They went down to the kitchen and Pat put the kettle on for a much-needed cup of tea. She made an orange squash for Abigail and gave her a Jammie Dodger biscuit from a tin on the counter.

Several women were sitting at the large wooden table, eating toast, drinking tea and puffing away on fags. They all said hello and introduced themselves, but their names roared over Kay's head and were lost amid the hubbub of chatter and the Bee Gees screeching 'Stayin' Alive' out of a transistor radio.

She observed her surroundings. The wood panelling on the ceiling reminded her of a log cabin or a sauna – not that she'd ever had a sauna, but she'd seen them on telly. It was a bit oppressive. The orange tiles were wet with steam and the place reeked of chip fat and nicotine. There were two fridges but only one cooker. The four electric rings were all in use – a large saucepan was sterilising baby bottles; another contained baked beans, and there was also a simmering pot of something that might be soup and a deep fat fryer on the go. It was only eleven o'clock in the morning, a bit early for chips, she thought.

'We cook for ourselves,' explained Pat. 'We tried doing big meals on a rota but it was a disaster. People forgot it was their turn, or they didn't like the food. Everyone's got different tastes. Now it's a free-for-all, but it kind of works. Just don't hog all the rings and don't forget to wash the grill pan after you've used it – it really pisses people off if it's full of sausage grease.'

Kay had a sudden pang for her sparkling surfaces at home. Her pristine oven that she cleaned after every roast, the brand-new microwave, which was great for frozen peas or heating up leftovers. They could do with one here, she thought.

Pat poured out the tea and slopped in some milk. 'These are the rules,' she said. 'Just a few, sweet and simple. No drinking – alcohol, I mean – no violence, no bringing men back: boyfriends, husbands, strangers, nobody. Do your bit on the cleaning rota, that's about it.'

Kay looked surprised, partly by the news that there *was* a cleaning rota. 'Why on earth would anyone want to bring men into the house?'

'We're not as secret as we'd like to be. Men find out, they hang around outside, wanting to make up. Sometimes the women let them in for a bonk. Verity draws the line at that.'

'Do they ever go back to their husbands?'

'Oh yeah, it happens a lot, but they often come back. That's up to them; we don't judge. Everyone has their own story, you know?'

There was a pause. 'I'm pregnant,' Kay said. 'Is that okay?'

Pat smiled. 'Of course! Congratulations. That is, assuming you want to keep it?'

'Oh yes,' she replied, although right this minute, she wasn't sure why.

It took Kay several weeks to adjust to life in Westhill House. Surprisingly, the most difficult aspect was not the mess or the dirt or the poor facilities, but the lack of privacy. There was literally nowhere, either in the house or its large garden, that wasn't constantly occupied by other women; unless you counted the toilets – only two of them for thirty-six residents! – and even then, if you lingered there for more than a couple of minutes, you soon had someone banging on the door.

Kay had felt lonely and isolated in her marriage, cut off from her friends, not allowed to work. She'd been imprisoned by degrees; she hadn't realised what was happening until it was too late. But now she longed to be alone, to hear only the sound of her own breathing, the scrape of her chair, her footsteps on the stairs. There was the beach, of course, that was deathly quiet, but every time she tried to leave the house, Abigail would ask if she could bring her new friends along to make mud pies or skim stones.

Abigail was part of a little gang now and had almost forgotten what it was like to go to proper school. On her birthday, Verity bought balloons and another mother called Alesha made little fruit jellies. Ms Gardiner – *You must call me Franny!* – turned up with a home-made cake and eight pink candles, and everyone sang 'Happy Birthday' with great enthusiasm and a terrible lack of tune, delighting Abigail, who blew out the candles so hard she sent hundreds and thousands scattering to the four corners of the kitchen.

'It was my best birthday EVER,' she said as they snuggled beneath their blanket that night, and it made Kay cry. A few women had moved on, or gone back to their husbands, and now they were sharing a bunk bed. She had her eye on the front attic room. There were no bunks up there, on account of the sloping ceiling, and fewer bodies meant less BO. But it was the sea view Kay longed for.

Sometimes, it all felt so normal, she forgot why she was living there. Nobody talked about the beatings, there was no comparison of bruises or one-upmanship – Franny would probably say one-up-*person*-ship – about who'd suffered the most. The women wanted to forget about the violence they'd been subjected to, but everyone knew it must have been bad – why else would they leave their homes and come to live like a load of sardines squashed in a tin? Life in the refuge wasn't easy. It was horribly overcrowded, washing facilities were inadequate, food was very basic, silly arguments broke out and there were a few rough characters Kay preferred to avoid.

They were living off charity – donations from the public that mostly came in the post: one-, five- or even ten-pound notes; sometimes just a fifty-pence piece taped to a piece of card. Last week they'd received a cheque for an astonishing fifty quid. To begin with, Kay had felt uncomfortable about accepting money from strangers, but when she read some of the accompanying letters, she was very moved. *I was beaten throughout my marriage,* one said. *If only there had been a place like Westhill House back then, I would have come to you like a shot. Keep up the good work, girls!*

'This is a squat, right?' she said to Verity one morning. They were sorting out the donations, putting the notes and cheques into piles. 'So that means we're illegal.'

'Technically, yes, but nobody's going to chuck us out,' Verity assured her. 'The police are telling women to come here now; they see what an important job we're doing. There are more and more refuges springing up all over the country. Some of them have proper local authority funding. It'll happen everywhere eventually.' Verity was always very optimistic about the future.

'I won't be staying much longer,' said Kay, feeling cautiously for her words. 'I'm going to apply for a council flat.' It was a plan she'd been nurturing for weeks. She was feeling stronger by the day, ready to strike out on her own.

Verity sighed. 'No chance, darling, not when you left the marital home of your own accord.'

'But he was going to kill me!'

'I don't doubt it for a second, but it won't make a jot of difference to the housing chaps. As far as they're concerned, you already have a home to go to. They don't even care that you're pregnant.'

She was four months gone now and showing clearly. Luckily she'd found a maternity smock in the clothes box, together with a size sixteen blouse. The pretty dresses she'd worn when she was carrying Abigail were still at her parents' house, but there was no way she was going to retrieve them. She'd had an upsetting phone call with her mother soon after she arrived at the refuge – 'Stop being so selfish, Kay,' she was told. 'Go home and look after Foxy. The poor man's falling apart.'

Verity reached across and patted her round tummy. 'You'll be fine here. We'll look after you. We're a community of women; you couldn't be in better hands.'

CHAPTER THIRTY-ONE

Stella

Now

I park on the concrete drive, next to the overflowing skip. I suppose I'm still paying hire charges on that, I think, making a mental note to organise its removal. But my mind is overcrowded with other, more important issues, and I know I'll forget all about it as soon as I enter the house.

It's late afternoon and I'm glad to be home, although somehow 'home' is not the right word for this huge, rambling house. The rooms are too big to feel cosy. It's never been somewhere I could shut the door, take my shoes off, collapse on the sofa and feel my shoulders drop. There's no sofa, for a start, and you can't get a warm, fuzzy feeling from a building site. But it's more than that – something to do with the atmosphere. No matter how many alterations I make, I'll never eradicate the house's history. It's written deep within the walls.

My thoughts have been slowly crystallising since the conversation with Molly. She said some harsh things, but I needed to hear them. That's what true friends are for, I guess. As I drove back via the Dartford Crossing, dwarfed by the vast expanse of the great bridge over the Thames, I left the past and re-entered the present, feeling a fresh sense of purpose as I approached Nevansey. I know what I need to do now. It's not going to be easy, but I can't let the situation drag on any longer. Lori and Abi have to go.

Taking off my coat, I sling it on the wicker chair, pausing for a moment to listen for clues as to what's been going on during my absence. I've only been away for a few hours, but it feels as if something has shifted. I think Abi was supposed to be interviewing more builders today, but I can't hear any footsteps tramping about upstairs or the low rumble of voices in distant rooms. Walking over to the doorway, I stick my head back into the hallway. Silence.

I go down the tiled corridor, narrowed by the stairs. The room Abi rather grandly calls the office is on my left, tucked into the belly of the house. Maybe she's in there, working on her laptop. I go to open the door, but it seems to be locked. I don't even remember seeing a key there, although I know all the doors in the house are lockable – we found a plastic box of keys when we moved in, none of them labelled. We never bothered to sort them out, just shoved them in a kitchen drawer.

The locked door bothers me. Is she just taking care of her valuables, or is there something in there she doesn't want me to see? I feel a prickle of irritation. This is *my* house. If anyone's going to lock doors, it's me.

Carrying on into the kitchen, I see that two mugs and two small plates have been washed up and are draining on the board. I touch the kettle – it's stone cold.

Perhaps Abi has persuaded Lori to go for a walk on the beach. I hope so; that would be a big step forward. Despite everything that's happened, I still feel a sense of responsibility towards Lori. She hasn't mentioned Darren for ages, but she hasn't forgotten about him. I know she's still frightened that he's out there looking for her. I sigh as I remember that ridiculous car chase on the way to Citizens Advice. How I used to look over my shoulder every time I walked down the hill, imagining him lurking behind cars, or hiding in one of the beach huts. The situation is a lot calmer than it was when she first arrived; she's recovering, little by little. I don't know if she's fully ready to leave here yet, but with the right support, it should be possible to reintroduce her to normal life.

A blast of air sweeps through the kitchen, sending a chill across the back of my neck. I turn sharply, half expecting to see somebody standing there. *Stop being so jumpy, Stella.* The back door must be open, that's all it is. Which means Lori and Abi are probably in the garden, having a smoke.

I go into the conservatory, and sure enough, the door is flat back on its hinges, kept in place by a brick. Mystery solved.

'Lori? Abi?' My voice seems to die on the breeze. Stepping out, I walk down the path of trodden-down grass, hugging myself against the cold and wishing I'd gone back for my coat. Strains of chatter and a clunking sound I can't quite make out are coming from behind the trellis of roses, long since lost to the wild.

I go through the wooden archway and reach the dilapidated old shed. There they are, right at the bottom of the garden. I halt for a moment, trying to comprehend what I'm seeing. Lori and Abi are heaving away with large spades, throwing clods of earth into a pile. Their backs are turned and their heads are down; they haven't noticed me. Both of them are wearing long black wellies and thick canvas gloves. They're working at a pace, their breathing laboured as they attack the heavy soil.

'What are you doing?' I say loudly as I approach.

They stop digging and turn around simultaneously. There's the same guilty expression on both their faces. They pull themselves upright and shuffle together, as if trying to hide something from my view.

'Hi, Stella!' says Abi breezily, waving with her free arm. 'You're back early.'

Too early for your liking, I think.

'I didn't say what time I would be back. What are you doing?'
I repeat.

'It was supposed to be a surprise,' says Lori, her face flushed
crimson, either with effort or embarrassment, probably both.

I walk right up to them and peer around the shield of their
bodies to look. There's a shallow hole in the ground, about a metre
long and half a metre wide. 'What's all this?'

'We're making you a pond,' says Abi.

'You said you wanted one,' Lori adds. 'You want to keep fish,
right?'

'Yes, but … there's about a million other things that need
doing first.'

'I know, but we can't do the other things, we don't have the
expertise.' Abi brushes mud off her coat.

'But you know all about building ponds?' I reply sarcastically.

'I've got one at home,' Abi smiles. 'I saw them do it. You dig a
hole, remove all the stones, then put a plastic lining—'

'Okay, fine, I don't need to know the details.'

There's a moment of stalemate as I stare down into the hole. The
soil here is a mixture of yellowish sand and grey-brown clay. A feeling
of unease spreads through me as I look up and meet their gaze.

'Building a pond is not a priority for me right now.'

The women exchange glances, then Abi says, 'Well, we've
started so we might as well carry on.'

'But I … I don't really want you—'

'You'll love it when it's done,' ventures Lori.

Abi nods. 'At least let us finish the hole.'

'Oh, do what you like,' I snap, nearly slipping as I swing
round on my heel and stomp back up the path towards the house,
kicking away the brick and slamming the door behind me. The
flimsy conservatory shudders, and for a second I think it's going
to collapse.

By the time I get back to my room, I'm shaking with fury. What possessed them to do that, for Christ's sake? It's just crazy. Why would I want a pond when I haven't got a decent kitchen or a proper bathroom, when all the floorboards are up and there's nowhere to relax? The only place I've got is this one room, where I have to eat and sleep and work, and even here there's damp under the window and the plaster falls off every time somebody bangs about upstairs. It's shit. Everything in my life is shit. I push my wicker chair over and my coat crumples onto the floor like a dead body.

I've got to be strong, I tell myself, pacing the room. Get rid of my guests, make contact with Jack. He can't be serious about this Pansy woman; he's just trying to make me realise how much he's hurting, how much is at stake. I so want him back. I'll sell the house if that's what it takes; who cares if I make a whacking great loss? It doesn't matter where I live, as long as I'm with him. I'll tell him the truth about my relationship with Mum and Dad. We'll make a fresh start.

I stop and lean against the mantelpiece, resting my forehead on the cool marble. I know where I want to be – in my favourite room, the little turret at the top of the house; up in the clouds, away from this chaos, away from Lori and Abi. I want to climb into the old armchair, curl up under the blanket and just watch the tide go in and out. I haven't been in that room for weeks, not since Lori arrived. I wanted her to feel that the top floor was her space, where she could feel private and secure. But this is *my* house, *my* space; it's time to reclaim old territory. Feeling defiant, I walk out of the room again and march upstairs.

The turret is warm, even though there's no heating. The circular window traps all the sunshine the day has to offer, and any heat in the house rises, coming to rest in this tiny space. I duck my head under the rafter, then turn to close the door. I'd lock myself in if

I could. I should have thought to search for the key in the plastic box. But I can't be bothered to go back downstairs.

There's not much air in here and my chest tightens as I cough drily. I run my fingers through the thick layer of plaster dust on the windowsill – the stuff gets everywhere. I open a window, letting in a sharp blast of sea air, take a few deep breaths, then shut it again. I sink into the saggy old armchair and cover myself with a blanket. This chair was the only piece of furniture the previous occupants left behind. I think the removal company must have forgotten about it.

It's late afternoon and the light is just starting to fade. God knows how long those idiots are going to stay out there excavating. I'll have to make them stop tomorrow; I can't let them go on digging, it's absurd. I should never have mentioned my idea to Lori. It was a stupid idea anyway. All of it was stupid. Two people do not need an eight-bedroom house, even if they are hoping to have kids, which, incidentally, only one of them was.

It's okay, Stella. Calm down. You're going to sort everything out, bit by bit, one step at a time.

I like it up here in my little cubbyhole. Maybe, once Lori and Abi have left, I'll move the bed up and sleep here. Just the mattress; there's not enough room for the frame. Might have to buy a single, in fact. I look down at the floor space, trying to calculate the dimensions, to see if a bed would fit. A circular mattress is what I need, I decide. That would be cool. I wonder if you can buy them, or if it would have to be specially made.

I sweep my foot in a circle around the window, tracing a line in the dust, and my toe catches on the edge of a small floorboard, flipping it up. Strange, I don't remember any of the boards being loose. This one looks as if it's been sawn in half, levered off and then put back. Throwing off the blanket, I edge myself off the armchair and lift it up. I lean forward, looking into the dark, cobwebbed cavity, poking at tiny pieces of rubble and bits of old newspaper. There's something at the back; I can just about see it. It's red, rectangular.

Lying down on my side, I stretch my hand under the boards and, after a short struggle, pull out a folder.

What's this? Some kind of diary? Study notes, perhaps? I sit up, settling on my knees, coughing as I rub a layer of filthy dust off the top. Maybe one of the women who used to live here wrote down her story and hid it here.

Feeling excited, I open the cover and read the front page.

Highly confidential material. If this book is found, please return to: Dawn Watson, Pathways Family Therapy Centre, Magnolia Gardens, Tunbridge Wells, Kent.

Who is Dawn Watson, and why has this book been hidden here?

I feel my heart pounding as I turn the page and start to read.

CHAPTER THIRTY-TWO

Stella

Now

Pathways Family Therapy Centre
Client: Lori Mattison
Ref: 1306 M
Therapist: Ms Dawn Watson
<u>Session 1: 5 March 2015</u>

Lori presented as very nervous and unsure that she wanted to be here. I told her that it had taken enormous courage for her to come to the centre to see me and reassured her that we would take the sessions at her pace, not mine. They were solely for her benefit and she could withdraw at any time. She asked immediately about confidentiality and I told her that I would not be sharing information with anyone unless I had concerns about her safety or that of her children. In this case, it might be necessary to have discussions with her GP, the safeguarding lead at her children's school, or Social Services, but I would inform her of this in advance whenever possible. This seemed to make her a little more comfortable. She understands that the school is already involved, as they made the referral, and emphasised that her main concern was her husband not finding out.

Lori is very slim and small in stature, with short dark hair. (Note: she was wearing a lot of make-up, which could possibly have been hiding facial injuries. Also a long-sleeved tracksuit top and jogging bottoms that may have been concealing cuts or bruises.) She appeared to be in reasonable physical health, although seemed lacking in energy. She spoke very quietly and I had to ask her to repeat herself several times.

We went through some general details first to put her at ease. Lori is twenty-seven years old and has been married to Darren for nine years; they met at school. They have a son, Jamie, aged eight, and a daughter, Casey, aged six. Lori works at the local supermarket on a zero-hours contract. Before she had children, she was training to be a hairdresser but never got beyond junior level due to her first pregnancy. Darren works as a loft insulation installer and runs his own business. They are not in receipt of any benefits – Lori said they could do with some extra cash but that it is difficult making claims because Darren is self-employed. They live in rented accommodation – a three-bedroom town house. She said she hated living on the Garrick Lees estate because there was a load of drug dealing going on right outside her front window. She would like them to move and buy a place of their own, but said there was 'no chance'.

Her parents are still alive, but she was vague about how often she sees them and how much they are involved with the grandchildren (maybe not involved at all?). She has brothers and sisters, but none of them live locally. I got the impression that she is lonely and quite isolated. Her main focus in life seems to be her children.

I tried to move the conversation on to more personal matters. According to the referral letter, staff at the school have been concerned about Lori's children for a while. Recently there were a number of violent behavioural incidents at school involving her son. Her daughter has recently shown signs of withdrawal and non-engagement with classmates. Both children have higher-than-average levels of absence. I began by asking Lori what sense she could make of Jamie's behaviour. How long had it been a problem? Was he behaving the same way at home as at school?

Lori clearly felt uncomfortable about answering these questions. She maintained that she didn't know why he was 'playing up' at school and that he wasn't a problem at home, although Darren 'keeps the kids on a tight leash' and they know not to make him angry. She said she was worried about her little boy and didn't know what to do; that's why she'd agreed to take part in the therapy sessions. I asked if she ever discussed the matter with Darren, but she said no, 'there would be no point'; he'd just get angry with his son for getting into trouble and it would make things worse.

I asked if there been any recent changes at home, any difficult or upsetting events that she was aware of. She became extremely agitated at this point but said she couldn't think of anything.

I asked Lori why she had only agreed to take part in therapy sessions on the condition that Darren didn't know (see referral letter). Did she think he would be cross if he found out? She said yes, he liked to keep family matters private. I asked if there was anything going on in the family that would embarrass him if other people found out about it. She said there wasn't, but she tensed visibly and I suspected I had touched a nerve. I was tempted to delve further, but decided Lori would not be receptive at this stage.

I asked what she was hoping to get out of our sessions together. She said she didn't know, she just thought it would be good to have someone to talk to – especially about the kids. She was upset that they were having problems at school and wanted to help them.

Time was up. I told Lori that she'd done extremely well, that I'd really enjoyed talking to her and hoped she would come and see me at the same time next Thursday. She reacted well to my praise and said 'it wasn't as bad as I expected'. She confirmed that she wanted to carry on. By the end of the session, she seemed slightly more at ease, and I felt that we had already established a positive rapport. Overall, a very encouraging start. I think Lori and her children could benefit hugely from therapy sessions with me, and I look forward to resuming our conversation next week.

CONCLUSION

This first meeting with Lori convinced me that that the referrer's suspicion that DV is taking place within this family is quite possibly a correct one. From observations by school staff about the children's changed behaviour, and Lori's presentation, responses and reactions, particularly her fear of Darren finding out about the therapy, I would conclude that there is a definite possibility that she is experiencing physical and psychological abuse and that her husband is the perpetrator. It is also possible that the children are being abused, or at least witnessing assaults on their mother. However, when Lori is clearly so scared of Darren, it is not going to be easy for me to draw her out. I anticipate that this will take more than the full six sessions allowed under the scheme.

My fingers are trembling as I turn over the next page. More notes from further sessions with Lori. And not just six of them, either. I flick forward – there are reams of the stuff. Session 8 ... Session 12 ... Session 17 ... Pages and pages of handwritten observations, passages underlined in red, huge asterisks and exclamation marks in the margins, and at the end of Session 4, the word *BREAKTHROUGH!!!* scrawled large across the page.

I sit back on my haunches, breathless. This is private information, I shouldn't be reading it. And yet something's not right, not making sense. I turn back to the opening pages and re-read the therapist's notes, more slowly this time. A sick feeling hits my stomach as I reach the second paragraph. *Lori is very slim and small in stature, with short dark hair.* And then, a few lines further on: *Lori is twenty-seven years old.*

That's not correct. Lori is short and quite dumpy, and her hair's a mousy blonde. There's no way she's in her twenties; she looks more like early forties. I check the date at the top of the page. These sessions were conducted three years ago. I suppose she could have put on weight since then and bleached her hair. Women who have a hard life age more quickly, but even so ... The description doesn't sound like the Lori I know.

I need to put this book back where I found it and get out of here, but before I do ... I whip my phone out of my back pocket and quickly snap photos of the first few pages. Then I push the treasure back into its dark and dusty hiding place and replace the loose board.

Walking quickly downstairs, I hurry into my bedroom and shut the door behind me. I type 'Pathways Family Therapy Centre' into Google, and the website comes up immediately. It's a private practice: *Quiet, relaxing rooms in a calm out-of-town setting. Space for reflection, sharing, or just being ... We always have time for YOU.*

I click on 'Meet Our Therapists' from the menu, my heart stopping for a second as I stare at the screen. A photo of the woman I know as Lori looks back at me – skin fresh, hair neatly bobbed, a sympathetic-looking smile fixed to her face. Underneath it is the name 'Dawn Watson', and a description: *I am a qualified and fully accredited therapist with many years' experience in both the public and private sector. I have worked with a wide range of client groups, including families and couples, and am very responsive to individual needs. I have particular expertise working with survivors of domestic violence.*

I will always listen to you and never judge. My aim is to guide you to making the decision that's right for you, whatever that may be.

The woman who knocked at my door, bruised and bleeding and asking for help, who's been living as a guest in my house for the last few months, is an impersonator. She isn't Lori, victim of domestic violence, but her therapist, Dawn Watson.

My mouth goes dry. I feel suddenly dizzy. My heart is banging against my ribcage like a wild animal trying to escape. I've got to calm down, think ... Lori – no, *Dawn* – is outside in the garden with Abi. And who the hell's Abi? She must be in on it – whatever 'it' is. What the fuck are they doing here? What is it they want?

All I know is, something really bad is going on here. A sting, a scam, a crime – and stupid, gullible Stella is the target. Jack was right all along; he knew the situation didn't smell right. That's why 'Lori' was so adamant about not going to the police, because she wouldn't have been able to prove her identity.

Turning back to my phone, I quickly type the name Lori Mattison into the search box. There are hundreds, thousands of results – links to Facebook, Instagram, Twitter mostly, none of them likely to be the Lori Mattison I'm looking for. But then, a few entries down, I see a headline, and my blood freezes in my veins.

Jury take just forty-two minutes to convict young mum's murderer.

I click on the link and it takes me to a local online newspaper for the west Kent area.

A judge described the brutal murder of twenty-eight-year-old mother-of-two Lori Mattison as 'one of the most extreme cases of domestic violence I've ever seen' as he jailed husband Darren Mattison for at least twenty-four years. The court heard that Mrs Mattison suffered horrific injuries in the attack, with her whole face caved in by almost a centimetre, her jaw broken in two places, fractures to both eye sockets and evidence of strangulation. Mattison had denied her murder but it took a jury just forty-two minutes to find him guilty.

Mary Oyelowo, prosecuting, said that the victim had been receiving counselling for the past year. After years of violent abuse, she had been encouraged to press charges against her husband, although no prosecution took place. The couple's two children had been previously removed from the home by Social Services and were in foster care at the time of the fatal attack. Darren Mattison had recently enrolled on a perpetrator rehabilitation scheme and the victim had been working 'extremely hard' to rebuild the relationship in order to be reunited with the children.

Judge Laurent Ritherden, jailing Mattison for life, told him: 'You pretended to the authorities that you were genuinely committed to changing your ways, when in fact you were simply waiting for the moment to take revenge on a warm-hearted and gentle woman who was trying her best to keep her family together.'

The defendant, who wore a black T-shirt and had heavy tattoos on his neck and arms, showed no reaction.

I fling the phone onto the bed and march out of the room in the direction of the garden. Blood is rushing through my head, my fists are clenched, and I've never felt so angry in my entire life. It's time my guests told me the truth.

CHAPTER THIRTY-THREE

Stella

Now

I crash through the archway, pushing aside the thorny rose branches, and march past the shed. Lori – Dawn – and Abi are still digging, their spades squelching into the heavy earth. 'Okay, so what's going on?' I demand, hands on hips, my body shaking with anger.

Abi looks up. 'We're making you a pond, you already know that,' she says patronisingly.

A scoffing sound bursts out of my mouth. 'Yeah, right. Who the fuck are you anyway?' The two women exchange the briefest shadow of a glance. Dawn opens her mouth to speak, then closes it again.

'I know who *you* are,' I say, turning to the woman I've been sheltering for the past couple of months. 'You're Dawn Watson. A therapist at the Pathways centre. Jesus, a therapist? You should be struck off!'

There's a sharp intake of breath. Dawn and Abi freeze. It's as if I've just tossed a hand grenade into the space between us. They stand there staring, waiting for it to explode.

'You're mistaken …' Abi begins, but Dawn shakes her head. She drops her spade and it clangs on the hard earth.

'How did you find out?'

'I found your file under the floorboards.'

'I see.'

'What was it, a kind of crib sheet to help you get in character?'

'No, it was—'

'Don't answer that,' warns Abi.

Dawn bows her head. 'They're personal notes I made on a very difficult case I was involved in. It was a terrible tragedy.'

'Lori Mattison, yes, I looked her up on the internet. I know she was murdered by her husband, Darren.'

'I'm really sorry, Stella. I didn't want to do it.'

'Do what?' I say. 'Pretend to be a dead woman?'

Abi, who has been edging her way around and is now standing with her back to the archway, blocking my exit, intervenes again. 'Don't say another word, Dawn.'

Dawn starts to cry. 'I'm so sorry, so sorry. I betrayed you, I betrayed my profession.'

Abi rolls her eyes to the skies. 'Nobody wants to hear your bleating. Just shut up.'

I'm shaking my head in disbelief as the events of the past weeks rattle through my brain. 'I don't understand. You turned up on my doorstep covered in blood. You were genuinely hurt. Why did you do it?'

Dawn looks away from me. 'It was an awful thing to do, I know. I didn't want to do it. She forced me.'

'What was the plan? To steal from me?'

'No! Nothing like that.'

'Then what? I need an explanation.'

'Dawn, if you say another word, you're really going to regret it,' says Abi threateningly. 'Shut up now. Go back to the house. I'll deal with this.'

'No, I'm staying here. We can't treat Stella like this.'

I swing around to face Abi. 'Did you help her with the injuries? She couldn't have done them to herself ...' A flicker passes over

Abi's face. 'Yes, you did. What's the relationship here, are you a couple?'

'It's none of your business.'

'We're sisters,' mumbles Dawn.

'I told you not to say anything,' Abi grunts.

'Sisters?' I look from one to the other. Two people could not look more unalike. And yet it makes sense. Abi the older, the bully, always in charge. Dawn the younger, the fall guy, the patsy, always getting the blame. 'But why target me? What's so important that you had to put on such a performance?'

'We're not going to tell you anything, so don't waste your breath. There's a way out of this. Just do what I say and you won't get hurt.' Abi steps forward and I instinctively move back, my feet sinking into the muddy earth at the edge of the hole.

'I'm sorry, Stella,' mumbles Dawn. 'I messed up. I was supposed to get in and out quickly, only it didn't work out—'

'Jesus Christ,' Abi roars. 'Will you just shut it! Let me deal with this, like I always have to.'

'But it's over, Abi, can't you see? There's no way out now.'

There's a long, cold pause as the three of us assess our position. Dawn's frightened and unsure, but there's a look of grim determination on Abi's face. Her heavy eyebrows are knitted together, her dark eyes shining fiercely. She's manoeuvred around me perfectly, cutting me off from my only means of escape. I glance at the high wall running along the bottom of the garden, the strong fences on either side. The excellent security of the house's former life is working against me now. I'm trapped.

'I've had enough of this. Let me pass, please,' I say, trying to sound irritated rather than terrified. 'It's cold and I want to go back inside. I don't understand what's been going on, but let's sit down and talk about this like civilised human beings.' All I can think of is my mobile, lying on the bed. Why didn't I bring it outside with me? Actually, why didn't I just call the police and let them deal with it? Why did I ever open the door and let the two women into my life?

'We can't let you go,' Abi replies. 'Not now.' She takes another step forward, brandishing the spade, and I lean away from her, almost losing my balance. The ground is slippery, the hole behind me about three feet deep. I sense it gaping beneath me, root tendrils reaching out, winding around my ankles, preparing to drag me in.

Is *that* the plan? To kill me and bury me in the garden? Maybe this isn't a pond, was never meant to be a pond. It's a grave. They've been digging it for me.

My stomach cramps. I feel sick … faint … I start to sway.

'What are you going to do, Abi?' Dawn whispers.

'Be quiet, I'm thinking.' Her eyes flicker over me as she calculates the options.

'Please don't … It wouldn't be right, she doesn't deserve it. Let's just stop now, yeah? Call it a day.'

'We can't!'

My pulse is racing, my heart galloping in my chest. But I have to stay calm and use my brain. Abi's raving mad, but Dawn is scared. The situation's getting out of control and she doesn't like it. She doesn't want to hurt me. I've got to get her on my side … talk my way out of it somehow. But Abi's the dominant one. If she makes an attack, Dawn will be too scared to stop her. I'll just have to scream my head off and hope somebody hears.

'Look, we've got a problem here,' I say, trying to steady myself on the slippery ground. 'Let's not make it worse. We've become friends over the past few weeks. Just tell me what's going on and we can sort it out. You know you can trust me. I've never let you down, have I? Dawn – when I thought you were Lori, when I believed you were really in need, I helped you. Took you in, gave you a home, did everything I could to support you. I even took your side against Jack.' A sudden image of him flashes into my mind and I almost lose my balance. If only he were here now, we could deal with this together.

'It's true.' Dawn, who is standing on the other side of the hole, looks pleadingly at Abi. 'She's a good person, she's on our side. If we tell her, she'll understand.'

'Jesus Christ, you're such a fool,' snaps Abi. 'It's a trick, you idiot. If I let her go, she'll call the police straight away. Think of the consequences! Is that what you want? For everything to come crashing down? After all these years?'

'No, but … Oh shit, what are we going to do?'

'There's no choice, Dawn. You have to face up to it.'

Dawn crouches and puts her hands over her face. 'We can't … we can't … it would be …'

Abi rolls her eyes. 'Stop being such a baby. You've always been a wimp, ever since you were born.'

'And you've always been a hard bitch!' shouts Dawn. 'I hate you, you know that. I hate you! You made me do this, you forced me, like you always do. I was trying to help you, I wanted you to get closure, but you're a lost cause, you're just an evil—'

'Evil?' Abi laughs. 'Thanks for the in-depth professional analysis, sis. Always welcome, especially from a failed therapist.'

'I didn't fail.'

'It was your fault Lori was murdered.'

'That's not true!'

'Yes it is. You treated her for months and couldn't make her see sense. She wouldn't get rid of Darren.'

'She was finally going to leave him; that's why he attacked her.'

'Then it was your fault both ways.'

'I didn't kill her, *he* did!'

For a split second neither of them is looking at me or even thinking about me. It's my only chance. I move forward and lunge at Abi, head down, arms reaching to grab her by the legs and tackle her to the ground, but she sidesteps me and I fall flat on my face, smacking into the soggy earth.

There's a moment's silence. I slowly lift my head, spitting earth from my mouth. Then I hear a loud screech like an angry seagull, and something hard, sharp and horribly cold crashes into the back of my skull.

CHAPTER THIRTY-FOUR

Kay

Then

She could honestly say it was the first time since she was fifteen that she'd been happy. Nobody would understand, Kay thought, as she put down the cleaning box and started hoovering. They'd think I was mad to love living in a squat with a load of strangers, although they weren't strangers any more; they were her closest friends. If her parents could see her now – and she had no intention of that happening – they would have a fit. And yet she'd never felt more at home, more respected, more valued. She felt free.

It was her turn on the cleaning rota – communal room, downstairs bedroom, office, conservatory, hallway and stairs as far as the first floor. She was supposed to be working with Alesha, but Alesha had had to take her son to the doctor's this morning. Kay didn't mind. She quite liked working by herself; it gave her time to reflect.

She lifted the sofa cushions and put them on the floor, then vacuumed up all the peanuts, biscuit crumbs, shreds of tobacco, sweet wrappers and countless strands of hair. She patted the cushions into shape and put them back. Then she cleared the coffee table of dirty crockery and gave it a polish, emptied the stinking ashtrays, tidied the toys into the corner, wiped down the marble mantelpiece, hoovered the floor as best she could, then opened the windows and let in some sea air.

It didn't matter that by the end of the day it would all be messy and dirty again.

She unplugged the hoover and trundled it into the hallway. Verity was in a meeting with fundraisers, so she couldn't clean the office, and Franny was running a lesson in the conservatory for the kids. It was the summer holidays, but the learning continued. Abigail was there, sitting next to her beloved teacher – she behaved as if Ms Gardiner belonged to her and her alone. Kay had thought Franny's presence a real bonus at first, but the situation was becoming awkward. Abigail was reluctant to share. She'd been quite mean towards the other children, and that wasn't kind, especially when they were newcomers who were frightened and confused about the changes in their lives. Franny had had a quiet word with Kay about it last weekend.

'You really must enrol her at the local primary in September. It's a nice little school. Several of the long-term residents send their kids there.'

Kay rested the hoover pole against the side of the stairs. That was what she was now – a long-term resident. There was no escaping the fact. And she loved living in Westhill House. It was Abigail – or Abi, as everyone seemed to call her these days – who was unsettled.

It wasn't just the schooling that was causing a problem. Abigail was playing up like she'd never done before, falling out with some of the other girls, cheeking Kay when she told her off. She was learning some choice swear words too, which wasn't her fault – several of the women found it impossible to control their language in front of the kids. Sometimes Kay overheard her bossing the younger ones about, using phrases she'd learnt from her stepfather: 'Why are you such an idiot? Why don't you just do as you're told?'

Then there'd been the drawing incident a few weeks ago. Abigail had ripped off the wallpaper in the space between the top and bottom bunks where they slept and drawn these horrific pictures in indelible felt pen. They showed a man holding up a stick and striking a woman, with a little girl standing to one side looking on. There were red scribbles and big drips of what Kay could only assume was supposed to be blood. It was extremely worrying to think that such images had come out of her daughter's head.

Kay had been really upset, and angry with Abigail, who knew full well she wasn't allowed to draw on the walls. But Verity had taken the opposite stance. 'She's getting it out of her system,' she'd said. 'That's a healthy reaction; it means she'll be able to heal.' Kay wasn't so sure. Maybe the damage had already been done and could never be repaired. The pictures had been immediately covered up with fresh wallpaper, but they were still there, just as the memories were still prickling beneath Abigail's young skin.

Kay crouched down – tricky with this growing bump – and started tidying the pile of shoes and boots, putting them into pairs and placing the odd ones to one side. It pleased her to arrange the pairs in a row along the side of the hallway, but they never stayed like that for more than five minutes. Change was the norm here. There were warm hellos and fond farewells almost every day. You never knew who was going to be sleeping in your bedroom, or sitting next to you on the sofa. The only constant was the unconditional love and support shown to every single woman. You couldn't put a price on that.

The baby wriggled and kicked out for space. Kay leant on the windowsill and heaved herself to her feet. *Take it easy*, she said under her breath. She didn't want to overdo it. A small group of them were going out tonight – Alesha, Pat and a woman called Babs, who'd turned up a few days after Kay with a fractured collarbone. Another group were babysitting their kids, the idea being that they would return the favour next Saturday. Verity encouraged the women to go out and enjoy themselves, even gave them a bit of cash to spend, but not enough to get drunk on. Kay was really looking forward to it; she couldn't remember the last time she'd had a girls' night out.

She'd already picked some clothes from the jumble box to wear: a cream polyester top with sparkly shoulders and a patterned cotton skirt, elasticated at the waist. They were okay, not her usual style, but big enough to accommodate the bump. It wasn't as if she was going out to attract a man ...

Nine hours later, hair up, make-up on, dressed in her second-hand glad rags, Kay linked arms with the others and walked down the Esplanade towards the pier. Pat had a new perm – one of the women in the refuge had done it for her earlier in the day. Alesha was wearing a halter-neck top and jeans that showed off her figure. Babs had brushed her hair and changed her T-shirt, which for her was quite a lot of fuss. They were a motley crew, their ages ranging from twenty-four to over forty, with different backgrounds and different outlooks on life, but they had one thing in common. No man was controlling them any more. They could do what they bloody well liked.

It was August, high holiday season, the weather a typical patchwork of dull, mild days, bursts of hot sunshine and miserable downpours. It had been dry and quite warm today, but clouds had gathered late afternoon and there was no sunset to marvel at. A cool evening breeze was playing across Kay's bare forearms. Should have brought a cardigan, she thought.

The hotels and guest houses were bunged with families, which surprised her, given how muddy the beach was and how freezing the sea – not even a tropical heatwave could warm it up. Nevansey was past its best – if it had ever had a best, that is. It was okay for a day trip, but not for a proper holiday. Not when you could buy packages on the Continent for the same price, sometimes cheaper.

They arrived at the pier, then stopped, unsure of their plan. The Esplanade expanded here, almost became a Spanish plaza. It was heaving with people, families mostly. Pat and Alesha lit up fags and Babs announced she was starving and went to buy some chips.

Kay stood quietly, people-watching. She saw little children being shouted at or begging their parents for candyfloss; elderly couples taking an evening promenade. Teenagers were smoking – even snogging – in the shelters, feet up on the benches, covering them with their mindless graffiti, no doubt. The Oyster Catch pub opposite was overflowing with drinkers. Men in their twenties and thirties were gathered on the pavement, beer glass in one hand, fag in the other, taking the piss out of each other at the tops of their voices, whistling at passing totty.

Living in the refuge, it was easy to forget that the world was still spinning in its usual fashion. Everything had changed for Kay, but in reality, things were just the same. There would be current or future wife-beaters here among the irritable dads, the elderly husbands, the joshing blokes, the randy teenage boys …

'We're going on the machines,' said Alesha, nudging her out of her musings. 'Coming?'

'Okay, as long as you don't waste all your money.' She wasn't a fan of arcades, but didn't want to be a spoilsport. They already seemed to have lost Babs. Oh well, I expect she'll catch up, thought Kay, entering the hellish din that was Vegas Amusements.

She stood next to Pat and watched her feed ten-pence pieces into a one-armed bandit. The noise was deafening – a cacophony of clanking, clattering, whizzing, whirring sounds, dreadful pop music, and beneath it, the relentless hum of electricity. Kay rested her hand on her bulge. God only knew what the baby was making of this. The bright flashing lights were making her temples throb. She couldn't bear it.

'That you, Kay?' said a familiar male voice. Her heart missed a beat and she whipped around. For a fraction of a second she thought it was Foxy standing there, but it was his brother – tall and stocky, wearing a tight white T-shirt and combat trousers. Micky's face had turned green under the lights, making him look a bit like the Incredible Hulk. But he didn't seem angry, just surprised.

'What you doing here?' he shouted as coins cascaded into the machine behind him and a loud cheer went up.

She couldn't speak. Her eyes flicked around nervously. Was he on his own or was he with Foxy? Perhaps they'd spotted her entering the amusement arcade and were mounting a two-pronged attack.

'He's not here,' he said, reading her mind. 'I'm with me mates, we just came down for a night out. Can we talk? Somewhere quiet?'

'I'll be outside,' she told Pat, who was too busy nudging up a row of lemons to respond properly. Alesha was similarly engrossed at the grabber, trying to win a teddy for her little boy. Babs was nowhere to be seen. Some bodyguard, thought Kay. But she felt all right. She was strong now, she could cope.

They left the arcade and stood by the sea wall. It was almost dark now, and the crowds had thinned.

'You're pregnant,' he said, staring down at her bump.

'Really?' she replied sarcastically, then caught his expression – he looked genuinely taken aback. 'He didn't tell you?'

'No.' He shuffled his feet, embarrassed. 'Er … whose is it?'

'Your brother's, of course. What do you think I am, Micky, a tart?'

'No, no, I just … He never mentioned it. He said …' Micky sighed. 'He said you'd gone off with another bloke.'

'He always was a liar.'

'I know.'

'I left because I had no choice. I thought he was going to kill me.' How much easier it was to admit now. She no longer felt ashamed or in any way to blame.

'I kind of knew something was going on,' Micky said, reaching for his cigarettes. 'I tried to stop him but it made things worse; he thought we were shagging.' He offered her one but she put her hand up to refuse.

'Not fair, is it?' she said. 'Everyone thinks you're the bad 'un because you've done time in jail, but Alan's the real villain and he gets away with it.' He didn't reply to that.

'He still loves you.' He pulled on his fag, puffing smoke rings into the sky.

'He doesn't have the first idea what love is,' she retorted.

'That's not true. He adores you, he's obsessed, can't function without you. He's gone to pieces. Walked out on his job, hit the bottle. Now he's behind on the rent. If he doesn't pay up, he'll be evicted at the end of the month.'

She shrugged. 'Like I care.'

He took another couple of puffs, then stubbed his cigarette out with his heel. 'So, where you living? Here in Nevansey?'

'I'd rather not say, if you don't mind,' she answered.

'Can't be easy with a kid to look after and another on the way. How do you manage?'

'I'm getting by. I'm actually happier than I've ever been. And no, I'm not with anyone else, if that's what you're thinking. I'm done with men.'

He raised his eyebrows. 'Where you living? Council give you a place?'

'I don't want to say.'

'You must be living somewhere – can't be managing on your own. Come home, give him another chance. He needs you, Kay. He's learnt his lesson, he won't do it again.'

'You're wasting your breath.' Pat and Alesha had just come out of the arcade and were looking for her. 'I've got to go,' she said, waving at them to come over.

Micky set his jaw. 'That baby needs a father.'

'No it doesn't. Besides, he told me to get rid of it.'

The girls ran up to greet her. 'We lost all our frigging money,' cried Alesha. 'Didn't even win a bloody teddy.'

'You're a quick worker,' said Pat, looking Micky up and down.

'Remember the house rules!' Alesha wagged her finger. 'No drink, no violence and no men!' The women cackled raucously.

Micky looked at the two of them curiously, then back at Kay. 'You living in a hostel? YWCA?'

'It's a secret, so get lost,' said Alesha – stupidly, Kay thought.

'Oh, I know … You're in one of those places for battered women. I've read about them in the paper. Is there one in Nevansey then?' He looked around, as if expecting it to pop up before his eyes.

Kay had had enough. 'Please don't tell Alan you saw me,' she said, her tone as serious as it could be. 'You'll be putting my life in danger.'

'You can't have a baby in a place like that,' he said. 'It's not right. Come back with me, we'll go to see him together. He'll be over the moon that you're back. You'll sort it out, I know you will.'

'Who is this?' said Pat, suddenly sharpening up.

'My brother-in-law. But it's okay, I'm not going anywhere.' Kay put her hands on Micky's shoulders and looked him straight in the eye. 'Please! Promise you won't say anything. I'm begging you. For all our sakes.'

CHAPTER THIRTY-FIVE

Stella

Now

I open my eyes to darkness. Where am I? I feel so cold. I'm lying on my back, arms at my sides, feet together. Can't seem to move my limbs. There's a wet, burning pain spreading across my skull and drilling deep into my brain. When I try to lift my head, arrows of fire shoot down my spine. I feel woozy; want to be sick.

There's something sharp scratching my neck. I think it's a tarpaulin; it crackles every time I try to move. I'm all wrapped up, like a caterpillar in a cocoon, with only my head poking out. My hands are tied together with something thin and sharp that's digging into my wrists. I can feel the same soreness around my ankles. Plastic garden ties, perhaps, the ones that are impossible to get off without a very sharp knife.

I can't touch my face, but I know it's covered with mud or blood – maybe a mixture of the two – plastered over my cheeks like a beauty mask and left to dry. There's a musty smell deep in my nostrils, like old dry earth. My tongue is coated in grit and sand, grains of it stuck between my teeth. I'm so thirsty … I try to swallow, but it turns into a cough, making my whole head throb with pain.

It's totally dark here, not a chink of light coming from anywhere. The surface beneath me is lumpy and hard. And it's so very cold. Am I underground? Please God, don't let me be underground. Waves of panic instantly rise from my guts and I instinctively start to struggle, but it's no use, I'm all bundled up. Can't breathe properly, can't fill my lungs. I gulp for air, but every little movement is excruciating.

Blinking, I try to widen my eyes. No … not underground. Not even in a box. There's space above me, the air choked with dust. As my pupils dilate, dim shapes emerge from the blackness. I look from left to right, up and down, stretching the limits of my peripheral vision. Dark objects loom ominously from the shadows. A pile of logs, I think. Metal shelving? I start to make things out on the shelves: plant pots perhaps, hessian sacks. Tools fixed to the wall. Empty jam jars. Wooden boxes. A tall block that could be a stack of chairs. A rectangle that might be a window. Hard to see from this position, flat on my back on the ground … Don't know where I am.

But not underground, not buried alive. I breathe out slowly. Thank God. For a moment I thought …

No, don't think. Don't imagine what might have been or what might be yet to come. Not dead. Not yet. But badly hurt. There's blood pooling underneath me. I can feel it dripping down my neck, soaking into my jumper. I can smell its sticky sweetness, like treacle. I was hit on the back of the head; I can just about remember that. There's a wound there, I can feel the open flesh stinging. It could be deep. Probably got concussion too. That would account for the nausea, the dizziness, the intense, pulsing headache.

I should be in hospital, not rolled up like an old carpet waiting to be slung on the dump. Is that what they're going to do with me? Are they out there now in the darkness, digging, measuring up the space, making sure it's long enough to take a body, deep enough to put off the rats and foxes?

Stop imagining things. If you carry on like this, you'll have a heart attack. You're not dead yet.

Surely they won't bury me alive. They're not inhuman. Desperate, yes, scared, yes, but evil? That's what Dawn said about her own sister, but even now I can't believe it. They're not behaving rationally; they're being driven by some other incredibly powerful force that I can't comprehend.

My eyes are adjusting now and I can see my surroundings more clearly. I'm in the shed; of course, that makes sense. I've been dumped on the floor between a rusty lawnmower and some logs, bound with garden ties and wrapped in a tarpaulin fastened with some old ropes. Everything they needed readily to hand.

It's pitch black outside. Completely quiet. Although if I listen really hard, I can just about make out the sound of the wind and the sea grinding over the shingle. Must be high tide.

'Help,' I squawk uselessly. I've no idea what time it is, but it feels late. Nobody will be able to hear me. Not in the middle of the night; not even in the daytime.

I sink into the sticky pool of blood beneath me, taking stock. I'm injured and weak, tied up, locked (probably) in an old shed. The garden is huge and well protected. We're on a corner plot, next to a side road that hardly anyone uses. The house on the other side is a holiday let, closed for the winter.

Frankly, it's not looking good. I could bleed out, slip into unconsciousness, become dehydrated, develop an infection, starve. I could be dead in hours, or it could take days. But I mustn't think like that, can't surrender. I have to stay alive, and the first job is to keep awake. Mustn't drift away … Concentrate on the pain, embrace the agony, use it as fuel to give me energy.

I know there's no way to escape – I can't free myself from my bonds, can't smash the window and crawl out. My only hope is that Dawn will come and I can persuade her to take pity on me. I don't want to see Abi, my spade-wielding executioner. If the door opens and she's standing there, I'll know it's the end. It's Dawn I need to work on. No, not Dawn exactly – I've no idea what makes her tick, and besides, she's too frightened of her sister.

It's *Lori* who can help me. If she goes back to being the Lori I know, if she channels her spirit, thinks about what she would have done, even just for a few moments, there's a chance I'll be saved.

But if I die here, some might argue that I deserved it.

My mind scrolls back over the years, moving faster and faster until I'm seventeen and in the house I shared with Mum and Dad and the foster kids. I'm lying on the bed with a file of notes open, trying to memorise Shakespeare quotes but nodding off in the warm sunshine streaming through the window. I'm studying for my A levels, trying to concentrate on getting good grades so that I can go to university and leave this shitty life behind me. I have an offer from Queen Mary, but it's too high – I'm going to have to perform out of my skull to achieve it.

My bedroom door is closed and firmly locked. Beyond, the house is shaking with the thumping play of the foster kids – two noisy fighting sisters and a toddler who is constantly having tantrums and refuses to eat anything but bread. And Kyle, of course. He's new, arrived a few months ago. He's fourteen going on twenty-three. Mum and Dad never tell me the details, but Kyle was happy for me to know that his mother's a drug addict and he's been in and out of care since he was six years old. In a couple more years he'll be flung out of the system and left to fend for himself, but until then, he's the responsibility of Social Services, which is where my parents come in.

I hate Kyle. I hate the way he soaks up all Mum and Dad's attention, hate the way they believe his lies. He's supposed to go to some special educational unit for challenging students; a minibus comes every morning to take him there and bring him home in the afternoon. Most of the time he refuses to get out of bed, claims he's ill or that he's scared to go because he's being bullied by the staff. It's all rubbish, of course, but my parents believe him.

'He's had a rough deal out of life,' Mum says. 'We have to give him a chance.'

Kyle's room is next to mine. He's got it all to himself at the moment, because the other boy who was staying with us has gone back to his mum. His name was Billy – he was okay, I didn't mind him. But Kyle's nasty. He says he can get me drugs – weed, skunk, ecstasy tablets, whatever I want. I told Mum and Dad but they said he was just 'playing the big man', not to take any notice. But Molly saw him in Basildon shopping centre the other weekend and said he was hanging around with some dodgy older guys who looked like they could be dealers. He's not supposed to go to Basildon; that's where his mum is. He was sent to our leafy suburb to give him a chance of a 'normal life', whatever that means. If this is normal, then give me abnormality any day.

I turn my attention back to my *Othello* quotes.

Oh, beware, my lord, of jealousy!
It is the green-eyed monster which doth mock
The meat it feeds on.

I accept that I'm jealous of Kyle – jealous of all the foster kids if truth be told. Okay, yes, it's stupid to be jealous of someone who's been tossed around between homes and carers, expelled from several schools. Apparently it's not his fault that he's so vile. But why does he have to be put in my family? And why does he have to play his disgusting music so loudly when I'm trying to revise?

Kyle has a face like a raw potato, all pockmarked, with hairs sprouting in odd places. He thinks he's so hard. Dad reckons he's 'naturally intelligent', but as far as I can see he's got the concentration span of a gnat. He's always going on about porn and asking me to have sex with him. The idea makes me want to puke. I've been locking my bedroom door for years, but now I put a chair under the handle too. Last week he offered me a fiver for a blow job. When I told Mum and Dad, they said he must have been joking, because as far as they knew he didn't even have a fiver.

'You're grown up now,' Mum said. 'Surely you can deal with a young boy like Kyle.' *Young boy.* She sees all her foster kids through rose-tinted spectacles. To her, they're innocents; their sins belong to society, not them. Mum and Dad are about as naive as Othello, and we know how badly that ended.

Then must you speak
Of one that loved not wisely, but too well.

Oh yes, there's plenty of love in our house, but very little of it is directed at me. I'm not speaking to Mum and Dad at the moment. We had a huge row over Kyle's blow-job offer and I went and stayed at Molly's house for two nights. When I came home – reluctantly – I begged them to send him away. I told them I was frightened to have him in the house. 'He's dangerous,' I said, but they wouldn't have it. Around them he's all please and thank you, never puts a foot wrong. It's a game for him. Free food, free accommodation, two gullible carers who don't ask questions. At least that's how I see it. As far as I'm concerned, Mum and Dad are being conned. If Kyle doesn't leave soon, I'm going to fail my exams and then I'll never leave this hellhole.

There's a rattling outside, like a padlock is being undone. The sound brings me sharply back to the present. My muscles tense as the door squeaks open and a beam of bright light shines across the floor, blinding me.

CHAPTER THIRTY-SIX

Stella

Now

'Stella?' Dawn's voice.

I try to answer, but my mouth is too dry to speak. She walks into the shed and crouches beside me, her face lit from beneath by her phone, making her look skeletal and sad.

'Are you okay? I've brought you some water.' She lifts my head and I gasp with pain. 'I'm so sorry,' she says, and I wonder what she means – what exactly it is that she's sorry for. I take a few sips from the mug and the water dribbles down my chin. 'Thank God you're still alive. I was terrified I'd find you … you know …'

The cold liquid tastes exquisite as it travels down my parched throat. She puts the mug on the floor, then kneels down next to me. The torch on her phone goes off and we're plunged into darkness again. She doesn't put it back on. I think she prefers it this way. She can't bear to see me trussed up like a piece of meat, my face covered in mud, hair matted with blood. A body waiting to be buried, the grave freshly dug.

'I'm so sorry,' she repeats. 'This wasn't meant to happen.'

'Police. Call the police,' I reply. My voice is croaky but the words come out strong. 'Now. Police, ambulance. Before it's too late.'

'I can't! I want to, but I can't.'

My eyes start to readjust to the darkness. I can see her out of the corner of my right eye, hands in her lap, head bowed, her lank hair hanging like a veil over her face.

'Abi's going to kill me,' I say flatly. It's a statement, not a question. Why else would she have rolled me up in this tarpaulin and bound it with ropes? I'm a glitch in the operation, collateral damage, an unfortunate mistake. A sacrifice for the greater evil. 'Listen to me, Dawn. It's not too late, you can stop her.' She moves her head from side to side, as if the answer has got stuck and she's trying to shake it out. 'I know it seems like there's no way out, but actually it's easy.'

'Everything's gone wrong,' she cries. 'It's out of control.'

'Just call 999 and it'll be over. That's all it will take.'

'I can't! Daren't.' Her voice recedes into the gloom. I shift my shoulders, trying to relieve the pain, but it makes no difference. The back of my head is sticky with blood, my hair glued to the sheeting. The plastic crackles with every tiny movement.

'What's Abi doing?' I say.

She looks up. 'She's asleep – said she was exhausted. I don't know how she can sleep when you're lying here, but that's Abi for you. Hard as nails.'

'You're not hard, though, are you, Dawn? You care about people, you care about me. You don't want me to die, I know you don't. But if you don't act very soon—'

'I can't, all right?'

'You can! You can make it stop.'

She sighs heavily. 'You don't understand.'

'Try me,' I say. 'Tell me about it. Go on, you might as well.'

There's silence. Silence and darkness. All I can hear is the sound of our laboured breathing. I know Dawn wants to unburden herself and let all the poison out.

She clears her throat, then slowly starts to speak. 'I never wanted to trick you. It was Abi's idea, she said it was the only way.

I had to "create a character", somebody who would be convincing. She made me pretend to be Lori. I didn't want to do it, it felt bad. But I knew how to be her. I knew how she spoke, how she felt. I'd spent hours and hours listening to all the terrible things that had happened … I was very emotionally involved. And in a strange kind of way …' She hesitates, twisting her fingers in her lap. 'I know this sounds weird, but it was as if I was bringing her back to life, giving her a second chance.'

'Well you did a good job,' I say crisply. 'Completely convinced me.'

She lets out a small, breathy huff. 'Almost convinced myself sometimes. I liked being her, it was almost easier than being me, you know? I wanted to keep her safe in the house, out of danger. I was never going to send her back to Darren. I wanted her story to have a different ending … That sounds ridiculous, I know, but at the time it made sense. It was the only way I could justify what I was doing – to myself, I mean.'

'It has a kind of logic, I guess,' I say. 'Did Abi beat you up so you'd look the part?'

'Yes, I think she enjoyed it, taking out all her anger on me. I thought it would be the worst bit, but it wasn't. Lying to you, that was the worst. I couldn't believe how kind, how generous you were. You totally trusted me; it broke my heart. I kept thinking, if only Westhill House was still a women's refuge, if only the real Lori had knocked on your door, you would have saved her.'

'So you knew it was wrong yet you carried on. Why? Did Abi make you; was she threatening you?'

'She's always been the boss, ever since we were kids,' Dawn says, her voice getting smaller. 'She became impatient because nothing was happening, I wasn't doing what I was supposed to do, so she turned up pretending to be my friend. I had to go along with it. I was sure you'd smell a rat, but you didn't. I almost wanted you to chuck us out. You're too kind, Stella, you know that?'

'I'm not kind,' I say. 'I was trying to be kind, that's not the same.'

'No, you're a really good person,' she insists. 'I'm a coward, the lowest of the low. I never should have agreed to it in the first place, should have left weeks, months ago. I only stayed on because I was scared of Abi.'

'But what were you supposed to be doing here?'

'I can't say.' She speaks abruptly. 'I've already said too much. If Abi finds out ...' She drifts off, presumably imagining what her sister might do to her.

But I need to understand what this is about. 'It was a scam, right?' I press. 'Somehow you found out I'd inherited a lot of money. You wanted to gain my trust and sympathy, then ask me for financial help so that you could "leave Darren"? Was that it?' No reply. 'Or you were going to worm your way into my confidence, then hack into my bank accounts and clean them out?'

'No.' She almost laughs. 'Nothing like that.'

'So what is it you want? What has got so out of control? What's so important that it's worth killing me for?'

'It's *not* worth it,' she says. 'Killing you would be the stupidest thing of all. I keep telling Abi that, but she won't listen. She says we're in too deep now and can't go back. I don't know what to do.'

I almost feel sorry for Dawn. She's so weak and I need her to be strong. If only I could touch her, I think. If only I could reach out and place a hand on her arm, or give her a hug and tell her everything will be all right. Let her collapse onto me, take the weight of this burden off her shoulders. But I can't move. The ties around my wrists seem to dig even deeper into my flesh.

'You'll get caught,' I say finally. 'Too many people know about you. Jack will tell the police, they'll track you down. Nobody's going to believe that I just disappeared, wandered off into the sunset ...'

'I know.'

'You'll get the blame, not Abi. And it's not fair, because none of this was your idea.'

'Yes, yes, I know! But I went along with it. I've done terrible things too.'

'We can sort this out. Just call the police now. I'll back you up, say you were coerced.'

She shifts onto her heels and stands up. 'I'd better go.' She touches her phone and it illuminates a path to the door. I can't let her go. If she leaves now, I'm lost, and the next person to come will be Abi.

I lift my head and a huge wave of pain breaks over my skull. 'I'm going to die! You don't want that – Lori wouldn't have wanted that. You tried to save Lori and it didn't work. Do you want my death on your conscience too?'

'Stop it!' She gags like she's about to be sick.

'Why are you trying to protect Abi?'

'It's not just her.'

'What do you mean? Who else is involved?'

'Can't say. I've got to go.'

'Alan? Is he part of this?'

She freezes at the sound of his name. 'No. Why would he be?'

'I overheard the two of you talking. Something about Foxy?'

Her fingers are on the door handle; she tries to pull it open, but the wood is swollen and resists.

'Who is he?'

'It's nearly light. Got to go.' She turns away.

'Please help me. Please! You can't leave me like this.'

She wrenches open the door. A shaft of grey light floods the space for a few seconds, then disappears. I hear the door shutting, the padlock clunking tight. I lie back on the hard, cold floor, my body throbbing with pain as I listen to the seagulls squawking in the new day.

CHAPTER THIRTY-SEVEN

Kay

Then

She sat at the kitchen table and let the jolly chaos unfold around her. Kids were fighting over hats and gloves, their mothers scolding as they buttoned up coats and pushed wellies onto wriggling feet.

'Can I have a toffee apple, Mum? Pleeeeeease?'

'If you're good.'

'Who's got the sparklers?'

'They're in my bag. Anyone seen my woolly scarf?'

'You've got one more minute or we're leaving without you.'

It was Bonfire Night and everyone else was going to watch the fireworks in Nevansey Park. The council organised a display every year, apparently, and the whole town attended. There would be mobile burger vans, fairground stalls and rides – dodgems, a carousel, swing boats and giant whirling teacups. Kay had been to look at the bonfire earlier in the week, an enormous stack of wooden pallets, precariously arranged like that game where you had to pull the straws out and try not to knock the tower down. On the top, somebody had fixed a guy – he was wearing a suit and tie and looked strangely respectable. Pat said he looked a bit like her husband, who worked in a bank. They started singing an old song from their schooldays, specially adapted for battered wives.

Build a bonfire, build a bonfire put your husband on the top!
Put your boyfriend in the middle and we'll burn the rotten lot.

Kay had been looking forward to Bonfire Night. She had some happy childhood memories associated with the event – parties in neighbours' back gardens mostly. Sweet, innocent times, before she grew up and it all went wrong. But unfortunately she had to stay at home this evening. Abigail had come down with a nasty cold and high temperature, and was lying in bed dosed up to the eyeballs. She'd been asleep for hours, poor thing, and Kay knew she would be devastated when she woke up and discovered the fireworks had been and gone.

The party still hadn't left the house. 'You can't go out in that, you'll catch your death,' Babs was saying to her teenage daughter, who was a punk.

Pat's voice rang out from the hallway. 'Are we going or what?'

Kay laughed quietly to herself as the kitchen finally emptied and the gaggle of women and kids trooped out of the door. She breathed in the silence for a few moments, then stood up, putting a hand out to keep her balance. Her belly was so huge, her legs could barely support her weight. She felt like a piece of badly designed pottery, likely to topple over at any moment and break into a thousand pieces.

Collecting up the dirty mugs and plates, she waddled over to the sink and made a pile. It was a shame to be missing the fun, but Pat and Alesha had kindly promised to come and relieve her in time for her to watch the second display at nine. In the meantime, she would enjoy the peace and quiet. In all the months she had lived here, she had never once been in the house on her own, not even for a few minutes. Even now she couldn't claim complete solitude, because Abigail was ill upstairs.

She started washing up, soaking her hands in the hot soapy water and thinking about her daughter. She'd picked up the germ at her new school; it was doing the rounds. There seemed to be one problem after another. When Kay had told her that she was going back to school, Abigail had immediately presumed she meant her old one, where Ms Gardiner taught and all her friends were. Even though several of the other refuge kids already went to the new school and liked it there, she had set her mind against it, refusing point blank to go. It was only Franny who had persuaded her to give it a try.

'I'll still come at weekends and you can join my lessons then if you like. But only if you go to school in the week.'

A deal was struck, although Abigail was convinced that she'd got the bad end of it. She'd been difficult from day one – not paying attention in class, being rude to the teachers, skulking in the corner of the playground, determined not to make any new friends.

Kay placed the clean mugs on the drainer, sighing as she reflected on how much her little girl had changed. She'd always been near the top of the class at her old school, a good reader for her age, with a talent for maths and a keen interest in every lesson, regardless of the subject. But those months off school had taken their toll, despite Franny Gardiner's best attempts to plug the gaps. Abigail no longer seemed to care about having approval from her teachers. It was true that the refuge kids were a wild bunch. They stayed up far too late and were always charging around, screaming at the tops of their voices. But it was impossible to stick to a calming routine of baths and bedtime stories when you were sharing with so many other families. Kay had tried, but had given up after a couple of weeks – she simply didn't have the energy to battle through. In the last few months, she'd watched her daughter unravel like a piece of knitting. She didn't know what to do with her, and it was going to be even more difficult when the new baby came. She hoped Abigail wouldn't turn out to be the jealous type.

It was three weeks until her due date, not long to go now. Everyone in the house was excited, with some convinced she was having a girl and just as many others certain it was a boy. Several of her friends were knitting squares to make a patchwork baby blanket, and Verity had moved her and Abigail into the round room at the very top of the house in preparation for the new arrival. It was a thoughtful gesture, although Kay suspected it was mostly for the benefit of her roommates.

The turret room had fantastic views over the beach and towards the pier but it was too small for what would soon be three of them. Still, she wasn't going to complain; there was nowhere else to put them. Verity had dreams of turning Westhill House into bedsit units, maintaining a communal lounge and kitchen downstairs. But they would need to be able to buy the place legally first, and that was proving to be quite a challenge.

Kay swept the crumbs off the breadboard, washed the knife and put it on the drainer, then wiped down the surfaces. After checking on Abigail, she would switch the telly on and watch a programme of her own choosing, then get ready to go out.

The first firework display seemed to have started – she could hear rockets whizzing and bangers exploding. If she went up to the top floor and looked out of the back windows, she might be able to see some of it.

She turned the lights out in the kitchen and went into the chilly hallway. For once, all the coat pegs were empty and the mound of footwear had been reduced to a few odd or broken shoes. She was about to climb the stairs when there was a loud knock on the door. She sighed. Either one of her friends had forgotten something, or it was a new arrival. She knew what to do if it was the latter. Invite her in, make her feel at ease, give her a cup of strong sweet tea and call Verity.

Without thinking about it, she opened the door wide, gasping as she saw Foxy standing there. He looked haggard, like he hadn't been sleeping, and there was a stain on his jacket.

'Kay, it's you.' His eyes flicked over her, resting proprietorially on her round belly. She immediately felt sick and light-headed.

'Who told you I was here?' She knew the answer; there was only one person it could be. Over two months had passed since she'd seen Micky in Vegas Amusements. She'd felt frightened at first, but as the weeks had passed, she'd gradually relaxed into the idea that he'd kept her secret. Clearly she'd been wrong.

'I'm very worried about you,' he said. 'So's everyone else. Your parents, Micky, all our friends. I've come to take you home.'

'I'm already home, thanks.' She started to close the door, but he stepped forward, putting his foot in the way. This tiny act of aggression was enough to make her feel faint. She gripped the edge of the door, steadying herself. All the bruises that had faded, all the cuts and burns that had healed suddenly felt vivid and sore.

'Aren't you going to let me in?' he said, smiling. 'I'm freezing my balls off out here.'

She pushed the door against his foot, and it bounced off. 'No men allowed. It's the rules.'

'All right. Put your coat on and we'll go for a drink.'

'I can't. Abigail's sick, I've got to stay and look after her. Nobody else is …' She bit off the end of her sentence. Bad move to let him know she was on her own.

'In that case, it won't matter if I come in for a few minutes, will it?' He walked forward, banging the door against her stomach as she quickly backed away. 'At the fireworks, are they?'

'They'll be back any minute,' she said.

Foxy shut the door behind him, then walked up and down the hallway, poking his head into the two front rooms like he was spraying his territory. He whistled through his teeth. 'What a dump.'

Better than living with you, she thought, but kept quiet. Her body was responding badly to his presence. Her heart was racing and she had pins and needles all the way down her left arm. It was very peculiar.

He strode past her into the kitchen and she followed, even though she wanted to run into the street and cry for help. But she couldn't leave him in the house with Abigail.

'Make us a cuppa, will you? I've been wandering around for hours looking for this place.'

She automatically reached for the kettle. 'How did you find it?'

'I saw a load of women and kids come out the front door; they looked like a right bunch of man-haters.' His lip curled; he was deliberately provoking her.

'So what do you want, Alan?' she said, calling him by his proper name. No more Foxy, no more Squirrel, no more hubby darling.

'I told you. I want you to come home. I need you.'

She frowned. 'I thought you were being evicted. Micky told me,' she added at his surprised expression.

'I've got another month's grace, on account of the baby,' he said. 'The landlord's a harsh bastard, but even he couldn't turf us onto the streets with a newborn just before Christmas. No room at the inn and all that.'

He looked down at her bump and she put her hands against it protectively. So that was why he wanted her back.

'Changed your tune, haven't you?' she said. 'Last time we spoke, you told me to get rid of it.'

He shrugged, as if he could barely remember the occasion. 'I was shocked, that's all, but I've got used to the idea now. I love you, Kay. My whole life's fallen to pieces since you left. I lost my job, I owe money. You've got to come back. I need you.'

For what? she thought. To do his cooking and cleaning, washing and ironing? To give him sex on demand? To be his punchbag? She would rather die than go back to that life.

'I can't. Sorry.'

'You what?'

He moved towards her, pushing her against the worktop and putting his hands on her shoulders. Her swollen belly was a buffer between them, but she could still feel his hot breath on her cheeks and smell the minty gum he always chewed. She held onto the edge of the counter as images from the past flashed into her brain.

'Please don't hurt the baby,' she said.

He looked at her as if she was mad. 'Me? I would never do that. I know I was hard on you sometimes, but it was only because I love you so much. I wanted our life to be perfect. Every time you let me down, it made me angry, because you kept spoiling things.'

His logic was perverse; she understood that completely now, saw through all the self-justifying lies. Why had she put up with it for so long? Well, it was over now, she was a new person. She'd worked hard, made sacrifices. It was a struggle, but she would get there in the end. Right now, she had to protect herself, her daughter and her unborn child.

'I'm sorry I let you down,' she lied. 'I tried, but it just didn't work out. I think it's best we go our separate ways.'

He dug his nails into the tops of her shoulders and lowered his voice to a growl. 'You're my wife. If I say you're coming home, you're coming home.'

He lunged forward and kissed her hard, shoving his tongue into her mouth. She stretched her hand back, feeling blindly with her fingers. The bread knife was on the drainer; if she could just reach it … He had his hands on her breasts now – they hurt madly but she let him manhandle her while she grabbed the knife and slowly brought it round and up until the blade was pointing at the side of his neck. She prodded him with the cold metal tip and he flinched.

'What the fuck?'

'Get your hands off me.'

He took a sharp intake of minty breath, then released her. 'Put the knife down, Kay,' he said. His tone was almost dismissive. 'Stop playing silly buggers.'

'I'm serious. Get out now, or I'll call the police.'

'Ha! Call them!' he said mockingly. 'Who are they going to believe? I'm not the one holding a knife.'

She waved the blade in his face. 'I mean it. Go.'

'All right, all right …' He backed off. 'Calm down, will you, or someone's going to get hurt, and it won't be me.'

'I wouldn't be so sure about that.'

'What's got into you? Have you gone mental? I've come here to put things right, for the sake of our family. I'm offering to take you back—'

'Go. Now.' He took a few steps backwards into the corridor and she followed him, holding the knife out in front of her. Her arm was steady; she'd never felt so powerful and in control. 'Get out,' she said, pushing him towards the front door. 'I never want to see or hear from you ever again.'

CHAPTER THIRTY-EIGHT

Stella

Now

'Stella? ... Stella?'

I blink my eyes open, but the light is too strong and I instantly close them again. The outline of a window scars the inside of my eyelids. Where am I? No longer in the shed, I think. I hold my breath, letting my senses do their work. Gone is the smell of damp earth, replaced by something sharper, like disinfectant. The air is warm but still, almost stuffy. I press my back downwards, testing the surface. It's soft and springy. I'm not lying on the ground, but in a bed. Hospital, perhaps?

Somebody is touching my hand, over and over, rubbing their fingers across my knuckles in nervous, repetitive strokes. I realise that my wrists are no longer tied.

'Jack?' I whisper. 'Is that you?' There's no reply, but whoever it is keeps on stroking, to calm themselves as much as me, I think. Please let it be Jack sitting at my side, patiently waiting for me to sit up. My spirits rise. I picture his face, his kind brown eyes and straggly beard, hair flattened by the beanie he always insists on wearing. I've missed him so much. But then I remember that the voice I just heard was light and thin, too high-pitched to belong to a man. Not Jack, then ... I feel instantly bereft.

Who is holding my hand? A nurse, perhaps. Yes, it must be a nurse.

Some hours, maybe even days ago – I've completely lost all sense of time – I dreamt that I was thrown into a handcart and wheeled away on cobbled stones. The uneven ground rattled my bones, made me cry out weakly with pain. Whoever was pushing the cart thought I was dead and I couldn't make them hear me. They were taking me to be buried in a pit. I was trying to shout at them – 'I'm alive, still alive!' – but no sound would come out of my mouth. Maybe it wasn't a dream; maybe that was me being rescued, pushed on a trolley, loaded into the back of an ambulance …

'Stella? I'm going to clean you up a bit, okay?' The voice belongs to an older woman, and for a brief, delirious moment I think it's my mother talking to me. I'm so confused, I don't know if I'm asleep or dreaming, dead or alive. She wipes a cold wet cloth over my cheeks, rubs at the corners of my mouth as she used to when I was a child. The cloth smells of aloe vera. Its coldness stings me awake.

'Open your eyes, love,' she says gently. I flutter my eyelids and stare into her face. It's not my mother, of course. Nor is she wearing a nurse's uniform. I've never seen this woman before and yet she is instantly recognisable, an older version of somebody I know. Either I've travelled forward in time, or I've been lying here like Sleeping Beauty for years.

'Dawn?' I croak. My tongue is parched, the roof of my mouth scaly.

'No,' she smiles. 'I'm Kay, her mum. Everyone says we're carbon copies of each other.'

'Her mum?'

'Yes, love. You're safe now, everything's going to be all right.'

'Where am I?'

'In bed, in your room.' She screws the baby wipe into a ball and throws it in the bin next to the bed. 'I've cleaned your wound and put a bandage on. I don't think it's too bad.'

I slowly lift my hand and prod my forehead. My head is swathed in soft crepe. The stickiness at the back of my skull has gone, but it still feels unbearably tender.

'Did Dawn call you?'

'Yes. I came straight away.' She sits on the edge of the bed and takes my hand again, rubbing it as if trying to remove a stubborn stain. 'I'm so sorry for what you've been through. It never should have happened. But you'll be all right, you'll heal. You just need to rest up, take it easy for a few days.'

'Did you call the police?'

She bites down on her lip before answering. 'You have to understand … my daughter's not a well person – Abigail, I mean, not Dawn. She didn't mean to hurt you; it was an accident.'

I start to shake my head in denial, but pain rolls behind my eyes, making me stop. 'It wasn't an accident. She wanted to kill me. She'd already dug my grave.'

'No … you misunderstood. You challenged her and she struck out. She was frightened and panicked. I'm not excusing what she did. She shouldn't have tied you up like that, it was really bad of her, but she wasn't in control of her actions. Dawn tried to stop her, but when Abi's having one of her—'

'Where is she?'

'Upstairs. Dawn's looking after her. She's taken her medication and she's resting now. I won't let her come anywhere near you, don't worry.' She smiles at me again – a sort of anxious, pleading smile that says: *Please don't ask any more questions, please let's pretend that everything's fine.*

But it's not fine. It's anything but fine. I'm grateful to this woman for making her crazy daughter see sense, for rescuing me from the shed and bringing me into the house, for tending to my wounds and taking care of me. But it's not enough. Something serious happened here; it can't just be swept away.

'I should be in hospital,' I say. 'My head is really hurting. I probably need stitches or something. I may have concussion.'

'You're okay, I checked your pupils. And you're not bleeding any more. It's just a small cut. I'll get you some paracetamol.' She reaches down for her handbag and starts scrabbling around inside, like a squirrel looking for food. 'I've got some somewhere.'

'Can you call an ambulance, please,' I say, feeling my hackles rise.

'Oh, they won't come for something as minor as this,' she replies, taking out a sheet of tablets and pushing two through their foil casing. 'You're better off resting. The queues in A and E are horrendous.'

'If you won't do it, I will.' I ease myself onto my elbows and look around for my phone. I can't remember when I last had it or where I left it. My head swims and I feel sick. 'Have you seen my mobile?'

'Sorry, no. Here, take these.' She puts the tablets onto my palm, then passes me a glass of water. 'You need to rest.'

Anything is better than nothing, I think, swallowing them down. 'I need my mobile. I want to call for help.'

'It's really not necessary.'

'Yes, it is. I was attacked by your daughter, I'm lucky to be alive.'

'Please don't,' she says. 'Please, I'm begging you. They'll only get the police involved. It was an accident, a stupid mistake; she didn't mean it. Please don't call, you don't understand the trouble it'll cause. Everything will come out and ...' She starts to break up, like a bad signal. 'Please, please ... don't.'

But I don't care. Throwing off the duvet, I drag myself onto my side and sit up. My brain weighs a ton, the pain behind my eyes so strong that I can barely keep them open.

Got to get outside … call for help … Even if I collapse in the street, surely someone will find me.

I heave myself off the bed and try to stand, but my legs buckle under me and I fall back onto the mattress. Groaning, I attempt to get up again, but my head is reeling with nausea. It's no use. I'm too weak. I won't even make it as far as the door.

Kay stands over me. 'Please, just listen to me first. I'll tell you what happened, from the beginning. I'll tell you everything. Then you can decide what you want to do.'

'I know what I want to do. I want to call an ambulance.'

'I'm sorry, but I can't let you,' she says, her tone firming up again. 'Not until you've heard my story. This is all my fault. I'm the one who should take the blame – not Abi, not Dawn.'

I moan, collapsing backwards onto the bed. Why is she torturing me like this? I don't care about her story; I'm not interested in her excuses. The mattress depresses as she sits down. She tries to take my hand, but I snatch it away, turning onto my side and closing my eyes as her words drift into my brain.

'I had Abigail when I was just sixteen. It was a one-night stand, a holiday romance.' She sighs. 'Not even a romance, really. Just a moment of stupidity. My parents stood by me, but they never forgave me. I was damaged goods, my mum said – no man would ever want me. Then I met Alan Foxton; everyone called him Foxy. He was a right charmer, swept me off my feet, told me I was the most wonderful girl in the world, all that crap. I fell for it, didn't I? I was a single mum, trapped at home. I thought my life had ended. It made me vulnerable and I suppose he saw that.

'The violence started soon after we were married. I didn't understand at first, I thought it was all my fault … I was used to being in the wrong, getting the blame. I tried really hard to be the best wife I could be so he wouldn't get angry, but nothing I did made anything better. Because I wasn't the problem, *he* was.'

'Foxy …' I murmur. Alan Foxton. The man I let into my house, who was so supportive of Lori, who brought her sandwiches every day, gave her pretty things for her room. *What kind of man does that to his wife?* That's what he said, the hypocrite.

'I didn't tell anyone,' Kay continues. 'I was too embarrassed, too ashamed. There was no point in going to the police because they didn't get involved in domestics – it was as if husbands had a right to beat their wives up. I put up with it for a couple of years, not that long compared to what some women endure, but long enough for me. I was pregnant with Dawn, but Alan didn't want the baby. He hated Abigail, was sick with jealousy. I was scared. I knew that if I stayed much longer, he'd kill me. There was no choice. So we escaped and came to the refuge.'

'You lived here?' My senses prickle and I feel my brain stuttering into action. Pieces of the jigsaw are starting to come together. The battered wife, the monstrous husband, two half-sisters caught in the crossfire. And at the centre of the picture is my home, Westhill House.

I uncurl and turn over to face her. 'When? How long were you here?'

She nods slowly, remembering. 'We arrived in April 1978 and I left just before Christmas.'

'What was it like? I've always wondered. Tried to imagine … Sometimes it feels like the house is full of ghosts. Good ghosts, not evil ones.'

'It was a squat back then; we didn't have any proper funding, lived off donations from the public. It was terribly overcrowded, there weren't enough toilets – we must have broken all the health and safety rules. But for the first time in my life I felt free. The other women were so generous, so supportive. They came from all backgrounds – some were rough types virtually off the street, but we had wives of professional men there too. Bankers, teachers … everybody mixed in. We'd all been through the same hell, so we understood each other. There was no therapy like there is nowadays, not to speak of. We just lived together and gradually the scars – mental as well as physical – healed.'

'Sounds incredible … women together.'

'It *was* incredible. We had nothing, but we couldn't give a toss. Because we had our freedom, freedom from control, freedom from violence.'

She pauses, looking down at me. 'I'm so sorry, Stella. This shouldn't have happened to you. I know what it's like to be bruised and beaten, to feel sick with pain.'

'If you know, why won't you help me?' I say.

'I *am* helping you. But first you have to listen to me.'

'Okay. Carry on, then.'

'It happened on Bonfire Night,' she says. 'Everyone else had gone to the display, but I was staying in because Abigail had a fever – she was only eight, I couldn't leave her. There was a knock on the door and I just opened it without thinking, didn't even put the chain on. Alan was standing on the doorstep, said he'd come to take me home.'

Her voice starts to waver and she twists her fingers in her lap, just as Dawn used to do when she was being Lori. The likeness between them is extraordinary. Not just their physical features, but their gestures and mannerisms – the tilt of the head, the way they unconsciously slip their hair behind their ears; even the rhythm of their speech is the same. Then I think of how different Abigail is. The outsider, the misfit. I can imagine her at eight years old – tall for her age, solid-looking, long dark hair, sallow skin, thick eyebrows, her eyes an impenetrable brown. Intelligent, but a bit of a bull in a china shop, perhaps. Forceful and slightly defiant, yet also vulnerable.

'What happened?' I say.

Kay shudders, then takes a long inward breath. And I know that she's about to speak the unspeakable.

CHAPTER THIRTY-NINE

Kay

Then

'Mummy?'

Their eyes swept upwards simultaneously. Abigail was standing at the top of the stairs, barefoot in her pyjamas. Her cheeks were flushed and feverish; black curls stuck to her forehead.

'What are you doing?' she said, staring at the knife, which was shaking in Kay's hand.

'Go back to bed, sweetheart. You're not well.' She lowered the blade and put it behind her back. 'Back to bed now, there's a good girl.'

'Why's he here?' Abigail's finger pointed accusingly.

'It's okay, he's leaving. Go back to bed.'

She hesitated.

'Hello, Abigail,' Alan said, going to the foot of the stairs, blocking Kay's way. 'I hear you're a bit poorly.'

'Go away. I hate you.'

'That's not a nice thing to say to your daddy.'

'You're not my daddy. You're evil.'

'Now, now, don't be rude. I've come to take you both home.'

'What?' Abigail took a step down. 'Mummy – Mummy! I don't want to go.'

'We're not going anywhere, darling,' Kay replied. Her palms were sweating; she had to grip the knife handle harder to keep it in her grasp. 'Stay right there. Don't come down.'

But Abigail kept walking down the stairs. She was swaying with fever, her glittering dark eyes fixed on her stepfather. 'You hurt Mummy. I saw you do it lots of times. You're a bad man.'

'Abi, please, go back to your room – GO BACK!'

But she carried on plodding down in her bare feet. As she reached the bottom step, Alan lunged forward and scooped her into his arms. She kicked and wriggled, but there was no escape. He locked his arms around her body and held her tightly against his chest.

'Either you come now, Kay, or I'll take her with me,' he said.

'No! Mummy! Mummy!' screamed Abigail.

'She can't go out in her pyjamas, she's sick,' Kay wailed. 'She's got no shoes on.'

'You've got two minutes to get your stuff together – two minutes! Or we're leaving without you.'

'Let me go! Let me go!' Abigail pounded him with her little fists, sobbing hysterically.

Kay cried out. 'Don't hurt her … I'll do whatever you say, just don't hurt her.'

'Drop the fucking knife!' he ordered.

The knife. She'd been holding it so tightly it had glued itself to her hand. How powerful she'd felt just a few moments ago, brandishing it in his face. But now he was holding a much stronger weapon: her beautiful daughter, whom she loved more than anything in the world. She loosened her grip and let the knife drop to the floor with a clang.

'Hurry up!' he barked. 'You're wasting time.'

'Just getting your things, darling,' she said to Abigail. 'I'll be very quick.' She tried to run up the stairs, but her huge belly held her back. By the time she reached the top floor, she was gasping for breath and the base of her tummy hurt. Downstairs, she could hear Abigail screaming and Alan shouting at her to be quiet. She was a fierce little thing when she was angry. Since playing with the other refuge kids, she'd become quite the tough fighter.

Kay picked a few clothes off the chair that was their only wardrobe, then gathered Abigail's trainers and her favourite teddy, shoving them into a plastic carrier bag. She could hardly breathe, her chest was hurting so much. If only somebody would come back now and rescue them. Pat and Alesha had promised to relieve her so she could go and catch the second firework display, but they must have forgotten. She paused to look out of the window and down into the street below. But there was no sign of anyone.

There was more commotion downstairs; it sounded awful. If Alan laid a finger on that girl, if he dared ... Kay grabbed a blanket and the bag, then lumbered down the top flight of stairs, her heavy breasts bouncing painfully, the baby on a roller-coaster ride.

As she reached the first-floor landing, she realised that the noise had stopped. Fear lurched in her throat. She took a few paces forward and leant over the banisters, gasping as her brain tried to make sense of what her eyes were seeing.

It didn't look real. A photograph, or a still from a movie, the horrific scene carefully posed.

Alan was lying on the floor of the hallway. He was crumpled onto one side, knees bent, not moving. Dark red liquid was pooled around his body. Abigail was standing by the door, her spotty pyjamas spattered with blood. She looked as if she was playing musical statues – frozen in mid action, arms slightly raised, mouth hanging open.

Kay felt herself starting to sway. She clung to the handrail to steady herself, then slowly descended, tread by uncertain tread.

'Abi? ... Abi, it's okay ... I'm coming. Mummy's here,' she said, her voice cutting through the silence. She reached the ground floor and edged past the pool of blood. When she reached her daughter, she put the blanket around her shoulders. 'Now you go and lie on the sofa for me, yes?' She gently pushed Abigail towards the door of the lounge. The child was like a doll, completely rigid, her limbs refusing to bend. 'Mummy will look after him. He's going to be fine, don't you worry. You lie down and rest, okay?'

Abigail allowed herself to be manoeuvred towards the sofa and let Kay lay her down and cover her with the blanket. It was as if she was sleepwalking. She didn't utter a single word, or make the slightest sound of protest when her mother left her side.

Kay went back into the hallway and bent over the body to check for a pulse. She couldn't feel anything. He was still warm, but he had that awful stillness dead people had. She'd seen it before, when her grandfather had had his heart attack and died in front of the whole family.

The knife was sticking out of his chest. It must have gone straight through his heart. How could Abigail have struck him with such force, how could she even have reached so high? It didn't make sense. She stared and stared at the wooden handle protruding from his shirt. This was the knife she'd washed up only this evening, that a few minutes ago had rested in her hand. How could this horror have happened so quickly?

She felt a terrible burning pain in the small of her back and stood up. The baby had never felt so heavy or so alive. Her stomach heaved and she clutched it, afraid that its contents would fall out.

It was her fault for dropping the knife when he told her to; she never should have left it there when she went upstairs. Shouldn't have picked it up in the first place. Only she hadn't thought, hadn't dreamt for a moment …

She tried to place herself in the drama. Abigail must have wrenched herself free and grabbed it. Or maybe Alan had picked it up and there'd been a tussle and somehow … But he was a grown man and she only a little girl. Could he have stabbed himself, fallen onto the blade? She couldn't believe Abigail had done it deliberately. Either way it must have been an accident – a horrible, horrible accident.

But that wasn't how it would look to the police. Kay could see that now. They would charge her with murder. She'd be locked away for life and Abigail would be put in care. And what about the child she was carrying? Would it be born in prison, then adopted by strangers? Anger started to burn deep within her, spreading like a fire all the way to her fingertips. She could not let that happen. After all she'd been through, all the suffering she'd endured at this monster's hands, after everything she'd done to build a new future for herself, she was not going to throw it away now. They would never take her children from her. She would flee, go into hiding. She would drown them all in the sea before she gave them up.

She looked down at the body and a fresh realisation swept over her. It was finished. Foxy, Alan, whatever she called him, was dead. He couldn't harm her any more. Relief flooded through her, drowning the anger. She retched violently and threw up onto the tiles.

But she had to act. Now, before any of the others came back. Her mind rattled through a list – grab clothes and supplies, gather Abigail up, call a taxi and just go. Go anywhere. But she was eight months pregnant, and she only had a few quid in her purse. Where would they go anyway? She would be a fugitive. Nobody would want to take her in, there was nowhere she would be safe. What were they to do, live in the woods in the middle of winter? They'd die of exposure.

Running away was impossible. The baby could come at any moment. She could feel it now, pushing its feet against the lining of her womb. A dull, period-pain-like ache was radiating from her lower back and wrapping itself around her body like a stiff rubber band.

She went back into the lounge to check on Abigail. The child had fallen asleep but was breathing fast, her eyelids flickering as if she was dreaming. Her face was warm and sticky with fever. Kay laid her hand lightly on the tiny ribcage, feeling her daughter's rapid heartbeat. Maternal love oozed out of her pores. She would not give up one life of imprisonment to replace it with another. It was over. They were free of him now. This was good. Something to be celebrated. She heard the crackle of fireworks outside; it seemed as if they were being set off for her.

Build a bonfire, build a bonfire, put your husband on the top …

She wouldn't burn him; that would be too difficult, too obvious. No, she would bury him instead. Bury him at the bottom of the garden and nobody would know, nobody would ever find out.

They found her by the shed. She was standing in the mud, cradling her belly, watching the fireworks with a strange look of elation on her face; she didn't respond when they called her name. Franny took her hand and led her slowly back to the house.

Pat and Alesha were there too; they'd come back to take over the babysitting, just as they'd promised, and Franny had come with them. They'd opened the front door and seen the body straight away. Pat went to call the police, but Franny stopped her. The man was quite dead; there was no saving him. And she'd just seen Abigail lying on the sofa, her pyjama top stained with blood.

Kay tried to tell them what had happened, only she realised that she didn't know, not with any certainty. She knew how it had started, but not how it had ended. 'I was upstairs,' she said. 'I heard noises, like a fight. When I came back down, he was lying there bleeding and Abigail was just staring into space.'

'What did she say?' asked Franny.

'Nothing. I don't think she understood.'

'Poor love, she must be in shock.'

'So what do we do now?' said Pat. She was sitting on the bottom stair, holding her head in her hands. 'If we call the police, they'll arrest Kay and she'll be put away – all on account of that bastard. They'll probably shut the whole refuge down and we'll be out on the street. It's not fair!'

'He deserved to die,' said Alesha.

'Yes, but what do we do?' Pat looked anxiously towards the front door. 'Everyone will be back soon. All hell will break loose. We can't let the kids see this. We have to get rid of the body and we have to do it bloody fast.'

Franny and Alesha gasped. It was unthinkable, and yet there was no other solution.

'I'm going to put him in the garden,' Kay told them. She'd planned it all when she went outside. There were some spades in the shed. The ground was soft; it wouldn't take long to dig a shallow grave.

'You can't do anything, not in your condition,' Alesha said.

It was true. The dull ache hadn't gone away; in fact, it was getting stronger. Her stomach had tightened a few times too, but she was ignoring it. The baby would have to wait.

'If we dispose of the body, that makes us an accessory,' said Franny. 'We could be convicted of murder. If we come clean and explain to the police that he attacked Kay and she was defending herself—'

Kay interrupted. 'They won't believe me. Look at him, for God's sake. There's a knife sticking out of his chest.'

'I know, I know, but—'

'We have to do *something*,' said Pat. 'Like now.'

Kay put her hands under her belly and let out a small groan. 'I'll take all the blame,' she said. 'If he's ever found, I'll say I buried him by myself. I swear to you on the life of my children ... I will never, ever tell anyone what happened.'

Franny pursed her lips. 'What about Abi? You can't expect a child to keep a secret like that.'

'She didn't know what she'd done,' said Kay. 'It was like she was in a trance. If she mentions it, I'll say it must have been a bad dream. A hallucination. Kids have hallucinations when they're ill, don't they? And she's had nightmares before. She's scared stiff of him – remember the drawings she did on the wall? If I deny it, she won't question it, she'll believe me. And if there's no evidence ...'

'I guess it might work ... We must make sure she doesn't wake up, give her some more medicine,' said Franny, but she sounded unconvinced.

'Come on, girls,' said Pat sharply. 'Franny, Alesha, you help me with the body. Kay, are you okay to clean up the blood? Throw the mop out when you're done, make sure you rinse the bucket out.'

Alesha nodded. 'I'm up for it. If Kay gets done for his murder, he'll have won. All the men who have battered us will have won.'

'I'm doing it for Abigail,' said Franny. 'Although God knows if we'll get away with it.'

'Thank you, girls, thank you ...' Tears glistened in Kay's eyes and her heart felt full, like a balloon that was about to burst. 'I promise I will never let you down.'

Pat started giving directions for lifting the body. 'I'll take his head, you grab his legs.' She turned him onto his back. Kay couldn't bear to see his face again, so she went into the kitchen in search of the mop and bucket.

As she ran the hot tap, a powerful surge of pain spread from her spine all the way through to her belly button, making her gasp and grip the edge of the counter. It lasted a few seconds, then slowly subsided. She knew exactly what it meant. The baby was on its way. One life had been extinguished and a new one was about to be born.

CHAPTER FORTY

Stella

Now

I lean back against the pillow, my mind whirring with what she's just told me. 'So let's get this straight … Your husband is buried in my back garden.'

'Yes, I'm afraid so. I never knew exactly where they put him,' Kay says. 'Somewhere down the bottom, by the shed, I think. I went into labour that night and was taken to hospital. Dawn was born early the next morning.'

The atmosphere is charged with the ghosts of the past. I feel them drawing closer, standing at the end of the bed, or pulling up a chair. They've sent their children into the other room to play, placed their hands over the ears of the babies. Everyone is gathered now. They want to know what happened next. You can hear a pin drop as they listen.

'But why did the other women help you get rid of the body?' I say. 'They were taking such a huge risk.'

Kay's face breaks into a sad smile. 'That's easy to answer. It could have been any of us in that situation – I'd have done the same for them. We'd all suffered terrible violence at the hands of our men. We were the victims, not the criminals.'

'But it was obviously self-defence, so why didn't you just call the police?'

'I didn't trust them; they'd let me down before. I was frightened they'd charge me with murder, and I didn't want to lose my girls.' She sighs. 'It was very different back then, Stella. Domestic violence was allowed to go on, as long as it was behind closed doors. The police didn't like to get involved; they saw it as a private business between man and wife. Horrendous, I know, but that's how it was.'

My thoughts return to the women who helped Kay cover up the killing. I've always thought I had close friends who would be there for me in times of crisis, but this is on another level. Would I have done the same for Molly? Would she have done the same for me? I instinctively feel that the answer is no. But then we've never been pushed to the limits.

'It's an ugly story,' Kay says. 'I'm sorry you had to hear it, sorry you had to endure all this. I promise, I had no idea what my girls were up to.'

I look at her, bewildered. 'I still don't understand.'

'I'll get Dawn to come down. She can explain.' Kay stands up and walks over to the door, opening it and calling through the gap. 'Dawn, love? Can you come and talk to Stella, please?'

I lean across and pick up the glass at my side. The water feels cool on my lips. As I swallow, I try to imagine how it must have felt for Kay in those first hours after Alan's death. She would have felt ecstatic to be free of her violent husband, then terrified that the body would be discovered, or that one of the conspirators would talk.

'I trusted them completely,' she says, as if reading my mind. 'I knew they'd never crack. Even so, we agreed it was best if we went our separate ways and didn't keep in touch. The girls went to other refuges, Franny took a job up north. I still think about those marvellous women every day. I owe them my life.'

'And nobody else in the house knew?'

'No. In a funny way, me going into labour helped. I'd just finished mopping up when some of the others came in. They laughed
when they saw me cleaning – said it was a sure sign I was about
to drop. I was a huge distraction. They called the house mother
and she put me in an ambulance. All that time, the others were
at the bottom of the garden, digging. It was such a chaotic place.
Nobody missed you if you stayed out; we were free to come and go
as we pleased. When they'd finished, they laid a load of crap over
the grave to hide it. Nobody ever went down there. The garden
was overgrown; we only ever used the top bit, to hang washing
out. The rest of it was basically a rubbish dump.'

And not much has changed in forty years, I think. I had so
many plans for my wilderness … A terrace with gentle steps
leading down to a beautiful lawn. A pergola, a vegetable patch, a
small playground, a pond full of darting fish.

'What did you do after Dawn was born?' I ask, turning away
from my musings on things that would never be. 'Go back to the
refuge and carry on like nothing had happened?'

She raises her eyebrows. 'No, it was too dangerous. I went
home, told the landlord that Alan had done a bunk – which he
believed, no problem. He felt sorry for me, let me stay on until
I got myself straight. I never went back to Westhill House – not
until today, that is.' She suddenly looks wistful. 'I loved it here.
I missed the place so much, missed the other women; I felt very
isolated on my own with Abigail and the new baby, but I couldn't
go back. I had to cut all ties with the place.'

'Nobody reported him missing?' It seems so strange to me
that somebody could disappear and the rest of the world barely
notice. I know people could go off the radar very easily in those
days, without the internet and social media tracking their every
move. But even so. If I vanished and nobody even raised the
alarm …

'Alan had lost his job, and he didn't have many friends. I used to think he was really popular, good old Foxy, Mr Charming and all that, but I realised later that that was *his* version of himself, not other people's. If anyone asked, I said he'd walked out on me and I didn't know where he'd gone. I reckon most of them thought, good riddance to bad rubbish.'

'Didn't he have any family who cared?'

'Just a younger brother. Micky knew what Alan was like; they'd fallen out over the way he was treating me. Alan was always manipulating him – it's how he was with everyone. Micky felt guilty because he'd told Alan where I was living. He came to see me a few weeks after Dawn was born. I have a feeling he suspected something awful had happened, but he didn't ask and I didn't tell. I gave him Alan's stuff – personal documents, certificates, passport … I didn't want them in the house. Then we said goodbye and I never heard from him again. I don't know how he ended up.'

But I do, I think. 'What was Micky like?'

She pauses to reflect. 'Spitting image of his brother, just a hell of a lot nicer. The boys had had a tough start in life. Micky got into trouble with the law when he was a teenager. But he was straightening himself out. He had a good heart. I'd like to think he made a go of it.'

'What did you tell Dawn about her father?'

'Obviously I couldn't tell her the truth,' she says. 'But she reached that age when kids ask questions so I had to say something. I told her he'd gone to Australia and died of cancer. She knew he used to beat me; I'd made no secret of it. I wanted her to know what men could be like. She trained to be a therapist, you know, so she could help women like me. I'm so proud of her.'

Right on cue, the door opens and Dawn enters. She looks at me timidly. 'How are you? All right if I come in?' I try to nod, but my head swims with pain. She crosses over to the bed and sits on the other side, and once more I'm struck by the physical similarity between mother and daughter.

'I've told her everything,' Kay says simply.

'You did what?!' Dawn's eyes open wide. 'Are you mad?'

'Don't talk to me about being mad … You're the ones who started all this.'

'But Mum … what about Abi? If she's arrested, she won't cope.'

'There's nothing we can do about that. Enough's enough. It's up to Stella what happens now.'

Dawn looks at me. 'What are you going to do?'

'I don't know yet,' I say. Their story is weighing heavily on me. 'Tell me more about Abi. She was the one who actually killed your husband. That's a terrible burden to carry for the rest of your life.'

Kay nods, putting her hands in her lap. 'I don't know exactly what she did, I didn't witness it. But she was clearly very traumatised. Didn't talk about it for days, and then she started saying stuff, talking about the blood, the man on the floor. It was obvious she remembered some of it. I told her she'd been very ill and had been hallucinating, that she'd had some awful nightmares but that was all they were – none of it was real. She believed me. At least, I thought she did.

'She seemed okay, at first. The damage didn't really show itself until she was a teenager. Then it was eating disorders, self-harming, aggressive behaviour, refusing to go to school, the lot. I sensed she'd remembered killing her stepfather but had suppressed it very, very deeply. I'd contributed to that, of course. I felt bad about it, but there wasn't a choice.'

Kay starts to cry, silent tears falling down her creased cheeks. Dawn stretches across the bed and takes her hand. 'It's okay, Mum, you did what you thought best.'

'I wrecked her life the day I met that man. I ruined everything.' She feels in her sleeve for a tissue. 'I'll never forgive myself.'

'I tried to give Abi therapy,' Dawn says to me. 'You're not supposed to treat members of your own family, but I knew she wouldn't open up to anyone else. She was very confused. She knew something very, very bad had happened when she was a kid and felt it had been her fault. I tried hypnosis. She had memories of a house full of women and my father turning up one night, and of being very frightened. It sounded like a refuge to me, but Mum had never said anything about living in a refuge. We asked you, didn't we, Mum? But you said it was all nonsense.'

'Yes, that's true … I hated lying to you, but I was frightened too.'

'We did some searches, tried to find a record of my father's death in Australia, but we drew a blank. You kept insisting that he'd died of cancer, but you couldn't show us any proof.'

'I know, I know … I was so worried.'

'Abi started to remember other things – the house was on a hill, she had a round bedroom at the top, overlooking the sea … there was a muddy beach nearby, and a pier. Through my job, I was able to get a list of refuges in the area. Nothing fitted her description, but then somebody told me about Westhill House, which had just closed down after forty years. Started out as a squat, then was taken over by a charity and converted into proper safe accommodation. We went to have a look at it and Abi knew straight away that that was where she'd stayed. It was up for sale. We even posed as potential buyers so we could have a look around.

'Everything came flooding back. Abi had a panic attack there in the hallway. We had to make some excuse and leave; it was really embarrassing. After that, she became obsessed with this idea that she'd killed my father and that he was buried somewhere in the house or garden. She said we had to find the body and get rid of it before the new owner did.

'We couldn't buy the place ourselves, obviously. We kept an eye out; it didn't sell for ages. Abi had all sorts of notions about breaking in and squatting, but then the Sold sign went up. She decided she had to make a plan. I didn't want to get involved, but she was going crazy, and I was really worried about what she'd do if I refused. She got friendly with the estate agent, and he said you were a lovely couple, really nice people. That's when she came up with the idea of me pretending to be a victim of domestic violence. The rest you know …'

'Dawn's been explaining how wonderful you were to her,' says Kay, wiping the corners of her eyes with the tissue. 'You remind me so much of the women who worked in the refuge – their kindness and generosity were second to none. They took everything on trust, never doubted my story, never challenged me.'

'You're forgetting that I'm the one who's been abused here,' I say hotly. 'They lied and deceived me, manipulated me to cover up a crime. They completely fucked up my relationship with my boyfriend. And then, when it went wrong, they tried to kill me. If Dawn hadn't fetched you, I'd be in the ground now, along with your bastard husband.'

'Yes, yes, you're right, it was appalling what they did.'

'But Abi wasn't trying to kill you; that was never part of the plan,' Dawn assures me. 'She just panicked.'

'Yeah, but I almost died! Your sister needs help; you all need help.'

There's a pause, filled by the pain in my head. I feel dizzy, as if the room is spinning round, taking me forward in time, away from the 1970s and back to the here and now.

Kay takes my hand and grips it tightly. 'Now you know the truth, what do you want to do, Stella?'

'Mum, we can't let her—'

'I made a deal, Dawn. I'm going to honour it.'

'Abi will never cope in prison.'

I hold up my hand to silence them. 'Give me my phone, please.'

Kay looks sharply at her daughter. 'Do as she says.' Dawn stands and goes over to my desk, opening the drawer and taking out my mobile.

'Please, please don't do this,' she pleads as she holds it out to me.

My hands are trembling as I prod the phone into life. The battery has been running down; there's only ten per cent left, but that's enough to make a single, quick call. Nervous about the boulder I'm about to roll down the hill, but still resolute, I start to dial.

CHAPTER FORTY-ONE

Stella

Now

The doctor – a young man with owl-like glasses and a beaky nose – peels back the bandage and peers at my wound. I feel nervous under the bright lights of the cubicle. Will my account of what happened match with the physical evidence?

'How did you do this?'

'I was hit over the head with a spade.' I remember reading somewhere that the best lies are the ones based on truth. It's a technique I've used for years.

'Really? How come?'

'I was doing some gardening; it was an accident.' I flinch as he prods the tender skin at the back of my head.

'When did it happen?' He pulls off his rubber gloves and throws them in the bin.

'Yesterday afternoon.'

He frowns. 'You should have come to A and E immediately.'

'Sorry.' I don't offer any explanation for the delay. How could I tell him I spent the night tied up in a tarpaulin on the floor of the garden shed?

'Well … the wound looks clean and it's stopped bleeding, but we still have to be careful with infections. When did you last have a tetanus jab?'

'Can't remember. When I was a kid, I think.'

'Any fever? Headache? Sickness?'

'My head's sore and I felt sick for a while, but I'm a lot better now.' That's true. As soon as I entered the hospital, the pain in my brain subsided and I felt as if a huge weight had been lifted from my shoulders.

'Hmm.' He shines a torch into my eyes. 'I think you're okay. We'll give you a jab, get you stitched up and send you down for a scan, just to make sure there's nothing more serious going on.'

'Thanks.'

'Might have to wait a while, I'm afraid. Have you got anyone with you?'

'No.'

He stops writing his notes and stares at me for a few moments. 'And it was a gardening accident, you say. You're sure about that?'

'Absolutely.'

'It was quite a whack ... Who did it?'

'A friend. She was digging the flower beds and I stupidly got in the way.' It sounds like a lame excuse, but it's the best I can come up with. 'It was my fault.'

'Okay ...' He pauses again, as if searching for the right words. 'Look, I don't want to interfere, but ... if you want to talk to anyone about anything, we have specially trained staff here. I can refer you—'

'It wasn't domestic violence, if that's what you're getting at,' I say quickly. 'If it was, I'd speak up, don't worry.'

'Good ... Glad to hear it ... Well, you know where we are if you need us.' He smiles briefly, then puts his pen back into his top pocket. He knows I'm lying, covering up for someone else. I can almost see the questions popping out like thought balloons on either side of his head. *Why didn't she come to hospital immediately? Why is she here on her own?* He could easily be forgiven for assuming I was an abuse victim.

No, not a victim, a survivor.

*

Three hours later, put back together and re-bandaged, scanned and given the all-clear, I take a taxi back to the house. I'm still feeling weak and vulnerable, anxious about what's been going on in my absence.

The journey back to Nevansey seems to take for ever. I sit in the back seat, staring blankly out of the window, fingers gripped around my phone. A well of emotion is rising in my chest. I'm having to use all my strength to stop myself contacting Jack. When we first met, we were in touch several times a day, updating each other on our whereabouts, sending jokey messages or photos – amazing sunsets or just funny things we'd spotted in the street. Sometimes he'd just text, *I love you*, and I'd text back, jokily, *Who is this?*

Even though I know it's over between us, I still feel that urge to hear his voice, to listen to his calming tones and his consoling words. I desperately want to talk to him, but I daren't. If I told him what had happened, he wouldn't hesitate to call the police and have everyone arrested. There'd already be a tent over the burial spot in the garden, people in white suits taking photographs, journalists gathered outside the house, waiting excitedly for some gory news.

I didn't call the police when Dawn handed me my phone, although I was sorely tempted. I rang Alan instead. He didn't pick up – I knew he wouldn't – so I left a message he couldn't ignore.

'I know the truth about Foxy. Come over to Westhill House now.'

The taxi reaches the pier and turns left along the Esplanade. I look out of the window at the familiar view: the bank of pebbles pushed against the sea wall by the force of incoming tides, the swathes of dark brown mud as sticky as treacle, the black wooden groins rising out of the water like rotting teeth. It has a strange beauty all of its own.

I haven't used the beach as much as I thought I would. I imagined long romantic walks along the coast path, picnics in grassy dips, wild swimming. I was going to learn how to cook lobster and eat oysters. I wanted to submerge myself in the culture here, not be a down-from-Londoner, pushing up the property prices.

I'm not surprised to see Alan's battered white van parked on the driveway. I knew he wouldn't be able to ignore my message. I pay the cab driver, then walk up the steps to the front door. Fumbling in my bag for my key, I eventually find it and turn it in the lock. The heavy door creaks open, revealing the tiled hallway. Immediately I picture the body that lay there all those years ago, blood oozing out, pulse fading. I enter cautiously, feeling as fragile as a dead leaf blown in by the wind.

'Hello? I'm back.' I shut the door behind me and put my bag in my room. The house is quiet. Everyone must be outside. I walk down the corridor, through the kitchen and into the conservatory. The back door is open, held back by a brick and letting a cold draught into the house. I pause, resting against the frame, summoning up what little energy I have left to go into the garden.

It must have rained earlier, because the ground is wet and slippery. I follow the path of trodden grass down to the bottom, bending my head to go under the arch of the pergola. My stomach lurches as I reach the old shed, where I lay for several hours, certain I was going to die. I take a few more steps, then round the end of the building.

Kay, Abigail and Dawn are huddled together as if at a funeral, mesmerised by the hole at their feet, watching every cut of Alan's spade as he digs, throwing the clods behind him in a shower of mud. He's not Alan, of course, but Micky. But I'll never get used to calling him that, any more than I'll ever adjust to thinking of Lori as Dawn.

Abi is the first to react to my presence. She catches me in her peripheral vision and glances up. Our eyes lock for a second, then she looks away, embarrassed. I have no memory of her tying me up – probably just as well – but I do remember her lifting the spade above her head and crashing it down on my skull.

'Hello,' I say.

'Stella, you're back.' Kay responds instantly, stepping forward and holding out her arms. 'How did you get on at the hospital?'

'Okay, thanks,' I mumble. 'I'll live to fight another day.'

Alan looks up, wiping the sweat from his forehead with the back of his gardening glove. The air is spiked with cold, but he has stripped down to his vest, revealing ugly, tired tattoos on his forearms.

'Stella,' he says, panting with exertion.

My tone is chilly. 'So this is what it takes for you to reply to my messages.'

He rests the spade against the growing mound of earth. 'I'm sorry,' he says. 'Sorry for everything.'

'Shall we talk?' I nod towards the house.

He tugs off his gloves. 'Of course.' Stepping out of the pit, he picks up his sweatshirt and pulls it over his head.

'I'll take over,' says Dawn. She picks up the spade and starts attacking the earth.

Alan follows me back up the path and into the conservatory. The old deckchairs are leaning against the wall. I take one and flap it open, then lower myself onto the seat. He prefers to stand, sticking his hands in the pockets of his dungarees.

'You're Micky, is that right?'

He nods, chewing on his bottom lip. 'Yeah, but I've been Alan for nearly forty years now. I don't think of myself as Micky any more.'

'Why did you steal your brother's identity?'

He sighs, and rests his back against the brick wall. 'I got into some trouble when I was young, ended up with a criminal record. It made it hard to get work; nobody wanted to give me a chance. I was hanging around with a few blokes I'd met inside, and they wouldn't let me go, you know? I could feel myself being pulled back under.' He screws up his face, as if the remembering is painful.

'I knew Foxy was violent towards Kay. I was glad when she left him. I bumped into her a few months later in Nevansey – she begged me not to tell him where she was living, and I promised I wouldn't. I kept it a secret for weeks. But Foxy was falling apart, kept saying how much he loved her and wanted her back, vowed he was going to change, and like a fool, I believed him. Told him she was in the refuge. Worst thing I could have done, as it turned out.'

'How did he react?'

'He went mental, said he was going to drag her back by her hair if necessary. I should have warned her, but I didn't.' He sighs and looks down at his muddy boots. 'It was early December. I hadn't heard from Foxy for a few weeks, so I went over to the house. He wasn't there, but Kay was. She didn't have to say a word, I could see it in her eyes. She wasn't scared any more – she looked like a different person. I knew then that my brother was dead, and I didn't give a shit. As far as I was concerned, he'd got what he deserved.'

'Kay told me the two of you never spoke about what had happened.'

'We didn't need to; it was better left unsaid. She gave me a box of his things. I took it back to my flat and stuffed it under the bed, didn't know what else to do with it. About a year went by. Nobody reported Foxy missing, nobody seemed to care. I was having a rough time. I was trying to go straight but it seemed impossible. I needed to get away, turn my back on my past and start again. That's when I got the idea of becoming Alan Foxton – someone without a criminal record. Ironic, when you think about it. I moved to the Midlands and found a job on a building site. Worked my way up, got some qualifications. Married a lovely girl, had two boys of my own. I've been very lucky.'

'How come you came back here?'

'The past weighed heavy on me, Stella. The older I got, the more I started to worry about being found out. I had too much to lose. I reckoned that if Foxy's body was ever discovered, I'd be blamed. At the very least, I'd be charged with impersonation. I felt I had to do something about it once and for all. I didn't know exactly what had happened back then, but I had a pretty good idea that Foxy had met his death here in Westhill House. I persuaded the missus to move down …' He pauses. 'She knows nothing about this; she thinks I'm Alan, five years older than I really am … Anyway, we moved to Nevansey, and I was able to keep watch on the house. The refuge closed, then the place was empty for a couple of years. I knew someone would buy it eventually and was bound to want to do it up. I felt as if time was running out, that my whole world was about to come crashing down. Then you bought the house, and I realised I had a chance. If I got the building job, I could search for his remains and get rid of them. That way we'd all be safe.'

'Why did you leave so suddenly?'

'The police got in touch, said you'd been burgled. Apparently you'd given them my name as a possible suspect.' He looks away from me, out of the window. 'I don't know, I just panicked. I had a feeling you were on to me. The detective rang back later to say the stuff had been found and there'd been a misunderstanding, but I couldn't face coming back. I was in a right state. The missus thought I was having a nervous breakdown.' He sighs. 'Perhaps I am …'

At that moment, Dawn comes racing through the grass, her hands muddy, her face red with excitement.

'We've found something,' she says, panting. 'Come and see.'

Alan gulps. 'Is that all right, Stella?'

'Yeah, you'd better go.' I heave myself out of the deckchair. 'But leave me out of it. I don't want to know. As far as I'm concerned, you're digging a hole for a pond, nothing more. If there's anything you need to dispose of, I don't want to see it, is that clear?'

They nod in unison. Then Dawn grabs Alan's arm and they hurry back down the garden. A deep shiver runs the length of my spine. I close the door and walk into the kitchen, my hand shaking as I lift the kettle to make a cup of tea.

EPILOGUE

Stella

Three months later

The photographer screws on another lens, then stands in the doorway assessing the best angle for his shot. It won't be easy to take a picture of what will no doubt be called a 'feature fireplace' without also revealing the damp patch on either side. Our bed has been dismantled, the pieces stacked in the alcove. The mattress is leaning against the opposite wall, draped in a dust sheet.

'Such a pity you weren't able to finish the refurb,' says the estate agent, casting his eyes around. His name is Rahim; he's wearing a very shiny suit and looks about fifteen. 'What happened? Run out of money?'

I glance at Jack. We agreed in advance not to wash our dirty linen in public. 'We've decided that Nevansey is not for us,' I say.

'Miss the bright lights of London?'

'Something like that.'

The photographer nods at Rahim to say he's ready to move on. We started at the top and made our way down, so now there's just the rest of the ground floor to do. We cross the hallway and troop into the other reception room. Most of the boxes were shifted out weeks ago, either to Jack's new place or to Molly's house, where I'm staying temporarily. The smell of damp is unmistakable. There's a forlorn chill in the air, even though it's June and outside the sun is blazing.

Next we move on to the kitchen and Jack offers our guests a cup of tea.

'Actually, can I have a glass of water?' says Rahim, loosening his tie. The photographer doesn't respond; he's too busy taking close-ups of the retro seventies wall tiles. Jack opens three cupboards before he finds a glass. His unfamiliarity with the place betrays us, but if Rahim notices, he doesn't say anything.

'Shall we do the garden now?' he suggests, swallowing back the water. 'I know it's a jungle out there, but at least we can get some good shots of the back of the house.'

'Sure,' says Jack, leading the way.

I follow them out there, feeling increasingly uneasy as we walk down the garden. New growth has made the old path of trodden grass disappear. The flower beds are thick with green foliage; there are glimpses of purple and red blooms struggling to make themselves seen.

Rahim holds up a measuring device, but he can't see it properly in the sunshine so starts pacing the length out instead.

'It's a big old place,' says the photographer. 'I'll need to stand as far away as possible to get everything in. How far back does the garden go?'

'I'll show you.' Jack beats a fresh track through the long grass, holding back the spiky rose branches for us to walk under the wooden arch of the pergola.

A feeling of dread rises up from my feet, flooding my body, drowning me internally. There's a sharp pain in the centre of my chest. But I have to keep smiling and chatting, can't afford to show even a tiny spark of nervousness about coming out here.

Rahim is giving us the spiel about traction in the market. He enthuses about the property's potential, what a wonderful purchase it will make for the right people. I nod and make agreeing noises, but inside, my heart is aching. I believed we were the right people once – we were going to transform this tatty old shell into our forever home, the place of our dreams, where our children would play safely and happily. Foundations built on sand, as it turned out.

This is the first time I've come down here since that awful day. I try never to think of it, but deep down I know that they found Foxy's body, because a while later, I saw Alan walking in and out of the house, carrying rubble bags. He put them in the back of his van and drove away. I don't know what he did with his brother's bones. If it had been me, I'd have found a way to bury them at sea.

I linger by the shed, leaning against the wooden slats, pretending to be sunning my face when in fact I'm trying to keep my balance. My knees feel weak, ready to buckle under me, but I have to act natural, have to pass the test. Steadying my breathing, I round the end of the shed and walk the few yards to join the others. The photographer is foregrounding a blown rose, pushing the building behind it into a deceptive soft focus, while Rahim is trying to measure this last piece of land, adding all the distances together on his phone app.

'Two hundred metres give or take,' he says. 'Secure, not overlooked. South-facing too.' He taps away happily on his tablet.

'What happened here?' Jack says to me, quietly. He gestures at the expanse of freshly dug earth, sprouting with healthy-looking weeds.

My stomach roils and I feel myself sway slightly. 'Nothing.'

'I don't remember it being like this.'

'Why would you remember? You never came down here.'

'No … I guess not,' he concedes, but his face retains its puzzled look.

I force myself to look at the earth. I feel as if I'm staring down from a great height. The hole has been filled in, but the rubbish hasn't been put back on top of it. It looks like an abandoned vegetable patch at best and a grave site at worst. Alan didn't do a very good job of hiding their tracks. Everyone was in such a hurry to get out. Thinking about it now, I should have checked, should have made them replace everything exactly as they'd found it. But I didn't want to know. Jack is still staring at the ground. I consider telling him that I tried to dig a pond and then gave up, but decide against it. I've had enough of making up stories.

Shots taken from every conceivable angle, we tramp back to the house. The photographer stays in the conservatory, making sure he's got everything. Rahim tells me there's an agency agreement to sign, so we go back to the kitchen, where there's a surface to lay out the documents.

'I gather you've already vacated the property,' he says.

'Yes, you'll need keys.' Jack digs into his pocket and throws his set onto the counter.

Rahim explains the terms and conditions, but I'm not really listening, I just want to sign the documents and end this farce. Pretending to be the happy couple who are abandoning their half-finished house for no good reason is proving too great an acting challenge. We're not fooling anyone. Our broken relationship is as obvious as the cracks in the ceiling above us.

'You need to sign here … and here …' The agent hands me a pen and I scribble my signature. It makes me think of an old dream – Jack and I signing our marriage certificate – and my hand wobbles, making my name unreadable.

At last Rahim and the photographer leave. Jack closes the front door behind them and turns to face me. 'God, that was torturous,' he says. 'I hope you manage to sell it quickly.'

'I've put it on at rock-bottom price; can't do much more.'

'Are you sure you want to sell? I know how much this house means to you. It seems a shame.'

'No, no, I want to.' I smile. 'Thanks for coming today, it meant a lot to have your support.'

He shrugs dismissively. 'I still had a few things to pick up anyway …'

'Well, it was still good of you.' There's a long pause. 'Actually, it wasn't the only reason I asked you to come.'

'No?'

I reach out for the banister, steadying myself. 'I've, er, been seeing a therapist, and … well, it's uncovered a lot of very uncomfortable stuff from my childhood.'

'I thought you had a happy childhood.'

'No. Not really. My parents gave all their attention to their foster kids and ignored me. I was jealous, extremely jealous, and just horrible to everyone.'

He lifts his eyebrows. 'But you said they were wonderful.'

'They were, but I didn't see it at the time. There was this boy, his name was Kyle, he was fourteen, a nasty piece of work. I really hated him, I wanted him to go but my parents believed they were helping him. So I … er … I did this terrible thing.' My mouth dries. Dare I go on? Nobody else knows this – not Molly, not my therapist. But I'll never move forward unless I tell *somebody* the whole truth.

'Kyle was always going AWOL. Sometimes he'd stay out all night, hanging around in the park, getting off his head. One night when he was out, I nicked one of his smelly T-shirts, ripped it up and soaked it in petrol. My dad kept a spare can in the garage. Then when everyone had gone to bed, I stuffed it into a bottle, set it alight and made it look like it had been put through the letter box.'

'Oh my God, Stella …'

My hands are trembling, just as they did when I flipped Kyle's lighter on and held the flame against the cloth. I'm instantly back in the old house, running back upstairs in the dark and hiding in my room, heart pounding, waiting for the fire to take hold. I was going to leave it a couple of minutes, then raise the alarm and be the hero. I'd had it all worked out.'

Jack's brown eyes stare into mine. 'Was anyone hurt?'

'Luckily, no. Nobody believed Kyle's protestations of innocence – why would they? He was the son of a drug addict; he'd already been expelled from several schools. He was really angry that my parents didn't stand up for him. Ended up in a young offender institution and became a professional criminal.'

'And nobody ever suspected you?'

'No. I ruined his life, but I couldn't see that I'd done anything wrong – I felt even more justified because my parents were so upset about Kyle "betraying" them and paid no attention to me. I did badly in my A levels and had to go through clearing to get a university place. I cut off all contact with Mum and Dad, worked my way through college – supported myself, didn't ask them for a penny. I even wrote spiteful blogs about how awful it had been growing up in a family of foster carers – one of them won an award. That's what got me my first job in journalism. Mum and Dad were devastated when they found out, but I didn't care. We'd been estranged for over ten years when they died.'

He walks up and down the hallway, pulling his fingers through his hair. 'Why didn't you tell me any of this?'

'Because I was ashamed! They'd left me everything in their will and I couldn't understand why. I felt so guilty. I started to worry that Kyle had had my parents killed. He was in prison at the time, but he could have paid someone to do it. That would have made their deaths my fault too. I couldn't cope, couldn't live with myself. If I hadn't met you that day on the Tube, I think I might have jumped in front of a train.'

'I thought you were just grieving. I didn't realise ...'

'Of course you didn't. I was living a lie, even to myself. I fell in love with you immediately. You gave me a reason to build a future, but it meant rewriting the past, keeping secrets from you. I couldn't risk telling you the truth. I wanted you to think I was a good person, like my parents. I wanted to *be* a good person. Lori's arrival felt like a test. By helping her, I could change, even start to make amends. But of course, it all went wrong. I'm sorry, Jack, I'm so sorry.'

'I can't believe you didn't trust me enough,' he says. 'We loved each other, talked about getting married …'

'I know, I really messed up. I did to you what my parents did to me. I shoved you to one side, made you feel second best. I know how that feels. Which is why I don't blame you for cheating on me, or for leaving, even though it really hurt.'

He steps forward and gathers me into his arms. I rest my face against his T-shirt and tears roll down my cheeks, making a damp patch on his chest.

'I'm sorry too,' he says. 'What I did was appalling. There was no excuse.' After a few moments, I drag myself out of his embrace and we hold hands, fixing our gaze on each other. 'Neither of us behaved well,' he continues. 'But we could try again, forgive each other. Put all this behind us and make a fresh start.'

'But you're with Pansy.'

'Nah … that ended weeks ago. It was just a stupid fling. I never stopped loving you. I know you still love me too. You don't have to sell the house, I'll move back in …'

'We can't, Jack.' I lean weakly against the front door. 'It's too late.'

'No, it's not. We just have to be honest with each other, tell each other everything. No more pretending, no more lies.'

He's right, of course, it's our only hope. But it's also impossible. Jack knows the truth about me now, but I can never tell him what happened here: that Lori was a fake, that her sister attacked me. That forty years ago, a man was killed in this very hallway and buried in the garden. I can't tell him that Alan pretends to be his law-abiding, upstanding brother, who was in fact a violent bastard who deserved to die. Can't tell him about Kay, who has lived in fear every day of her adult life – first, afraid that her husband would beat her to death, and then afraid that his murder would be discovered. I can't pass that burden on to him. Can't take the risk.

'I'm sorry,' I say, finally. 'I do love you, but I know it wouldn't work.'

'Why not?'

'I can't explain. I just need some time on my own to sort myself out.'

He puts his hands in his pockets. 'We'll keep in touch, eh? Stay friends.'

'I'd like that.'

'Me too.' There's an awkward pause. I look down at the pattern on the floor tiles and he checks the time on his phone. 'My train leaves in twenty minutes. You driving back to Essex?'

'Yes. I'll lock up.'

'Take care of yourself, Stella. I worry about you.' He leans forward and kisses me chastely on the cheek. 'Think about what I said, eh, about staying. Don't rush to take the first offer.'

'I may not even get one … Go on, off you go, you'll miss your train.'

After he's gone, I go to the conservatory and lock the back door. Then I walk upstairs to the top floor. There's just one place I want to say goodbye to. My turret room, where I used to sit in the saggy old armchair and watch the sea.

I creak open the door and step inside. The room is hot and stuffy, motes of dust hanging in the shaft of sunlight bursting through the circular window. I go to the front and gaze out at the view – the glistening expanse of mud, the flat green sea, the wind turbines motionless on the horizon. The sunshine presses against my back, massaging my tense muscles, soothing me. I love this little room – so high up, so safe. It has always felt like a refuge.

For the first time, the house is completely empty. No boyfriend, no builders, no strange guests. Not even the ghosts are here. The spirits of all those women who knocked on the door asking for help are finally able to leave. They don't need to keep guard any more. There are no more secrets to hide. They can wander down to the beach, skim stones, dip their toes in the water, make sandcastles with their kids. They can walk along the Esplanade and go on the pier, try their luck in the amusement arcades, buy a cone of chips. No need to look over their shoulders. They're free now. We're all free.

A LETTER FROM JESS

Thank you for taking the time to read *The Dream House*. If this is your first Jess Ryder book, you might want to try my other psychological thrillers – *Lie to Me, The Good Sister* and *The Ex-Wife*. It's easy to get in touch via my Facebook page, Goodreads, Twitter or my Jess Ryder website. Or you can keep up to date with my latest releases by signing up at the Bookouture link below. Your email address will never be shared and you can unsubscribe at any time.

www.bookouture.com/jess-ryder

This story was initially inspired by my own house-hunting, and viewing a house that was opposite a women's refuge. I have long been interested in the issue of domestic abuse and this sparked some creative thoughts that eventually turned into *The Dream House*.

As a writer of psychological thrillers, I think very carefully about depicting violence in my stories, particularly violence against women. In this book, I wanted to confront the issue without falling into the trap of titillation, so have deliberately pulled back from graphically described physical abuse whenever possible. It cannot be entirely avoided, of course, but I've tried hard to take a responsible approach to this deeply concerning problem found in societies across the globe. The characters and story are entirely fictional, but if just one reader recognises elements of abuse in their own relationship through reading this novel, and is encouraged to change their life for the better, then writing it will have been entirely worthwhile.

Despite its serious themes, *The Dream House* sets out to be a dramatic and entertaining story with convincing characters, and I very much hope you have enjoyed the experience. If you feel able to write a brief constructive review and post it online in the appropriate places, I would love to read it. These days, book buyers are very much guided by the opinions of other readers, so it is very helpful to share.

With best wishes,
Jess Ryder

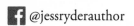 @jessryderauthor

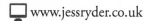 www.jessryder.co.uk

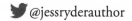 @jessryderauthor

Note: If you have been affected by the issues in this novel, further information and practical help for victims of domestic abuse in the UK can be found via the following links:

www.refuge.org.uk
(Refuge – including twenty-four-hour domestic abuse helpline)

www.ncdv.org.uk
(National Centre for Domestic Violence)

ACKNOWLEDGEMENTS

I would like to thank the following people who have helped me in the writing of this novel:

Brenda Page, my researcher, who never fails to give me the information I'm looking for, no matter how obscure, ridiculously specific or hard to find. I'm also grateful to her for picking up on my typos and errors in the early drafts.

Julie Lloyd, therapist, whose insights into the issue of domestic violence have been invaluable. I would like to stress that the therapist's notes in the novel are deliberately *not* what a reputable therapist would write!

The senior police detective who gave up her precious time to provide me with the lowdown on the role of the police in domestic violence cases and the current difficulties for women seeking help and protection in refuges. Any mistakes are entirely of my own making, or deliberate artistic licence.

Karen Drury (aka Sara Sartagne), fellow writer and long-standing friend. Also Fiona Eldridge – the two of you offer enormous support and have incredibly useful contacts!

My brilliant agent Rowan Lawton, who has such energy and passion for her writers' work and makes me feel very valued and supported.

My equally brilliant editor Lydia Vassar-Smith, who has an uncanny ability to ask exactly the right question at the right moment. Also the perspicacious Leodora Darlington and everyone on the Bookouture team – they work so hard for their authors and I really appreciate it.

Not forgetting Christine Glover, my media agent at Casarotto Ramsay & Associates, who is always looking for new opportunities for my work.

And as ever, my wonderful family – husband David, my parents and mother-in-law, my children and their partners. I'm lucky to be surrounded by some very strong, intelligent women, including many friends too numerous to mention here.

Made in the USA
Middletown, DE
13 June 2023

32514011R00201